MARIA R. RIEGGER

Thunderstruck

**Eighth
House
Press**

First edition

ISBN: 978-1-7339741-2-7

This book was professionally typeset on Reedsy.
Find out more at reedsy.com

Contents

IV SEPTEMBER

V OCTOBER

VI NOVEMBER

VII DECEMBER

I

JANUARY

Chapter 1

Monica's pulse raced and her palms became clammy in anticipation of the endeavor she was about to undertake. It made her anxious, more anxious than the decision to go to law school, and more anxious than giving birth to her son. Today's decision to go fully forward would be significant. Indeed, her decision this day would be a game changer, but in more ways than she could ever have imagined.

The group sat in the living room of Monica's townhouse in the Del Ray neighborhood of Alexandria. The closeknit band of those people closest to Monica included her husband, Christian, and fourteen-year-old son David. Also present were Nicole, a well-connected DC attorney and Monica's closest friend from law school, and Don, who had experience volunteering in political campaigns.

The living room was adorned with several science fiction posters, including Star Wars, Alien, Dune, and Mad Max. Monica's love of science fiction had influenced her son David; they always went to sci-fi movies together. Indeed, David had helped her decorate the living room.

Don sat next to Monica, and hung on her every word. "You do realize that this will be an uphill battle, don't you?" he told her.

Monica looked ahead, thinking. Indeed, the Eighth District

of Virginia, just a few miles outside of Washington, DC, was heavily Democratic. Any Republican would have a really tough time making headway with the population there. But Monica believed that she had a chance.

She nodded without looking at Don. "I get that. But you know me, and you know that as soon as someone tells me I can't do something, then it is a certainty that I will do it."

Monica's husband spoke up then. "Are you sure you want to do this?" he asked his wife. "Quit your job? Run in this election?" Even though he had been born in the U.S. to Argentine parents, he spoke with a slight *porteño* lilt.

In Monica's opinion, Christian certainly had the right to be concerned. Monica had served two terms as a delegate to the Virginia House of Delegates, the state-level equivalent to the U.S. House of Representatives. She had been able to work her full-time job at a large D.C. law firm while serving in that position. After all, a delegate's annual salary was only around $18,000. Plus, it looked good for her firm to have a local politician of counsel.

Monica currently planned to quit her day job as an attorney practicing corporate and transactional law. That meant that her family would lose about half of their household income. But she had spent years saving for this, and she and her husband had talked about it at length.

Christian had initially said that he was on board, but now appeared to be having doubts. His attitude annoyed Monica, but she was determined. If she was going to do this, run in this election, it was going to be now. She was forty-four years old, and felt the pressure of time.

"I've actually never been so sure of anything," she told Christian, tilting her head and brushing her thick, chestnut hair away from her face.

"Well," Don began, "a Hispanic female Republican may have a better chance than a white male Republican, that's true. Especially since Representative Hoffman is retiring."

Hoffman had been the congressman for the Eighth District since as long as Monica could remember, and she had grown up in northern Virginia. He was a staunch liberal Democrat, and to say that his district leaned heavily to the left was an understatement.

"You'll have to get through the primary first," Nicole said.

Monica smiled at her friend. Nicole was a registered Democrat, and had even done policy work for the Democratic National Committee. She was a member of the Democratic Freedom Caucus, and her libertarian leanings often brought her out of lockstep with other members of her party.

Monica was more of a libertarian, anyway, and championed freedom of speech and economic liberties. In that, she and Nicole agreed on most things. Monica had been overjoyed when Nicole had agreed to help with her campaign. It meant all the more to Monica since she knew that her friend was no doubt subject to criticism from her political peers.

Don would be Monica's campaign director, and Nicole would be her communications director. They would be her two right-hand people.

"I'm not too worried about the other Republican contenders in the primary," Monica said.

Indeed, she would be the only woman and hoped to get the female vote. She could also appeal to the many Spanish speakers in this particular district, and hopefully to the immigrant population in general.

Nicole turned to Don then. "Who's going to be running in the

Democratic primary?" she asked him.

Don rattled off a list of names. "I know more or less who all of them are, except for the last one, and that would be —" Don looked at the bottom of his notes. "Brian — Murphy."

Monica's heart sank and her stomach clenched. There was no way it could be the same Brian Murphy.

Don went on. "I think he's originally from —"

"San Francisco," Monica said absently.

"That's right." Don looked at her.

"And I think he works for a — like a — think tank, or something," she continued nervously.

"Yeah." Don's brows furrowed as he stated the name of the firm where Murphy worked. "Do you know him?"

"No," Monica lied. "I mean, I know who he is, that's all." All of a sudden Monica had a vision of running her hands through thick, dark brown hair. She shook her head to clear it.

To say that she hadn't thought about Murphy in a long time was a lie. However, she had pretty much blocked out the details of all the past memories.

Monica changed the subject slightly. "I have to say, I don't know why a guy from the West Coast would be interested in Virginia, I mean, in representing Virginia, you know?"

"Don't worry, for that same reason he most likely won't make it out of the primary," Don said.

Monica prayed that that would be the case.

Chapter 2

That same week, Brian Murphy met with the two men who would direct his campaign. Sean was a longtime friend of his, who worked for the Democratic National Committee, and who would be his communications director.

Mike was his campaign manager, and was a hard-hitting, soul-stomping attorney who worked for the litigation division in the D.C. office of a large law firm. Although Mike wasn't always the nicest guy, Sean had highly recommended him as necessary to get through the Democratic primary. Sean had also suggested that having an attorney on his team would give credibility to Brian's campaign, since Brian wasn't a lawyer himself. Brian trusted Sean's judgment. In fact, he was more worried about the primary than the congressional election.

"If you make it through the primary, you're home free," Mike said. He sat on the couch in Brian's rowhouse in Alexandria. "No Republican has any shot of winning this district. It's all populated by immigrants, Muslims, Somalis, Ethiopians, Hispanics. Not to mention the gentrified Old Town people, the yoga moms and such. And they never vote Republican. That's just a fact."

Old Town Alexandria was a historic section of the district that dated back to the 1700s. Politically, it leaned heavily to the left.

"As true as that may be," Sean said carefully, "It would be wise not to take anything for granted. Let's just focus on one thing at a time." He shifted his weight on the sofa and shuffled through some papers, looking for something. "Now, Hoffman's been in that seat since 1991. Technically, Mike is right in that it'd probably be extremely difficult for a Republican to be elected. However —"

"There are a lot of people who don't like Hoffman," Brian said, running a hand through his thick, brown hair. He usually kept his hair short and neatly groomed, as the wavy locks tended to get out of control. He reminded himself that he needed to get it trimmed soon, especially before making any public appearances.

Brian gave Sean a tight smile. "Who knows? People may be ready for a change. Constituents can be unpredictable." He stood up and stretched his tall, lean frame, then began pacing. It didn't do much to calm his restless energy.

"Well, you're the expert on elections," Sean replied.

Brian inclined his head in a noncommital gesture. For years, Brian had worked for a think tank in D.C., providing Democrats consulting services on how to manage local and statewide elections all over the country.

"Well," Brian corrected, "that's partly true. I only worked with Democrat clients. I don't know anything about being Republican."

"There's nothing to know," Mike scoffed.

"Who else is running in the primary?" Brian asked both men, his eyes lost in thought.

Sean looked at some papers and reeled off a list of names. "It's a grab bag of Democrats, some lawyers, some local career politicians."

"So who's running in the Republican primary?" Brian asked. "Not that we need to know that now. And assuming, of course, we make it that far." He felt confident, but knew the risk of taking something like this for granted.

Sean again looked at his lists. "Mostly local people we already know, although it seems like there's going to be one dark horse."

"Who's that?" Brian's interest was piqued, mostly because Sean seemed to be so intrigued.

"A woman, actually, the only woman running in the primary. Monica — Orellana." He pronounced her last name Orelana.

Brian's heart rate suddenly increased. He couldn't believe it. "Orellana," he corrected Sean's pronunciation, stating the double *l* as a "y" sound. "It's a Catalan name."

"You know her?" Mike asked incredulously.

"Yes — I mean, no," Brian said quickly, as an image ran through his mind of a chestnut-haired woman lying next to him, kissing his jaw and running her hand through his hair. "I know who she is."

"How do you know her?" Sean asked.

"Just — through friends. I don't really know her," he lied. "I only know who she is." He regained his composure. "She's an attorney, right?"

"That's right," said Sean. "And she's served two terms in the House of Delegates, so that's something."

"Sounds inexperienced," Mike said dismissively.

"I wouldn't call someone who was a state delegate inexperienced," Brian corrected.

"Well, you won't need to worry about her for very long," Mike said with a smirk. "No Republican lasts long in northern Virginia."

Brian wasn't so sure about Mike's statement, especially since he did know Monica. He knew her very well.

II

JUNE

Chapter 3

"You won, Mom! You won!" Monica's son David yelled his congratulations through the phone. His mother had called him first when she had found out.

"Yeah, I'm excited!" she told him. Monica had been waiting for the primary results in a rented office with Nicole, Don, and a couple of other assistants. Right now she was alone.

"So what happens now?" David asked. "What can I do? Can I help you?"

"Of course! I hope you will." Monica sighed. "Now I'm going to have to run in the general election. There will be a ton of campaign events; I hope you'll come with me. I'll also have to debate my opponent, but not for a while."

"Who are you running against?" David asked her.

"I don't know yet. I'm waiting for the results now."

The Democratic primary for this district had been much closer than the Republican one. Monica had been heartened to discover that some people had even remembered her from the pro bono work that she did with the local bar association. It had also helped that Don and Nicole had made sure people knew about her.

"Honestly, David," Monica said, trying to think realistically, "this is just one of many hurdles. It's probably even the least difficult one."

"Well, I'm proud of you, Mom," her son said.

Monica almost became tearful. David was easily one of the only people in her life who kept her sane. "Thanks, sweetheart. Look, tell your father that I'll be home later, and not to wait up."

David's enthusiasm made Monica happy, especially since her husband had been less than thrilled.

"You have no chance of winning this," Christian had told her. "I don't understand why you insist on doing it."

Of course you don't understand, Monica had thought. You resent my success, and you resent my ambition. You used to be ambitious, too, but now you just drift in life, as if you're in neutral.

Monica's phone blipped, bringing her back to the present. "Hey, your aunt is calling me on the other line," she told David.

"Okay, no worries. See you later, Mom!"

"Okay, bye, sweetheart. And don't stay up too late!"

Monica smiled and switched her cell phone to the other line.

"Hey!" she said exuberantly into her phone.

"Hey, hey!!" her sister said. "Congratulations!!"

Monica's sister was the only other person who kept her sane. "Valentina, ¿como estas?"

"Pues, super bien! Felicidades, mujer! I can't believe you won!"

At thirty-two years old, her sister was twelve years younger than Monica. Their father hailed from Barcelona, Spain and had immigrated to the U.S. with his family when he was a teenager. Their mother was also from a Spanish family, near Madrid, but had been born and raised stateside. Like Monica, her sister Val had long, curly hair. Unlike Monica, Val's hair was blonder. However, they had the same smile.

Their parents had apparently only planned on having one child. Their mother's second pregnancy had been a complete shock, but Monica could not have been happier to have a sibling, especially after being alone for twelve years.

Their parents had been much more lax with Val, and that may have been a factor in Val's more free-spirited nature. Where Monica was irreverent, Val was downright inappropriate. Where Monica got angry, Val got livid. With her family and friends, Val was outgoing, adventurous, and fiercely loyal.

At her job she was a consummate professional. Val was a surgical resident at one of the teaching hospitals in Washington, D.C. Like her attorney sister, she had the reputation of being a ballbuster.

"I can't believe it, either!" Monica almost shouted into the phone.

At that very moment, Don came rushing into the room. "Hey, boss!" he said to Monica, smiling suggestively.

Monica winked at him, then said into the phone, "Hey, Val, I should go. It's late and I have to talk to the gang here before I head home."

"No problem. Congrats again! And I love you!"

"I love you, too," Monica told her, then hung up. She turned toward Don.

"Congratulations," he said, rushing up to her, then stopping short a few inches from her.

"Thank *you*, for all your hard work."

"We should all go out for a drink tonight," Don said hopefully.

"I can't. I should go home. My family will be waiting for me."

"They'll understand if you stay out for a bit to celebrate."

"I can't tonight." Christian is going to be pissed off enough as it is, Monica thought. She believed he had honestly wanted her to lose.

Traditionally, the candidate's family stayed with the candidate on primary night, to (hopefully) celebrate the results together. But Christian had preferred to watch the results from home, and Monica had wanted to be with her team for solidarity. David had stayed home with Christian.

"Why didn't he come with you tonight?" Don asked.

"He has work, and figured David would be bored here." Monica realized how weak the excuse sounded.

"Gotcha."

Monica changed the subject. "Please start by working the donors. Money. We need money, Donald."

"I know, I know."

"Money talks," Monica said, "and shit walks."

Don laughed.

Nicole barged in just then, making Monica jump.

"What's going on, Nic?"

"Democrat primary results just came in," Nicole said breathlessly.

"And?" Monica and Don both asked together.

Nicole grinned broadly. "I think it's really good news for you."

The seconds seemed to tick by slowly. Monica held up her hands in a Spanish-style gesture of impatience.

"You'll be running against Brian Murphy."

Monica felt as if she had been kicked in the gut. This could not be happening. If someone had told her five or six years ago that things would turn out this way, she would have laughed in their face.

"I think that's good news, too," Don agreed. "From what I know, he's pretty much a political novice. And, like you said, Monica, he's from California, and you're a lifelong resident of this area. I mean, he's got basically no connection to Virginia. That'll work against him."

16

"Okay," Monica pretended to agree, nodding her head. "Look, you two. It's late. We're all tired. Let's get some rest and meet tomorrow morning. We'll need to rent an office on a more long-term basis, among other things."

"I'm already working on that," Don grinned broadly.

"Excellent," Monica said. After hugging both of them, she went to the bathroom and splashed cold water on her face. She felt a bit nauseous.

Monica took a few deep breaths and began to calm down. Then there was a sharp knock on the bathroom door. She almost jumped out of her skin.

"I'm heading out, Monica," Nicole said through the door.

"Okay, see you soon," Monica replied. She had her hand on the doorknob when her cell phone blipped.

Monica looked at her phone. She had a single text message from an unknown number.

Monica stood silently for a moment, reading the message.

Hey, this is Brian. We should probably talk.

Monica realized that she had been holding her breath. She let it out in one sharp exhale and felt as if she were about to faint. When she had recovered, she texted back.

Call me tomorrow on my cell.

Monica looked up from her cell phone and into the mirror, staring at her own reflection. She took a deep breath and recited aloud a verse that she had been citing since college, since she had first read the science fiction novel *Dune*. The verse was known as the Litany Against Fear. She almost always recited it when under pressure.

"I will not fear," she paraphrased, "I will face the fear."

She inhaled and exhaled deeply one more time, and headed home.

Chapter 4

Monica's team didn't waste any time. It was June, and that left little time until the November congressional election. The day after the primary results came in, Nicole, Don, and Monica met at Monica's house.

"Okay," Don began, "I've got a couple of places here that we could rent to use as your campaign office."

Monica and Nicole looked over the locales and narrowed it down to two of them.

"The rent on these seems high, but it's competitive for the area, and the size is about right," Nicole said.

"I'm okay with either of them. You guys pick," Monica said. "And Don, how is the list of volunteers coming? Make sure you include the Republican National Lawyers Association, Federalist Society, law school Republican groups, etc."

"Will do," Don answered, smiling. "You're the boss."

Monica sighed. "I'm going to be honest with you guys. I've been thinking a lot about this." In fact, it had kept her up most of the night. "I'm not really sure how much money we'll be able to raise. I mean — the establishment already thinks this is a lost cause because of the voter makeup of this district."

"Hey, it's been done before," Don said confidently.

"True," Monica said. "I think we'll need to do more of a grassroots, boots-on-the-ground approach. But, honestly, I'm not sure how well that will work in northern Virginia."

"I agree that we should follow that strategy," Nicole said, while Don nodded. "If people know you, and you have strong ties to the community, then they will be more likely to vote for you."

"Here's the thing that worries me," Monica said. The pessimistic, risk-averse attorney took over. "We need to start that sooner, not later. But — the sooner we start it, the sooner the other side will know what we're doing, and they'll take action. Then the Democratic machine will kick in, and they'll be flooded with money."

"Not necessarily," Nicole countered. "The thing is, Monica, they're going to be expecting an easy ride. They expect to just cruise to victory in November, so the party will divert money to other candidates. And frankly, I want them to *think* they have an easy ride."

"I want to take a scorched earth approach," Monica said.

"What do you mean?" Don asked, pensive.

"An all-out blitz. Ads, endorsements, interviews with people who know me —"

"Pro bono clients," Don added.

"If they're willing to be interviewed, yes. Campaign stops, conferences, address the local bar associations — he's not an attorney, remember?" Monica sighed. She couldn't bring herself to say Brian's name. "Also, town hall meetings, all that."

"Don't forget the debates," Don said.

Monica's gut wrenched again. The idea of having to appear on stage, on television no less, debating Brian, was more than she wanted to think about at that moment.

"Can you get me on national news shows? And radio?"

"I can do that," Don said, nodding fiercely.

"Let's do all that."

"Scorched earth," Don echoed, smiling. "I like that."

"Also," Monica pondered. "I want to have meetings with the volunteers so that we all know how we're going to explain our positions. How we can answer questions when we go door-to-door." She turned to Nicole. "Nic, remember in law school, when we did mock trial? We were taught to always anticipate the one question we did not want to be asked, and then to make sure we had an answer for it."

Nicole nodded, smiling.

Monica went on. "We need to instruct the volunteers on how to address all the issues, how, when they go door-to-door, they can articulate our position. The Democrats have been controlling the rhetoric for far too long in this district. And remember —"

"We know, we know," Don said. "You're not a social conservative."

"Yes, but we need to put the social conservatives at ease, too."

"We'll do that," Don said.

"When this campaign is over, I want to have spent every penny," Monica said with determination. "It makes no damn sense to have money left unspent."

"Totally agree," Nicole said.

"And if the President campaigns with him —" Monica said. "I mean, I don't see why he wouldn't; it's right here in his own backyard."

"That will only happen if he thinks he's in trouble," Nicole told her.

Monica frowned. "I don't want him to *think* he's in trouble. I want him to *be* in trouble."

Monica's cell phone rang. She picked it up, and her chest tightened. It was Brian.

"It's Christian," she lied to her friends. "Hold on a minute. I'll take this upstairs."

As she went up the stairs to her bedroom, she answered. "Hello?"

"Hey." The voice was calm, nostalgic. Her heart wrenched. It had been a very long time since she had heard it.

"Sorry, who is this?" she asked, although she knew perfectly well who it was.

"It's Brian."

"Oh, hey. I was surprised when you texted last night. How did you have my number?"

"I've always had your number."

Monica ignored the hidden implication in that statement. "Well, what can I do for you?" she said instead. Then she couldn't resist. "It's about 2:30 in the afternoon. Are you just waking up? That's about right for you Millennials, isn't it?"

Brian chuckled lightly on the other end of the phone. "No, I've been up for a while."

"So spill it."

"We should talk, don't you think?"

"About what?"

"Come on, Monica, this isn't easy for me either."

She resented his matter-of-fact tone. "As I recall, it was very easy for you." Both the screwing and the leaving, Monica thought.

"Look —"

"No, *you* look," Monica said angrily. "It's all in the past. I don't want to relive it —"

"I'm not asking you to. Let's just meet and talk and decide, between just ourselves, how to handle it."

"You mean — meet — just you and me?" She hesitated.

"Just to come to a decision on how we're going to handle it, that's all."

"So no one knows? I mean, no one on your end?"

"That's right."

Monica sighed, then couldn't think of anything to say.

"Hey," Brian started, "please just — just meet me, just the two of us — we won't tell anyone we're meeting — just to decide, like, just to strategize —"

"I don't know." She didn't like the duplicity of a secret meeting; it made her feel guilty all over again.

"Please. We can meet wherever you want. Besides — I just want to know that you're okay."

Monica wanted to believe that. "Don't talk like that, Brian. We both know it's not true." But he *had* saved her number.

"It would be better for your campaign anyway, if you decided sooner rather than later how you were going to handle this."

While Monica resented his attempt to convince her, she knew that he told the truth. She remembered something he had said, when they were together, about how to deal with issues like that. You needed to have a strategy; then it was less likely that the shit would hit the fan. She told herself that that was why she wanted to meet with him.

"Okay," she said softly.

Chapter 5

"Tell me everything you know about Brian Murphy," Don said.

Monica almost jumped off the sofa. "What do you mean?"

"Well, you seem to know more about him than Nicole and I do."

Monica relaxed a bit. "I mean, he's from San Francisco, he's about ten years younger than me. He's an atheist —"

"How do you know that?"

"I just remember."

"I thought you didn't know him that well."

"I *don't*. But there are things that I remember." Like that he would touch my hand sometimes, and that he wouldn't eat when he was stressed, and would get really skinny, thinner than usual, and then I would worry about him, Monica thought.

"He's an only child. He's kind of hipster, like most Millennials, I guess," Monica continued.

"He doesn't appear to be *that* hipster," Nicole said then. "Not by how he dresses and stuff."

"Well, he went to school in Seattle," Monica said, then regretted it.

"How do you know *that?*" Nicole asked, curious.

Monica shrugged. "I looked it up online," she lied.

Nicole looked at Monica over her thick-rimmed glasses.

"He's just a typical liberal Democrat — I don't know what to tell you guys." Monica chewed a nail. "He's pretty type A — as far as I know," she added quickly, then tried to cover. "That bit of knowledge may come in handy during the debates, I don't know —" Her voice trailed off. She remembered that he could also have a temper if people pushed him too far, but she didn't say that.

"Okay, well, we'll keep digging," Nicole said. "The fact that he's from the West Coast should work against him here. I mean, you've been in the Virginia House of Delegates for two terms and he's never even held public office."

"Hopefully voters will see it that way," Monica said.

"He's married, right?" Nicole asked.

"Lives with his girlfriend," Don said. "I just found that out recently. Her name's Abby something or other."

Monica sighed. So he was still with the same girl, she thought. Brian's girlfriend was a sore point for her for many reasons.

"I heard they've been together a long time," Nicole said. "Don't know why they aren't married."

Monica found the subsequent silence uncomfortable. "How are we doing on the volunteer list?"

"Good!" Don said animatedly. "We're also going to distribute the usual stuff, bumper stickers, yard signs, you know —"

"Okay, great. Who's going to be managing our finances?"

Nicole replied, then spent the next thirty minutes going over the most important members of Monica's campaign staff and their tasks. Her team was coming together, bit by bit.

Chapter 6

"I think you know more about this woman than you let on at first," Mike said to Brian.

This *woman?* Brian thought with annoyance. He shrugged. "I've just been doing some research, that's all."

Mike, Brian, and Sean were at Brian's rowhouse. They were beginning to outline campaign tactics, and were reviewing their list of potential big-ticket donors.

"So what have you found out?" Mike pressed.

Brian looked at Sean, who had his arms crossed. "Well, she's a Latin Catholic; her parents are from Spain; she's fluent in Spanish. That will certainly help her in this district. She grew up in the DC area. She has a younger sister." He sighed. "She's married, with a kid."

"She's pretty hot," Mike said irreverently.

Brian rolled his eyes. Why did Mike have to say that? he thought. Now all he could think about was Monica naked, with her full breasts rubbing against his chest.

"We shouldn't talk about her in those terms," Brian told him. "People will say it's anti-feminist."

"But it's true. Don't tell me you don't agree."

"Even if it's true, we shouldn't say it," Brian snapped. It didn't seem right to talk about Monica like that with Mike.

"He's right, Mike," Sean said. "It's not appropriate." Sean gave

Mike a chiding look, which looked strange on his youthful face. Sean's blue eyes showed with something short of disdain.

Then Sean seemed to remember something. "Oh!" he exclaimed. "And I know her communications director. Nicole Simms. She does, or did, policy work with the DNC. We worked together in the past."

"That's absolutely brilliant," Brian said in admiration.

"Doesn't having a Dem as her communications director hurt her credibility with Republicans?" Mike said.

"Probably not so much in this District," Brian answered, pensive. "She's likely banking on the fact that even if it bothers some Republicans, they would still vote for her over me. Anyway —" he remembered a conversation he had had with Monica years ago. "Monica would say that Nicole is politically very similar to her and that she's really a libertarian calling herself a Democrat."

"Why would a DNC attorney be helping a Republican?" Mike couldn't believe it.

"Not everyone is as polarized as you," Sean said, then turned to Brian. "They're close friends from law school. And Nicole has a very good reputation with Democrats; she's honest and respectful, even of the other side."

"Well, I don't like it," Mike insisted. "It gives Monica credibility with Democrats."

"That's why it's so brilliant." Brian raised his eyebrows. He remembered telling Monica at one time that most people outside of the D.C. bubble were not partisan, and tended to vote for the candidate rather than the party. He smiled, then continued. "I'm telling you, Monica won't go down without a fight."

"How do you know that?" Sean asked. His eyes held a loaded

question.

"I know enough about her to know that she's pretty aggressive."

"Based on what my attorney colleagues say about her, that's mostly true," Mike agreed. "It's still going to be an uphill battle for her. I'm not worried."

Brian shook his head and pressed his lips together. "Maybe you should be."

Chapter 7

Monica had agreed to meet Brian at 9:30 that night at the pier in Old Town Alexandria. It was more of a trek for Brian than for her, but Monica didn't care. He had said that they could meet wherever she wanted, and she had taken that statement at face value.

Monica sat waiting on a bench on the pier. The sun had set a while ago, and the air was a bit cooler. After strategizing with Nicole and Don most of the day, she had run home and changed into jeans and a black V-neck T-shirt. She leaned against the back of the bench, refusing to look around for Brian. If he wanted to talk to her, then he could find her.

She was anxious to see him; she couldn't help it. But the entire situation sucked. She hated the fact that she was forced to have contact with him.

"Hey, there." The tone was friendly.

Monica turned her head and there he was, in work clothes, khakis and a long-sleeved shirt and tie.

"Hey," Monica said back, exhaling.

She couldn't believe how good he looked. He was in his thirties now, and his dark, wavy hair was exactly as she remembered it, if a little more trimmed. She was reminded how his high cheekbones and straight nose gave him a patrician look, which somehow made him seem older.

28

He was trim, but his fitted dress shirt suggested that he was muscular rather than skinny. He gave her a rare smile, one that she had once pretended was reserved only for her.

Monica couldn't help smiling back, even if weakly.

"You look great," Brian told her.

"Thanks," she said, a bit taken aback by the compliment. "Sit down," she inclined her head to the bench. He sat, with about two feet of distance between them.

"Thanks for coming out here," she said. Now that he was here, she felt bad that she had made him come all this way to meet her.

"No problem."

They both gazed at the Potomac in silence for a few moments.

"So how have you been?" he asked. He turned his head toward her, but she didn't look at him.

"Great," she said. "So this is the typical DC intrigue, right? Clandestine meetings? Jesus Christ," Monica sighed, shaking her head.

Brian chuckled a little. "For a Catholic, you're so blasphemous."

"Says the atheist. Anyway, you can hardly call me a practicing Catholic now, can you?" She chanced a brief glance in his direction and met his eyes, then looked back at the water.

"So is this how it's going to be?" Brian said carefully. "You constantly pissed off at me?"

"I would think so, yeah," Monica said without looking at him. "I mean, how would you expect it to be?" She still felt his eyes on her.

"I was kind of hoping we could be friends or —" he hesitated, catching himself, "at least civil."

His statement offended Monica. He hadn't gotten in contact

with her during the past few years, which, in her mind, reflected that he had no desire to have any contact with her. He only had contact with her now because he was forced to. Just like before, she thought, when he had seen her only because he had needed to get laid.

She huffed and shook her head. "That's bullshit. Brian, we are running against each other in a congressional campaign. Even if we didn't have a past, we still wouldn't be friends. And — even if we weren't in this campaign — I still couldn't be your friend." She instantly regretted her last statement, because that meant that she still felt something, and she hadn't wanted to admit that.

Brian sighed. "I'm sorry to hear that," he said tightly as he pulled his tie to straighten it.

"Yeah, well, that's how it is," Monica said with resignation, then changed the course of the conversation, eager to get it over with. "So you said you haven't told anyone, right?"

"Right."

"Well, I haven't either." Monica looked at him. "So what are you thinking? That we just don't say anything, and pretend like it didn't happen, and hope that no one will find out?"

"That was pretty much my plan," he told her.

"So no one knows about it?" Monica asked again.

"No one."

"Wrong answer, Brian."

"You told someone?" His eyes widened.

"No, I've never told anyone. But your roommate saw me, remember?"

"Well, yes." Brian exhaled and seemed pensive. Then he looked at Monica. "He won't say anything."

"I wish I could believe that."

"Monica, it was a long time ago. I'm sure he doesn't even remember."

"Have you talked to him?"

"No, not for a long time."

"It's something we should consider, Brian. How to deal with it if people find out."

"I don't think that will happen."

"You know I'm a pessimist, so I have my doubts."

"And you know I'm one, too," he said. "But, lately, I've tried to be more optimistic."

Their eyes met.

Monica broke the moment. "Then I think we should plan for the worst-case scenario."

Brian grinned broadly. "You mean the zombie apocalypse?"

Monica couldn't help laughing. He had apparently remembered her predilection for science fiction.

"Exactly."

They looked at each other briefly.

"So, are we agreed then?" Monica began. "That neither one of us will say anything to anyone, and we'll just hope that no one finds out?"

Brian sighed. "Yes, I think so."

"Okay." That had pretty much been Monica's plan anyway. "But," she added, "what if people *do* find out?"

Brian sighed. "We'll do damage control. I mean — if people find out —" he struggled for words, "we'll just deal with it and move on."

It was the "deal with it" part that was so nebulous to Monica. She thought that if the worst happened, then neither side would want to dwell on it since both sides were involved. It was indeed a unique, and highly uncomfortable, situation.

Monica stood up, eager to get out of there, and Brian followed suit. They faced each other.

She wanted to reach out and touch his hair so badly.

"So you feel pretty good about this election?" Monica asked him instead.

"Yes," he said, smiling.

"I mean, you don't know much, if anything, about Virginia."

"You don't know much about elections." He suddenly appeared defensive.

Monica ignored his statement, even if it was not entirely true. She certainly did not have the campaign consulting experience that Brian had, but she *had* run for and held office.

"Well, you don't know anything about being Republican," she countered.

"And you know something about being Democrat?"

Monica nodded. "I had an excellent teacher." She looked into his eyes one last time and turned to walk away.

"It was good to see you," Brian called after her.

"Whatever," Monica said, giving him a half-wave without turning around.

As Monica ambled around before heading home, she got a call from Don.

"I'm working on some endorsements for you," Don told her right away.

"Awesome. Let me know what you need me to do."

"And I got a call from Sean today."

"Who's Sean?" Monica asked.

"He's Murphy's communications director. Nicole knows him. They both worked at the DNC together."

"What did he want?" Monica was automatically suspicious.

32

"He wants us to meet, kind of like an icebreaker."

"Why?" Monica's thoughts became frantic. She had just seen Brian, and didn't want to think about having to see him again.

"He says for goodwill, to avoid partisanship. But my interpretation is that it's a publicity ploy." He continued. "I think it means that they're a bit skittish about the election in general. I have a feeling that they want to size you up."

"So we won't agree to it." Monica's statement was not a question.

"But if we say no, then we look too petty. They will be seen as reaching out to us, across party lines, blah blah, you understand?"

"Yes, but I still don't think it's a good idea."

"Hey," Don said then.

Monica sighed.

"Do you trust me?" he asked.

"Yes," she nodded, even though he couldn't see the gesture.

"I think we should do it. Don't worry, no media, it will be lowkey. Just lunch or something."

"Let's do coffee, like, in the morning. Coffee and donuts or something," Monica negotiated.

"OK, you got it."

"Set it up then."

"You're the boss."

There was silence for a few seconds.

"Is that it?" Monica asked.

"Monica, how long have we known each other?"

Monica had met Don at a Republican National Committee event a couple of years ago. He was smart and had impressed her with his background in political organizing and campaigning. They had been friends for a while, and he had been eager to assist

THUNDERSTRUCK

in her campaign. Recently, he had been giving off a vibe that suggested that he was interested in her as more than a friend. She hadn't paid much attention to it since she was married and they were in the middle of a campaign.

She was surprised at the question, but too tired to protest. "I don't know, a couple of years. Why?"

"Is that long enough for me to ask you a personal question?"

"Shoot." Monica stifled a yawn.

"Maybe it would be better if Nicole asked you."

"*What?*"

"How's your relationship with your husband?"

Monica stopped walking, brows furrowing. "Why?"

"He wasn't with you on primary night —"

"What are you trying to say, Donald? Bottom line, please."

"It looks better if he's with you at campaign events. That's all."

"Gotcha."

"So if you can convince him to come out with you, that would be best."

"I got it."

"Thanks. That's all."

They hung up and Monica stood frozen, looking at the ground, thinking.

Chapter 8

Brian arrived home that night to a dark house. He lived with his longtime girlfriend, Abby. They had been together for eight years, and everyone wondered why they hadn't gotten married yet. They used to occasionally talk about it, but about two years ago those conversations had ceased.

Abby was either working late or out with her friends. They really didn't see much of each other. And when they were together, they were only physical a small fraction of the time.

Brian cared about her but didn't like being alone all of the time.

He ordered something for dinner, then his thoughts turned to Monica.

He couldn't believe how gorgeous she was, and how in control she seemed to be. She was the same as he remembered, confident, self-assured, always saying what was on her mind. He had always appreciated those traits in her.

And her eyes. He had always remembered looking into her sometimes golden, sometimes greenish eyes, especially when they were in bed together and she would wink and smile at him. When she smiled, she easily looked ten to fifteen years younger, especially since she didn't have as many lines around her eyes as he did.

He took a deep breath and instantly smelled a sweet, gingery scent, an olfactory memory from earlier that night when he had stood close to Monica. It had made him remember burying his face in her thick hair, with the scent of her lotion all around him.

At the moment, he lamented that they had stopped seeing each other. Most of all, however, he lamented the manner in which they had stopped seeing each other. He had no one but himself to blame for that.

Monica had been hoping that she would feel nothing, that she would see Brian, and that he would be just another man, another misguided Millennial.

But it hadn't been quite like that. She had felt things that she didn't want to feel, and she hated it. At that moment she hated him. She felt angry and hurt all over again.

When Monica lay down in bed that night next to her husband, she felt guilty. It didn't matter that they hardly ever had sex, or that he resented her successes, or that sometimes he took out his stress on her and their son by raising his voice. She knew that if she wasn't happy, she should just end it. They would both be better off that way, and David would live through it because he had two parents who loved him.

But Monica knew that it would hurt Christian. It was a horrible situation. If she left him, he would get hurt, and she would be a pariah. Their friends would probably hate her; Christian's family would ostracize her. And if she stayed, she herself would be stuck in an emotionless marriage, starved for intimacy and contact. Could she live with that for the rest of her life?

Monica looked at her husband's back. He appeared to be asleep. She thought about putting her arms around him from behind. In the past, she had loved to do that.

"I'm sorry I got back so late," she told him.

"It's okay." But she knew he didn't mean it.

Whenever she thought about leaving him, she would try to remember the beginnings of their relationship, when it had been better. And now, even though they had issues, there were still times when he was thoughtful. He would occasionally make her coffee when she was in a rush and would leave her the last of the fresh strawberries, which she loved. Monica always tried to let those memories carry her through the rough times. The problem was that the rough times had become more and more frequent.

Chapter 9

Don had scheduled a breakfast meeting with Monica's opponent and his two right-hand people.

Monica dreaded it. She was also constantly petrified that someone would find out about her past with Brian. Well, maybe their shared past could work to her advantage. After all, if the Democratic machine dug too deeply into her past, they would find out about Brian's. He thus had an incentive to keep it quiet.

"I still don't understand why we have to do this," Monica said in the taxi on the way over to Brian's campaign office. "I mean, I *understand*, I guess. I just don't see why we *should*."

"Would you please just smile and be nice?" Don said to her from the front passenger seat.

"It's not a big deal," Nicole assured her. "And Sean is really nice. I know him."

"But I heard the other guy's a real jerk," Monica said.

"And watch your language when we're in there," Don told her.

"Why?" Monica insisted. She had almost said, Brian knows I'm abrasive.

"Because we want them to think that you're this demure, docile woman. We don't want them to know yet what you're really like."

"And what am I really like?" Monica crossed her arms and

twitched her lips in an amused smile.

Don smirked but said nothing.

It doesn't matter, Monica thought. Brian knows what I'm really like.

They arrived at their destination and filed out of the car.

Monica wore a black suit with a pencil skirt. Her long hair hung in waves down her back and shoulders. She usually wore minimal makeup. Today, she only had on eyeliner and mascara.

They walked into the office and Don checked in with the receptionist. Monica looked around.

"These are your peeps," she said to Nicole, smiling.

"*You* are my peeps, friend," Nicole replied.

Monica laughed. "Did I ever tell you how much I appreciate you doing this for me?"

"You have."

"Well, I'm saying it again."

Nicole gave Monica a warm smile.

"You can follow me, please," the receptionist said to them.

The three of them followed her through the main office, which was a cube environment. As they entered, conversations seemed to hush, or at least lower in timbre.

Monica leaned toward Nicole's ear. "What's going on?" she whispered.

"For most of them it's probably the first time they have ever seen you in person."

"Ah." Monica thought of Don's comment about "sizing her up." She was afraid this invitation was no more than a mere ploy, but Nicole and Don had more campaign experience than she did, so she deferred to them.

They were ushered into an office with a large window, letting in plenty of sun on this summer morning. There was a large desk in front of the window, and a table laden with coffee and pastries.

Don stayed protectively at Monica's side. Her opponent turned around and greeted each of them in turn. When Brian shook Monica's hand, he looked into her eyes. Monica wanted to look away, but couldn't. She gripped his hand firmly, and tried not to look uncomfortable.

"Hi, I'm Sean." Monica was brought back to reality as Sean stuck his hand out toward her. She took it, gripping it as firmly as he gripped hers. Monica guessed that he was older than he looked. His skin was clear and smooth, and his eyes were bright and friendly.

"I think you two know each other, right?" Sean asked her, gesturing toward Brian.

"Ah, yes," Monica began, "just from — you know, D.C. circles." Then she remembered something. "And you know Nicole, I believe."

"Yes, from work. Although I must admit," Sean said, directing his gaze to Nicole, "it's a bit odd seeing you on the other side of the fence."

Monica thought she detected a hint of flirtation from Sean toward Nicole, but wasn't sure.

"Yeah, well," Nicole shrugged, "you know I'm not a follower. I go with the best candidate, not necessarily the one with the D behind his name." She gave Sean a winning smile, showing white teeth against her light brown skin.

"You always support candidates with little to no experience?" Mike asked. Monica caught Brian pursing his lips in apparent annoyance. He held up a hand and opened his mouth to speak, but Monica cut him off.

"Well, *you* obviously do," Monica said to Mike. "Just because he used to consult doesn't mean he has experience leading anything," she added as she jerked a thumb in Brian's general direction. "Plus, he's never held any office of any kind. Plus, to my knowledge he's never even lived in Virginia before. *Plus,*" Monica emphasized, raising her voice to cut Mike off from speaking, "when was the last time a Millennial ever *solved* anything?" Her last comment was a cheap shot, and she knew it. Because she knew Brian, and she knew that he was quite intelligent and a hard worker. She also knew that despite their different party affiliations, they actually agreed on some issues.

"Oh, and you *do* have leadership experience?" Mike was relentless.

"Okay, okay," Brian said, holding up his hands and asserting control over the situation. He looked at Monica. "I'm sorry for what he said. It was *not* appropriate," he emphasized, then glared at Mike.

"Look," Brian continued, spreading his arms out as he talked. "We just wanted to have you guys over today to say hi."

And to size me up, Monica thought. She crossed her arms and tried to look nonchalant, but realized that she probably came off as looking annoyed.

"Well, hi, then," Nicole said. Monica could tell that her friend had her guard up.

Brian smiled slightly. Seeing his smile again made Monica sad.

Suddenly she hated being there and wanted to leave. But she knew she couldn't, so she told herself that she could freak out later.

She accepted a cup of coffee from Sean, but refused any food. She had already eaten, and was too nervous and overstimulated, anyway.

The group made inoffensive small talk for awhile, and the morning continued without incident.

As Monica and her friends were poised to leave, Monica with one foot outside the door already, Mike asked her one last question. "So you feel pretty good about this campaign?"

She turned to look at him, smiling a bit deviously. "Oh, it'll be an uphill battle all the way. But who knows?" She shrugged. "Maybe I'll get a consulting gig out of it, or a pundit position on a cable news network. Don't worry about me. I'll be just fine."

After the door closed and they knew that the other three had left the premises, Mike turned to Brian.

"Man, she does *not* like you," he said.

Sean looked surprised. "That's funny. I kind of got the impression that it was *you* she didn't like," he said to Mike.

Mike grimaced. "With the way she berated his lack of experience?"

"That's just campaign talk," Sean said. "And she gave us a clue as to what she'll be focusing on in the coming weeks."

"That's no secret," Brian said, unimpressed. "You know she'll emphasize my youth, lack of connection to Virginia, no prior political office, all that stuff. And she would be right to focus on all that. If I were her, I would."

"Well, I will say," Mike said, "she's even more attractive in person." He whistled slightly.

"Stop," Brian said, annoyed. Something else bothered him. He didn't like the way Don had stood so close to Monica, hanging on her every word.

He likes her, he thought. He wondered how much influence Don had over her, and wondered how they had met.

"Never make those kinds of statements in public, Mike," Sean said with a serious tone. "The other side would have a field day with that, calling us chauvinists, and other worse things."

"All right, all right," Mike held up his hands. Then he walked toward the door. "I'm going to get the donor lists and take a look at the calendar. We're going to schedule some fundraising events soon," he said as he left.

After a few moments, Sean turned toward Brian. "So — Monica —"

Brian had been deep in thought, but at the mention of Monica's name, he looked at his friend.

Sean continued. "She's a firecracker, isn't she?"

Brian could tell that the question was serious, not meant as a joke.

"Yes," Brian nodded. "That's why I said that we should take her seriously." His voice had a guarded edge to it.

Sean lowered his voice and asked cautiously, "And I think you know her better than you said you did, isn't that right?"

Brian looked directly at him. "I don't know what you're talking about." His tone shut down all further questioning. Then he looked at his watch. "I'm going to go talk to Mike about those events."

Brian hurried out the door.

Chapter 10

The following Sunday, Monica, Christian, and David drove to Monica's parents' house. Her parents lived about half an hour away. Val was also going to be there, since she had one of her rare days off.

Christian drove while Monica looked out of the window.

"Hey, Mom?" David asked his mother from the backseat.

"Yes, sweetheart?" She looked back.

"Dad says you're going to be gone a lot, with the campaign and stuff."

Monica sighed. "Well, we'll have to do events, interviews, debates, things like that. But everything will be local."

"Can I come with you?" David asked.

"Why would you want to go?" his father said. "It will be boring."

Monica pursed her lips, feeling resentful. She hoped to fire up the crowds, make them see that she was a true leader. Her husband really had no idea what she was all about, she thought.

Although he agreed with her politically, for the most part, and he complained about the current state of the country, that was all he did, complain. When she had first talked about doing something about it, she had thought that he would be supportive. He ended up being only tacitly supportive. She had the impression that deep down he just wanted her to go to her

44

law firm job and bring home the big money. She had always been the breadwinner in the household, and she feared that he resented her for that. Not for the first time, she wondered what she was still doing in the relationship.

"No, Dad, I think it'll be really cool!" David pressed. "So I can go, right?"

"Of course!" Monica said with enthusiasm.

"No," her husband said at the same time.

David and Monica sighed simultaneously.

"Your father and I will talk about it," she told her son.

"He can't miss school, anyway," Christian went on.

"Well, he could at least come with me during the summertime." They pulled into her parents' driveway. Christian put the car in park and said to his wife, as if it were an afterthought, "Honestly, you don't really think you have a chance, do you?"

She looked squarely at him. "That's what they told Scott Brown before he won Ted Kennedy's old seat," she countered.

"Well, last time I checked, he wasn't Senator there anymore."

"So, what then?" Monica said angrily. "I'm just supposed to sit here and watch? It's bad enough we have a Governor who's from up north, who doesn't know the first thing about Virginia. What happens when all the money they're firehosing dries up, and there's no one left to foot the bill?" She bit her lip to keep from saying more, then opened the car door and got out.

Why did Christian have to say those things in front of David? she thought. Couldn't he at least wait until they were alone? It was bad enough they obviously had issues in their marriage, but they didn't have to air them in front of their only child.

Monica was happy to see her sister's car there. It was 2pm, Spanish lunch time. Her mother would have invariably prepared the typical Spanish midday meal.

As they entered her parents' house, Monica continued to turn over thoughts in her head. Even though her husband had been born in the U.S., in her opinion he maintained some of the typical Latin traits, many of which she found to be negative. The machismo, for instance, and the insecurity of dealing with an independent woman who always spoke her mind. At that moment, Monica pretty much decided that, once the campaign was over, however it went, she would seriously consider leaving him.

As expected, Monica's mother had prepared an incredible amount of food, paella, *tortilla de patatas*, salad and *escalivada*, a Catalan dish consisting of marinated vegetables.

Val arrived a bit late. When the sisters saw each other, they hugged for a long time.

"*¡Felicidades, mujer!*" Val exclaimed. "I finally get to congratulate you in person!" Val was taller than her sister, five feet ten inches as compared to Monica's five-foot-seven-inch height. And where Monica had hips and large, round breasts, Val was leaner. Part of that was due to the fact that Monica had given birth and Val hadn't, and part was due to the fact that Val's schedule was so crazy that she hardly had any time to eat. Val's curly hair hung over her shoulders in an unruly mass.

"*Has hecho muy bien!*" their father said, then continued in accented English. "The only woman in the race and you beat all the men. I love it!"

Monica smiled at her family's show of support.

"Well, don't assume I'll win in November. Odds are that I won't, so don't get too optimistic, you guys."

Her mother chimed in then, once again raining on Monica's parade. "Can you tell me again why you're doing this?" She held herself erect, chin up, staring haughtily at her daughter.

Monica's smile faded, and silence fell on the company. Her mother must have asked her that same question at least ten times.

"I've told you before, Mom," Monica said defiantly. "I'm tired of the same old policies, of the same old people in office. It's time for someone from the outside, someone who is *not* a career politician, to take charge and get things done."

"Yes, but, can't someone else run?" Her mother set a dish on the dining table, and Monica was unsure whether she was even listening.

Her mother had been quite attractive when she was younger, and even at her age still had much black hair mixed in with the gray. Indeed, she appeared much younger than her near-seventy years.

Monica didn't know why she even bothered explaining these things to her mother. She never seemed to actually hear her.

"I get it, Mom," Monica said, exasperated. "You think I should just be home, taking care of my family —"

"I didn't say that —"

"— like you did."

"Well, if that's how you interpret it."

Monica wasn't sure what bothered her more, her mother's passive aggressive behavior or the fact that she must consider Monica so stupid as not to notice.

Monica took a deep breath, consciously reminding herself, once again, that she was in charge of her own destiny.

"Anyway," she changed the subject, refusing to take her mother's bait, "my team has a tough road ahead of us. So don't expect me to win. It would be great — don't get me wrong — but don't expect it."

"Yes, but that other guy is too young, and has no experience," her father said.

That other guy, Monica thought sadly. That guy I used to sleep with, unload to when I had arguments with Christian, confide in when I was stressed. That guy who I —

"Valentina, you are so skinny," their mother said. "I'll give you food to take home with you."

Monica smiled. Their mother never called *her* skinny.

Monica's parents then took turns interrogating David about his school and friends.

Lunch was excellent, as always. Over espresso, Val asked a ton of questions about the campaign.

"So tell me about your opponent. Do you know him?"

I wish I didn't, Monica thought. "I know who he is. I don't really *know* him, though," she lied.

Lying to Nicole and Don had been bad enough, but lying to her sister, her alter ego, was like tearing her heart out.

"He's kind of cute," Val said, smiling.

Monica smiled sadly. She had thought so, too. "Well, he's about your age."

"He's that young?!" Val's eyes widened. "I didn't realize it."

"Why? You think he seems older than he is?"

"Yes, actually. Not so much his physical appearance as the way he carries himself."

Monica was intrigued, because that was what she had thought as well when she had first met Brian. She had been surprised when he had told her how young he was.

Monica wanted so badly to just call her sister later and tell her, I slept with him. I'm an adulterer, and I'm probably going to hell. I had a relationship with him that no one knows about. And Christian was being, as now, a jackass, and I didn't know if

I wanted to be married to him anymore, and when I had that affair I knew that in fact I *didn't* want to be married to him anymore. But then it ended and I didn't want to be alone, and I felt so horrible. And when it ended I cried every day for so long, and I had to hide it from everyone. I couldn't tell anyone. And now I'm forced to relive feelings I had that I had ignored, and it sucks.

But Monica couldn't say any of that; and she certainly couldn't tell her sister that and ask her not to say anything to anyone. Monica had almost told her sister on several occasions, both during and after the affair. She desperately wanted to, but she just couldn't. That would be unfair. Val had enough to worry about with her job and her finances and medical school debt. She didn't need to worry about this, too.

Monica listened, since Val was telling a story about having to bust some pharmacist's ass for writing the incorrect dosage on a medication that she had ordered for a patient.

"I mean, come on!" Val said. "How difficult is it to just write what I gave to you? It's all right there!"

"How mean were you?" Monica asked, smiling slyly.

"She cried. I kinda felt bad." Val scrunched up her nose.

"You shouldn't," Monica said. "Your patients depend on you for their health."

"It's just that I cannot stand incompetence," Val said with exasperation.

"And you shouldn't put up with it," their mother said.

"Oh, believe me, I *don't*," Val said, putting a piece of chocolate cake in her mouth.

"How is your job going, Christian?" Monica's mother asked then.

"It's going all right," he shrugged, and didn't say anything else.

He should not have come, Monica thought. I told him he didn't have to.

Christian didn't say much for the rest of the time they were there. Monica resented that but enjoyed the time spent with her family. Monica's father made her laugh constantly, while her mother appeared annoyed that she couldn't stop laughing. That made Monica laugh even more.

At the end of the meal, Monica's mother called for her usual toast. Monica rolled her eyes.

"*Siempre lo mismo,*" she said. "It's always the same one, Mom."

"Oh, come on," her mother encouraged everyone. "Raise your glasses. You know how it goes. *Salud, amor, y dinero. Y no necesariamente en esa orden!*"

Monica and Val always laughed at the toast in spite of themselves. *Health, love, and money, and not necessarily in that order.*

On the way back to their house, Monica was pensive. She wanted so badly to talk to someone, to ask whether the feelings she had about her marriage were normal.

Is it normal that I'm thinking about leaving Christian? Monica thought. Is it normal that we're hardly ever physically intimate, and that I'm always the one to initiate it, and is it normal that he doesn't want to hold me or kiss me passionately anymore?

That can't be normal, she thought. Just because we're in our forties doesn't mean we don't have a sex drive.

Monica and her family walked in the front door of their house.

"I'm going upstairs to finish my homework for tomorrow," David said to his mother.

"Okay, sure," she told him. "I'll do a light dinner later tonight." She smiled at him. David looked like his father, but had his mother's dark eyes and her personality. Sometimes she felt like

David understood her better than her husband did.

As soon as David was upstairs, Monica turned to her husband. She needed to say something.

"Hey, if you're going to criticize me, or my decision to run in this election, for the love of God don't do it in front of our son." Her voice was steel.

Christian looked at her, his eyes hard. "What do you mean?"

"Don't talk badly about me in front of David. I have complaints about you, too, but you don't see me airing them in front of him."

"And what complaints do you have about me then?"

"First, shouldn't you support me? When we initially talked about it, you seemed supportive of my decision to run."

"Well, that was before I realized that you were going to quit your job."

"Christian, we talked about that. And I have saved plenty of money to pay our bills during this campaign. So, honestly, I don't see what the problem is here."

"What about after the campaign?" he said, with an edge to his voice. "What will we do then?"

"Well, if I don't win —"

"You mean *when* you don't win."

Monica kept her cool. "*If* I don't win, I can get my old job back."

"You're sure?" Monica was pissed off that Christian didn't seem to believe her.

"Of course," she said. The truth was that her former boss at the law firm had told her that she would most likely be able to go back there, but it wasn't 100% positive. However, she did not tell Christian that. She was fairly certain that she would be able to find another law firm job, anyway.

There was a pause in their conversation and Christian turned away.

"What are you going to do now?" Monica asked him.

"I'm going to watch TV."

"Like every day, right?"

"Well, I'm tired," he said defensively.

"What the hell do you have to be tired from?" If he wasn't at work, she thought, he was watching the boob tube.

He turned back toward her immediately. "If you haven't noticed," he began sarcastically, "I run this house when you're out playing in the campaign."

That pissed Monica off, because she was the one who paid the bills and managed the finances. All Christian really did was go to work and come home, and cook once in a while.

"What the fuck ever!" Monica raised her voice. "Maybe you want to pay the bills then, or be in charge of our finances? And who took David to buy new school clothes? And who folds the damn laundry?!"

"What is *that* supposed to mean?" Christian's brows furrowed in anger.

"It means that you don't do shit. I do everything around here!"

"Watch your mouth!"

"Don't tell me what to do! And by the way," Monica added angrily, "you knew I was like this when you married me. So don't complain now!"

"What are you talking about?"

"That I'm ambitious, driven, that I have plans. I always do my own thing. And the thing is —" Monica almost choked up, because she remembered that Christian had been like that, too, when they had gotten married. They had talked about all the plans they had, graduate school, travel, and volunteering, among other things. "You used to be like that, too. But now you just drift through life. You didn't even say anything at my parents' house right now —"

"Honestly, what is there to say?" Christian seemed tired.

She looked at him, then shook her head incredulously.

"I don't want you to run," he said.

"But — we always talked about how things are going to hell in this country, and how we should do something about it —" Monica's voice trailed off. "I'm trying to do something about it. Aren't you excited about that?"

"Other people can try to do something. Not you, not if it means we don't see each other anymore."

Monica was shocked. "Christian, I need to do things. I have plans. I can't just do the daily grind anymore. It's not enough."

She meant that this marriage wasn't enough anymore. And from his reaction she figured that he understood.

"All right," Christian said. He seemed to deflate, his shoulders falling. After a few moments, he gave her his back. "I'm going to the store, we need a few things."

"We have stuff. We don't have to go to the store right now." But Monica understood. He needed to leave the house.

He had just given up. But she figured that that meant that she could, too.

Chapter 11

"Okay, Monica, we need to have a serious discussion." Monica was surprised at Nicole's tone. She looked at her friend. Nicole's eyebrows were raised and her lips were pursed.

The two women were with Don in Monica's new campaign office, in the Del Ray area near Old Town Alexandria, not far from Monica's house.

"What are you talking about?" Monica asked.

Nicole smiled. "Don't look so freaked out. I just meant — I know we initially talked about this before the primary, but —" she paused and Monica didn't like it. "We need to confirm."

Monica looked at Don, and by his expression she guessed that he knew exactly what Nicole was talking about.

Don didn't sugarcoat it. "Look, Monica, we just need to know if there's anything in your past that the other side could potentially find out."

"You mean — like, that they could use against me?"

"Exactly," Don nodded.

Monica forced a tight smile. "You're asking me if I have any baggage."

"Right," Don said, and he appeared glad that she understood without him having to explain more fully.

"Do I have any baggage?" Monica said slowly, pretending to

ponder the question, a finger to her chin.

The answer is Hell, Yes! Monica thought. I only slept with my opponent for a couple of years.

"No, of course not," she shook her head. "I've been married to the same man for a long time. I — I've had a pretty boring life, nothing exciting."

"I'm sorry, Monica, but you know we have to ask," Nicole told her.

"I know, don't worry," Monica said with understanding, shrugging her shoulders.

"So you're sure there's nothing?" Don asked again.

She looked at him. "Yes, I'm sure, not unless my sister has a criminal record that I don't know about. But that's highly unlikely," she joked.

"Okay," Don said, smiling. "Then let's talk about this district."

III

AUGUST

Chapter 12

Monica's campaign calendar filled up quickly, leaving her little breathing room.

Don had organized a townhall-style event at a local business. Monica arrived early, along with Nicole.

Monica was supposed to stand at a podium to answer questions from the attendees, mostly representatives from local businesses. Don had assured her that this would be good practice for her. In theory, this crowd wasn't supposed to be particularly hostile to her.

Nevertheless, she was nervous, and felt overwhelmed staring at the crowd.

I will let the fear pass through me, she thought, reciting the Litany Against Fear. Then only I will remain.

Monica began by taking a question from a young woman with dyed blonde hair. The woman looked directly at her as she spoke.

"What is your position on immigration?"

Monica answered with a line she had rehearsed with Don. "I absolutely support immigration. Most people who immigrate to this country come here to improve their situation, and we should all support that."

The young woman wanted to ask another question but Don moved on, enforcing the rule of one person, one question.

However, another member of the audience continued on that theme. "What do you think of illegal immigration?"

Monica considered asking the speaker to clarify. What do you mean, what do I think of it? she thought. It's a dumb question. However, she knew that answer would appear condescending.

"I support upholding our laws," she answered.

The speaker continued quickly. "Would you deport illegal immigrants?"

Don made a move to continue with someone else, but Monica stayed him with a slight hand gesture. She didn't want to appear afraid of the question.

"I am certainly sympathetic to people who immigrate here in search of better opportunities. My parents both immigrated here from Spain, which at the time was controlled by Franco, a totalitarian dictator. I have also assisted applicants for legal residence here on a pro bono basis. However, this country does not have the resources to have open borders. The process to immigrate here legally should be easier and more streamlined. For example, non-citizens who are married to U.S. citizens should not have to wait so long to come here. People should not have to wait for years. That time frame should be much shorter."

Monica was gratified to hear the murmur of agreement from the audience and some light clapping.

Don quickly moved on the next audience member.

"So people don't have the right to immigrate here?"

This was a loaded question, Monica knew. Technically, a non-citizen, non-resident alien does not have the right, under the Constitution, to immigrate to the U.S. Immigration law is largely under the purview of the executive branch; and the President could, theoretically, declare an indefinite ban on all immigration. Not that that would be good policy, Monica thought. But she knew that that reply would not sound appealing to the audience.

"People are welcome to immigrate to the U.S. As I said, immigration should be more streamlined, and the process should be faster, so that people should not have to wait as long. Also, the government should be educating would-be immigrants on the benefits of legal residence and becoming U.S. citizens. By becoming legal residents, they can work and pay into Social Security. By becoming citizens, they can vote. There are benefits to being a legal immigrant."

The event wrapped up without any major incidents. Monica breathed with relief as Don announced that they had run out of time and thanked everyone for coming.

Don approached Monica to remove her microphone. Once he did so, she asked, "what did you think?"

Don smiled broadly. "You did great."

Chapter 13

Monica walked along a near-deserted King Street in Old Town Alexandria. It was almost 10pm, and she had had a grueling day doing local events and talking to her campaign staffers about various issues.

Despite all that, she was not tired. Always a night owl, she needed some alone time to recharge and think. Her ears rang from the overstimulating events of the day. She had been around so many people, having to listen carefully and articulate well-thought-out answers. She felt worn out.

She would deal with her marriage to Christian after the campaign, she had decided. She lacked the energy to deal with him now. The campaign would be over in November. Of course, if she won, still a long shot in her mind, how would it look if she split from her husband while she was in office?

It seemed unlikely that things would go that way, she thought. Even if she did manage to pull a victory, maybe she and Christian would stick it out until she was no longer in office.

Assuming, of course, that they actually split. Thinking about splitting up and actually splitting up were worlds apart. Monica believed that most people fantasized about being alone and independent, or maybe that was mostly introverts. Extroverts seemed to be in relationships so that they were never alone again, so that they always had someone to do something with, and introverts —

Well, she supposed, introverts seemed to be in relationships to have someone who understood them, so that they never had to explain themselves to someone else.

So why was she always having to explain herself to her husband?

Monica approached the waterfront area, and had only passed a few people strolling. On a summer weekend, Old Town would be more active, full of life. But it was a Tuesday, and while many bars and restaurants were still open, it was definitely more of a ghost town.

Instead of heading straight on King Street to arrive at the waterfront, where she had met with Brian a little while ago, she turned left on Union Street. She had walked so far that her feet were sore. It was a long walk home, and she would need to call a car service.

"Funny seeing you out here."

Monica looked up automatically, her thoughts disturbed, and found herself staring directly at Brian.

"Hey," she said. "What are *you* doing out here?"

He shrugged, his hands in his pockets. "Just walking."

"Same here," Monica said after a pause.

"Anything particular on your mind?"

Monica stared at him, taken aback by the question. All of a sudden, his eyes softened, revealing small creases at the edges.

"Um, not really." Then she reconsidered. "Well — I do have a bit on my mind." She noticed that her shoulders were tense and dropped them. "Difficult to articulate."

"I understand," he nodded.

She noticed what he was wearing for the first time. Dark gray slacks with a vibrant blue tie.

"You just come from work?" Monica asked, then thought about how inane that question sounded. His "work" consisted of trying to beat her in a congressional election.

"Yes," Brian nodded. "Long day." He shrugged.

"Me, too." Monica considered for a moment. "How's it going?"

"Going okay."

Monica tried to suppress a smile. "I'm still gonna beat ya, though, so —"

"Oh, really?" Brian lifted one eyebrow and smiled, crossing his arms.

Monica was pleased at his defensive posture. What did he have to be defensive about?

"Oh, yeah. Not just beat you. Gonna kick you in the rear, which is fitting because —"

Brian chuckled, then hung his head to try to avoid laughing outright.

"What?"

Brian lifted his head. "I mean, you said 'rear.' Hehehehehe."

Monica threw her head back, sighing. "Oh come *on*. Beavis and Butthead is a Gen X classic. That was before your time. *You* can't lay claim to it. Do you see me making Dawson's Creek references?"

Brian's chuckle turned into laughter. "You're comparing Dawson's Creek to Beavis and Butthead?"

"No, I'm saying one is a Gen X show you know nothing about, and the other is a Millennial show *I* know nothing about."

"I've never watched Dawson's Creek," Brian insisted. "How do *you* know about it anyway?"

"I have a Millennial sister," Monica countered, taking a couple of steps forward and sticking her tongue out at him.

"Jesus, that explains it."

64

They looked at each other, their faces closer together. Monica shook her head in jest.

She saw the moment Brian's eyes changed, and, as he drew his hands up, her pupils dilated in fear that he would kiss her.

Instead, he took her hands and gently placed her palms against the sides of his face, which was uncharacteristic of him. Intimacy, true intimacy, when you let someone see you vulnerable, was never something that Monica thought had come naturally to Brian.

"You've been drinking, haven't you?" she said.

"No," he shook his head. "Well, I had one beer. Okay, two. Two beers."

Monica remained silent.

"I was just — just remembering."

Remembering what? Monica thought.

Then it dawned on her. She used to do that to him, put her hands on his face like that, just to look into his eyes.

A rush of emotional pain came over Monica, and she stepped backward until her hands were no longer touching his face. She dropped her arms.

"I'm gonna go," she said.

She turned around without giving him a chance to say anything, walking back the way she had come, and called an Uber as soon as she had put enough distance between Brian and herself.

IV

SEPTEMBER

Chapter 14

It was make or break time. During the past few weeks, Monica's team had organized events all over the district. Monica had made appearances at local businesses, volunteer organizations, and at several local events. She participated in meet and greets at local coffee shops. Monica used her Spanish a great deal and felt that she was connecting with voters.

It was starting to work, too. Informal polling reflected that she was gaining in the polls. Her message regarding immigration seemed to be making headway.

Monica's team still had a long road ahead of them. These next few weeks would be crucial and she needed to continue to progress in the polls. If everything went well, she would peak on Election Day, carrying just enough votes to eke out a victory.

Monica was at her campaign office, deep into a strategy session with Nicole, Don, and a couple of campaign staffers when her cell phone vibrated. She sneaked a quick glance and saw Brian's number.

"I should take this," she said to the others and quickly stepped out of the room.

She walked down a nearby hallway and whispered into her phone, "dude, this better be urgent."

"Yeah, well, it is," Brian said tersely.

"What?" Monica's stomach seized at his anxious tone.

"Look, I got a call from a friend of mine. I haven't seen him in a while but he's close friends with Ross."

"Ross?" Monica asked in confusion.

"Yeah," Brian paused. "My old roommate."

"Okaaaay," Monica dragged the word out, wondering about the possible significance of Brian's statement.

"Apparently, Ross told my friend that he's going to appear on CNN tonight."

"Okay, so?" She still didn't understand.

"Monica," Brian said carefully, "I think Ross may do a scoop on us."

Monica's heart sank at once. "What do you mean?"

Brian sighed. "He may reveal on CNN the fact that we used to — you know —"

"Seriously? Why would he care?"

"I don't know. Maybe someone convinced him to. Maybe he just wants his fifteen minutes of fame. Maybe someone paid him a lot of money. I don't know."

"This makes no sense. What's his motive?"

"I don't know —"

"You're sure he's going to say that?"

"No, I'm not —" Brian seemed to be at a loss for words, and his apparent lack of control frightened Monica even more.

"Well, what else could it be? What's his interview supposed to be about?"

"The thing is, he's not scheduled to be on any shows. My friend thinks this is a kind of coup."

"To shine the headlights on us."

"Right."

"But why?"

"I don't know."

"So how do you want to handle this?" she asked.

"I don't know."

"So tell me what you *do* know!"

"What would *you* suggest we do?"

"We do nothing, since if he does go on CNN tonight, it will probably be about something that has nothing to do with us."

Brian sighed. "Okay, let's wait and see."

They agreed and hung up.

A couple of hours later, Nicole interrupted Monica as she was reviewing her calendar to see where she could fit in a few events.

"Hey, Monica, come see this," she said, brows furrowed.

Monica walked into the main room with Nicole, where the staff had two televisions which were continuously on, tuned in to different news channels.

Monica saw the Breaking News headline and wondered what was going on. She faced Nicole for an explanation.

"Watch for a second," Nicole said.

The newscaster started speaking again. "To recap what we just announced a few minutes ago, tonight we are going to have a special guest on the late news hour. His name — Ross Goldman. The topic he's going to talk about — the congressional election in Virginia's Eighth District. Mr. Goldman has an inside scoop on the candidates, which he will only reveal — tonight. So make sure you tune in."

The newscaster's deliberate pacing of his speech for effect annoyed Monica. She turned to Nicole. "What's he going to say?"

Nicole shook her head, wondering. "I don't know. I was hoping *you* could tell me."

71

Monica exhaled.

"Do you know him?" Nicole asked.

"No," Monica shook her head. It wasn't the complete truth, of course. She knew who Ross was, even if she didn't *know* him.

Don stormed through the door just then, locking eyes with Monica.

"Did you see it?" he asked, motioning toward the television screens.

"Yeah," Monica nodded. "What's going on?"

"I don't know but I just got off the phone with a couple of people. Turns out that this guy used to share an apartment with Brian."

"Oh yeah?" Nicole raised her eyebrows. "When?"

"Few years ago. They were roommates."

When neither Monica nor Nicole spoke, Don continued. "It'll be interesting to see how this plays out."

"How do you think it will play out?" Monica asked cautiously, crossing her arms.

"Well, obviously, he's going to say something about Brian. Judging by the way they're building it up, something negative. That can only work out well for us."

"Don, they said he's going to say something about the candidates, plural," Nicole said, putting her hands on her hips. "I'm not sure what he's gonna say, but I'm not sure this is something we want."

"What could he say?" Don said, shrugging.

Then, as if choreographed, Don and Nicole both turned to Monica.

"Monica?" Nicole asked gently. "Do you know what this guy Ross is going to talk about?"

Monica sighed, then looked from Nicole to Don. "I'm not

100% sure, but I think it's going to suck for us."

Chapter 15

"What time is he coming on?" Don asked, throwing the door shut.

Monica jumped at the loud noise.

"8pm," Nicole answered.

The three had retreated into Monica's office.

"So we only have two hours," Don said, glancing at his wristwatch.

"What's going on?" Nicole looked at her friend.

Monica tried to control her breathing, which came out in loud exhales.

"I think I need a paper bag," she said.

Don left immediately and returned with one. Monica sat at her desk chair and breathed into and out of the bag for several seconds until she was calm enough to talk. As she started to calm down, she thought about whether she should tell them everything. If it turned out that Ross was going to talk about something other than the affair, she would have alerted Nicole and Don for nothing. However, shouldn't they know about the affair anyway?

Monica gazed up at Nicole.

"If you have something to tell us, say it now," Nicole said.

Monica took one more deep breath, then said, "I had an affair with him."

"With Ross?" Don asked.

"No, with Brian."

"What — ?" Nicole started.

"Holy fuck," Don said, pivoting on his foot and running his hand through his hair.

"And you tell us this *now*?!" Nicole raised her voice.

"Ssshh," Monica whispered urgently, "they're all going to hear you outside."

"Does it matter? Everyone is going to know in about two hours!" Nicole said.

"How could you not tell us?!" Don was incredulous.

"What the hell was I supposed to tell you guys? That I used to bang my opponent — oh, and that, by the way, I was *married* at the time?!" She made it sound more casual than it had actually been for her.

"I don't believe this!" Nicole said, her hand to her forehead.

"Yeah, something like that," Don said to Monica, his hands on his hips, glaring at her.

"I was too embarrassed! Don, I couldn't believe it when you told me Brian was running in the primary, and then when he won!" Monica looked at the ceiling, then back at her friends. "It was unbelievable! This shit doesn't happen in real life!" She didn't know why she was surprised. After all, she totally deserved it.

"Monica, we asked you," Nicole said, "we asked you if there was anything like this in your past —"

"Honestly, what would you have said if I had told you that I had had an affair with *my opponent in a congressional race?*"

Nicole ignored the question. "And, by the way, you're married!" she said. Monica didn't like her friend's accusatory tone. She had always thought that her single friends would never have understood her situation with Christian. She realized that she had been right to think that.

"You wouldn't have understood, anyway," Monica said defensively.

"Well, friend, you never gave me much of a chance to understand, did you?"

Don faced Monica, and she noticed that he seemed to have regained most of his control.

"Okay," he began, "tell us everything. First, when did it start?"

"We don't have time for this now," Monica replied.

"She's right," Nicole agreed, nodding her head at Don. "We need to focus all our resources right now on making sure Ross does not get on the news tonight."

"Oh, and how are we gonna do that?" Don asked, annoyed.

Nicole turned to Monica. "How does Ross know about you and Brian?"

Just like that, Monica noted, Nicole and Don switched to damage control mode.

"Ross was Brian's roommate at the time. He saw me there."

"But you could've been just visiting him or something. Just because he saw you in his apartment doesn't mean you were sleeping with him."

Monica looked at Nicole hard. "The time of day would've given it away. Plus —" she paused. "He saw me leave Brian's bedroom."

"Who else knows about it?" Don asked.

"No one, as far as I know," Monica replied. "I never told anyone, and I doubt Brian did either."

"But Ross could've told someone," Don said.

"Wait," Nicole held up a hand. "Ross saw you, but did he know who you were?"

Monica looked at Nicole again. "Nicole, you don't remember Ross Goldman from law school? Tall, lanky, long hair, awkward-looking?"

"Wait, what?"

"He was the teacher's pet in our constitutional law class?"

"*That* guy?! You're joking," Nicole said.

"I wish I were."

"Fuck," Nicole whispered. "Well, the cat's out of the bag now."

"Not if we make sure he doesn't get on the news tonight," Don said.

"What's the damn point, Don?!" Nicole said. "He'll either do it tonight on the news or in the papers tomorrow. What do you wanna do, put a bullet in him?"

"We can't do that," Monica said, as if it were seriously an option.

"No, but we can delay him, until we figure things out, and until we can get our story out first."

"A mea culpa," Nicole offered.

"Exactly."

"Okay," Nicole sighed. "Let's give it a try."

Chapter 16

For the next two hours Monica, Nicole, and Don were on the phone, frantically trying to reach anyone who could prevent Ross from going on the news. Nicole had promised exclusive interviews with Monica, and other favors, but they made no progress.

About ten minutes before 8pm, the staff started to gather around the television screens in the main room.

Monica's heart was sinking faster than an anchor. She had come to the conclusion that the only reason Ross would be doing this interview would be to "out" her and Brian. Despite what Don had said, in her mind there could be no other explanation.

But why? Monica thought. Why does Ross care about this?

Her hands were sweaty and her pulse raced. She ran into the bathroom five minutes before the broadcast was set to air, and splashed cold water all over her face. Luckily, she was the only person in there. She looked into the bathroom mirror. She was nauseous and, for a second, thought she would vomit. Then her phone blipped.

It was Brian.

Hey, just hang in there.

She wrote back.

I am freaking out here!

Brian's answer came a few seconds later.

I know. I am too. Just relax and we'll deal with it.

Easy for you to say, Monica thought. You're not married with a kid. You most likely won't be abandoned by your party because you don't conform to some stereotype. This isn't going to affect you half as much as it's going to affect me.

Monica arranged her hair and freshened her lip gloss, then checked her watch. It was three minutes until eight o'clock.

She left the bathroom and walked into her office. Don and Nicole stood there anxiously. The three of them would watch the interview on the flat-screen TV in Monica's office. The rest of the staff were watching just outside Monica's office, in the main room.

Monica stood right in front of the TV, next to Nicole, who turned toward her.

"Put your game face on," Nicole told her friend. "Let's see what he has to say first."

"Why would he do this?" Monica asked in a whisper.

Nicole shrugged. "Who knows? He was probably paid to do it."

"By whom?"

"You got any enemies?"

"Nobody that would do something like this, not that I know of. Anyway —" Monica paused, thinking, "this hurts both me and Brian. So what's the point?"

"Maybe Ross wants his fifteen minutes. Maybe he wants a news anchor position."

Monica shook her head. She took her suit jacket off; she had already sweat through the armpits of her blouse. She kept her arms glued to her sides so that no one would notice.

The program started just as Don came over to stand on Monica's other side.

The host did the introduction. Ross didn't look much different from how Monica had remembered him. His black, curly hair showed a bit of gray, but, as with most men, it made him look distinguished. He had gained some muscle and was now quite attractive with large, dark eyes.

Ross introduced himself as an attorney working for the DC office of a large, national law firm.

The host went right into it. "So what made you agree to give this interview? What do you have to say that is so important?"

"Well," Ross began. He had his hands clasped, and wore a serious expression, as if what he were about to say were a matter of national security or something.

Monica pursed her lips. She hadn't known Ross well in law school, but she knew enough to know that he had always thought too highly of himself.

"As you may know, I used to be Brian's roommate," Ross began, "before he moved in with his current girlfriend. And —" he appeared to be weighing his words.

Monica bit a fingernail. She and her friends were glued to the screen.

"I think that the public has the right to know what Brian was — is like, and I think the public also has the right to know what his opponent is like."

Monica's heart sank to the floor. Any small hope she had had that Ross was going to say something else was completely dashed.

Her mind raced. No, no, no, no, no! she thought, as if she could will Ross into shutting up.

"So," the host continued, with a dramatic pause. "Let me get this straight. You have something to tell us, something that involves both opponents in the congressional race in northern

Virginia, specifically the Eighth District of Virginia, which is right outside of Washington, DC. Is that right?"

"Yes, that's right," Ross said, still looking serious.

"Let me just lay this out for our audience. Democrat Brian Murphy is running against Republican Monica —" he struggled with Monica's last name. "Orellana." Photos of the two of them were displayed on the screen. Monica didn't like her photo, but she never liked her photos.

The host continued. "I think that's how you say her last name. Anyway, Representative Hoffman is retiring, and the seat is open. That's what we've got."

"Right," Ross nodded

"So what do you have to tell us that is so important?"

Monica stared bug-eyed at the screen. She wanted to run away but her legs wouldn't move.

"Well," Ross punctuated slowly, and that pissed Monica off. Get the fuck on with it, she thought. "When I was Brian's roommate —"

"No," Monica said aloud.

"— this was several years ago —"

"How many years ago exactly?" the host asked.

"About five or six years ago," Ross answered.

"So what happened about five or six years ago?" the host pressed.

"No!" Monica's voice grew louder.

"— Brian and Monica had an affair."

"Fuck!" The exclamation automatically escaped Monica's lips and she was certain that everyone in the outside office had heard it.

She heard gasps from outside her office and cringed. Don and Nicole remained stonefaced, listening.

The host asked Ross how long the affair had gone on.

"I'm not sure exactly, but I think at least a few months," he answered.

Monica huffed loudly. She knew that Ross had no way of knowing how long it had gone on, since she trusted that Brian had never said anything to his roommate. After all, both she and Brian had had significant others at the time.

"Brian had a girlfriend at the time —"

"The same girlfriend he lives with now?" The host had obviously done his homework.

"Yes," Ross said, nodding. "And Monica was married."

"How did they meet?" the host asked.

"I'm really not sure." Ross look puzzled.

"So how do you know they had an affair?" the host pressed.

"I saw her leaving his bedroom, in the morning. I mean —" Ross appeared to be choosing his words. "There could be no other explanation for that."

"And you're sure it was Monica Orellana who you saw leaving?"

"Yes. I knew who she was because —"

"Fuck," Monica said again.

"— I went to law school with her."

"Oh, fuck!" Monica lost it. "*Fuck you*, Ross!" she exclaimed, pointing furiously at the television screen.

"Monica!" Nicole was right there.

Monica put her hands to her face. Her heart pounded in her chest and her ears rang. Suddenly, she wondered how Brian was handling this right now.

Monica raised her head. "I don't want to see anyone right now except you two."

Nicole nodded.

Even though she was experiencing sheer panic, the rational part of her attorney mind came through a bit. "Don, you're going to have to talk to everyone. Keep them busy. Give them something to do. Tell them not to say anything to the outside world. Just — just for a little while."

Monica looked around and she thought she would cry. "Guys, please — don't hate me."

Monica noticed then that her cell phone was vibrating. She picked it up from her desk and saw that her husband was calling her.

"Fuck! That's Christian," she said. "I — I can't talk to him right now."

Suddenly, the reality of the situation hit her. She had just been talking with two of her friends, but soon all kinds of calls would come pouring in.

Her phone vibrated again. When she looked at it this time, she felt relief. It was her sister, the only person she wanted to talk to right now.

"Hey," she said into the phone, on the verge of tears.

"What's going on? Are you all right?" Val was all concern.

The sound of Val's voice, and her comforting tone, was exactly what Monica needed right now.

"Val, I am so sorry!"

"For what?"

"Did you see the broadcast just now?"

"Yeah. So it's true?"

"Yes, it's true! I know you must think the worst of me."

"What — well, I was surprised, but — why wouldn't you have told me about something like that?"

"How could I — I didn't want to burden you — I didn't want to stress you out — and it's not like you think. I was so lonely

83

—"

"Hey, Monica —"

Monica started to cry. "Just tell me you still love me."

"Jesus, Monica. I'm your sister! I will always love you. How could you think otherwise? Whatever you were feeling — it's okay —"

"Monica," Don whispered. "We've got to deal with this here."

Monica heard the bustle of activity outside her office.

She steeled herself. "Look, Val, I have to go. We'll talk later, I promise. I love you."

"I love you, too! Deep breath!"

Monica heard the smile in Val's voice and smiled herself, despite the circumstances. She still had her sister.

Monica hung up. There was a loud knock on the door. Everything was happening so quickly that she didn't have time to think.

"What? What?!" Monica yelled, fraying at the edges. Nicole jumped.

Nicole's assistant barged in, opened his mouth and then stopped when he saw the tears on Monica's face.

"What?" Monica said again.

"Murphy is on the phone. He wants to talk to you."

Monica took a deep breath. "Okay. Send the call over here. Everyone out —"

"Monica, I should be here —" Don began, shaking his head slowly.

Monica cut him off with a hand gesture. "We'll talk in five minutes. Just — please give me five minutes." Monica wasn't sure if Don was concerned about the campaign or was jealous, but there was no time to wonder about it.

Everyone else filed out, and Monica was alone in her office.

Her office phone rang and she picked it up.

"Hi," she said.

"Hey," Brian said. "I tried your cell but it was busy."

"Yeah, my husband called, then my sister called."

"So you talked to him?"

"No, not yet. I'm ignoring his calls for now. Have you talked to your —" Monica couldn't say the word "girlfriend."

"Not yet," Brian said.

"How did your team take it?" Then Monica had a thought. "Are they there with you now?"

"No, it's just me. Sean appears to be calm but Mike is raging. He may even quit, I don't know."

"Look, I only have a few minutes. What are we gonna do?"

"Monica, the press will be calling, if they're not calling already."

"Yeah."

"What do you think we should tell them?" Brian asked.

Monica noticed that Brian had also used the term "we," but didn't have time to think about what that meant exactly.

"Oh my God, I have no idea. What do you think?"

"I don't know either."

"Brian, I'm not ready to give any kind of a statement. I should talk to my husband first, out of respect for him, if nothing else." She was struck by how hypocritical she sounded mentioning the words *husband* and *respect* in the same sentence. "What do *you* think?"

"I don't know," he said tersely.

"Hey," Monica said. "Are you all right?"

Brian paused for a moment. "Not really, but — I'll survive. What about you?"

"The same." She tried to think. "Look — maybe we should say no comment for now, and that we'll issue a formal statement later. That would buy us time, wouldn't it?"

"That actually sounds like a plan. You were always better at thinking under pressure, anyway."

His comment made Monica sad; being reminded of their previous relationship always made her sad.

"Should we say that we'll issue a joint statement?" Brian asked.

Now she knew that he wasn't thinking clearly. That was definitely not something that the Brian she had known would suggest.

"It's probably not a good idea to say that we'll issue a joint statement, since that suggests that we're admitting to the — relationship. I don't think I'm ready to do that yet. I mean — I don't see any way of not admitting it, frankly, but — not yet."

"Yes, you're right."

"So let's just say no comment for now, and that we will each be issuing our own statements a little later. How does that sound?"

"That's perfect." He paused. "Thank you, Monica."

"No problem. Of course, I have no idea what we'll say in our statements."

"I don't either."

"I think this is the best we can do for now."

Don barged into her office. "Monica, I need you," he said urgently. "The press wants a statement."

She sighed heavily.

"We'll talk later," she said into the phone.

"Okay."

She hung up with Brian, and turned to Don.

"Tell all the journalists that we have no comment for now, and that we'll issue a statement shortly," she said with as much determination as she could muster.

"How shortly?"

"Don't say when. Just say that a statement will be forthcoming."

"Is that what Murphy's gonna do?" Don seemed suspicious.

"Yes." Don continued to look at her, so she said, "I'm not ready to say anything else right now."

His expression seemed to soften a bit, and Monica wondered, not for the first time, how he really felt about her.

"Okay," he agreed. "Then we should talk."

Monica nodded. "Tell everyone that when their work is done, that they can go home, but tell them not to talk about this to anyone, and that we'll issue a statement soon. Of course, that doesn't mean that they won't talk, but we can't do anything about that, can we?"

Don shook his head.

Monica went on. "After you've done that, and told the press what I said, get Nicole and we'll talk."

Don nodded and started to leave.

"Hey," Monica said.

Don turned back toward her.

Monica sighed and shook her head. "I'm sorry." She wasn't sure what she was sorry for, that she hadn't told her team, or that she wasn't as perfect as Don seemed to think she was.

Don nodded in response.

Monica managed a weak smile. Then her phone vibrated.

It was Christian again. "It's Christian," she told Don. "I need to take this. We'll talk in five, okay?"

"Okay." He left.

Monica answered, her heart in her throat. "Hi."

"Oh my God, I have been trying to get hold of you!"

"I'm sorry, Christian."

"What the hell is going on?!" he yelled into the phone. He had every right to be furious, she thought.

"I'm sorry," Monica repeated.

"Tell me it's not true. Tell me you didn't screw that guy!"

Monica felt exhausted all of a sudden. And there was no point in denying it. "I'm sorry, Christian, but it's true. I — I had an affair with him."

Everything got very quiet, and Monica knew that meant trouble.

"For how long?" he asked.

"Two years."

The silence dominated the room. Monica couldn't think of anything else to say. "Look —" she stammered, "I'll be home soon, and we'll talk."

"The only reason I will be home when you get here is because I don't want to leave our son all by himself." Then he hung up.

Monica was frozen for about five seconds, then tried to rally her energy. That was easier said than done. Her pulse increased and her heart started to palpitate. She walked to her office door and opened it. Everyone stopped what they were doing and stared at her.

The silence allowed her to hear the pounding in her ears. Monica suddenly had an extreme onset of nausea. Her stomach heaved and her head ached. She ran through the room and to the bathroom, shoving the door open. There were two young women in there chatting, gossiping about her, no doubt.

She didn't make it to the toilet, and threw up right there over the sink. At that moment, Nicole came in after her.

"Get out of here!" she raised her voice to the two women.

Nicole stood next to her friend and held her hair back.

After a few moments the nausea subsided a bit. Monica ran the water and washed her mouth out. "I don't know — what the fuck to do —" she sobbed, her chest heaving.

"You talked to Christian?" Nicole asked gently.

Monica nodded.

"How did he take it?"

"How do you think?" Monica managed to choke out.

"What did Brian say when you talked to him?"

Monica's heart wrenched a little when she thought of how stressed Brian had sounded. She didn't know why she cared.

She dodged Nicole's question. "We're not going to make any comments for now, until we all figure out what to do."

"Look, we'll deal with it," Nicole said.

Monica looked at her friend in the mirror.

"You helped me through law school when I had several meltdowns," Nicole continued, "even though you were always so together." She smiled. "So I'll help you now."

"I wasn't together," Monica said. "I just hid my anxiety really well." Her nausea subsided a little more. "But thanks, Nic."

"And God knows, you're not the first candidate to have had an extramarital affair."

"But I'm probably the first to have had one with my opponent."

Nicole considered, shrugging. "That's probably true."

"Well, we both know I already had a snowball's chance in hell." Monica attempted a chuckle.

"So we might as well go down fighting," Nicole smiled. "Like you said, maybe we'll get a book deal out of it, or positions as cable news contributors."

Monica laughed. "We could do worse."

"You know we could." Nicole smoothed her friend's hair.

Monica's expression turned serious as she looked back at Nicole's reflection.

She felt the need to be completely honest with her friend. "I loved him, you know?"

Nicole's face turned pained. "Why didn't you end up with him, then?"

"It's complicated," Monica said, her voice shaking.

"Did Brian know that was how you felt?"

"No," Monica said softly, shaking her head, then she half-smiled, a sad smile. "Besides, you know it's almost always the woman that gets her heart broken, never the man. I don't give a fuck what those stupid songs say."

"I know." Nicole sighed. "And I'm sorry."

"Yeah, I am, too." Monica was far away for a few seconds before she straightened her back. "Tell Don we can talk whenever you guys are ready."

Chapter 17

Brian wasn't doing much better than Monica at the moment. He had been ignoring Abby's calls while Mike and Sean, especially Mike, berated him.

The television was on and the commentator appeared to be relishing the juicy bit of news on a relatively slow news night.

"Both campaigns of the candidates running for Representative Hoffman's old seat in the Eighth District of Virginia must be in disarray tonight, and I imagine both campaign teams are in total damage-control mode —"

"Let's recap for any audience members who just joined," the host cut in then. "It has just been revealed by a former roommate of Brian Murphy, the Democrat running for Hoffman's old seat, that he had a long-term affair with his opponent, Republican Monica Orellana. Ms. Orellana is a married DC area attorney, and is ten years older than Murphy —"

They are absolutely loving this, Brian thought. And how do they know that the affair was "long-term?" Ross had no idea how long they had seen each other. Brian wondered again about Ross' motives.

The host went on, excited. "We have just received a response from both campaign teams. They have no comment at the moment, but will soon be issuing statements."

"That's to be expected," the commentator was saying. "They

are both working on their strategies, buying time —"

Mike was so loud now that Brian was sure that the entire staff could hear him outside of the office.

"First of all, how the *fuck* does it occur to you to bang a married woman when you want to run for office?!" Mike was saying.

Brian was worn down, but refused to take Mike's barbs. He stood up and looked at Mike.

"I guarantee you I was not thinking about that at the time," he said coldly.

"Of course, you were thinking with your dick!"

Not entirely, Brian thought. It had felt good to be with Monica. She understood me, more than Abby ever did, he thought. Instead of explaining all that, he glared Mike into silence.

"How old were you when the affair started?" Sean was more logical, methodical. He would try to figure out the best damage-control strategy.

Brian sighed. He figured it was a semi-legitimate question. He thought for a moment. "Twenty-six."

"And you were definitely with Abby at the time?"

"Yes," he said softly.

Sean looked at Mike, and they had a conversation as if Brian weren't even there.

"It shouldn't be too difficult to label this a youthful indiscretion," Sean said carefully.

"Maybe." Mike's face was still red. "But if we had known about this beforehand, we could have planned for it. Now we're doing this on the fly. Makes it more difficult."

"True. But you know she's not going to release any dirt about him," Sean said matter-of-factly.

Mike raised his eyes. "You sure about that?"

"You can never be 100% sure of anything," Sean admitted.

"However, any statement she makes or anything she releases about him, it will reflect on her as well. I guarantee you she will think of that. From everything I see, she's very intelligent. Not only that —" Sean paused.

Mike looked at him intently. "What?"

"I know Nicole, and I know she'll think of that. Those women are like sisters. Nic will do everything possible to protect Monica."

"She won't quit?"

"No way in hell."

Thank God, Brian thought. Monica needed supportive people around her, in case her marriage imploded. At that moment, Brian felt horrible about that. Her marriage may end because of him, and because of what Ross had done, but mostly because of him. He began to pace, thinking.

"So," Mike said to Sean, "should we ask him?"

Sean shrugged, slightly annoyed. "Might as well. We should know sooner rather than later." Both men turned to Brian.

"So what happened?" Sean asked carefully.

"What do you mean?" Brian stopped pacing, crossed his arms, and looked at Sean.

"With Monica." Sean paused. "We need to know everything."

Brian's face hardened. "Well, I'm not telling you everything." As far as he was concerned, they didn't deserve to know everything. It was extremely personal to him.

Mike opened his mouth to speak, but Brian interrupted him. "Both of you look at me and you just see some jackass who cheated on his girlfriend. And you think that Monica was just some older woman desperate for affection, and she just wanted to hook up with some young guy. But —" he shook his head slowly. "It wasn't like that." It may have started somewhat like that, he thought, but all in all it hadn't been like that.

"Then what was it like?" Mike asked impatiently.

Brian stared at Mike coldly. "If you think I'm going to tell you details of when she and I were together, that's not gonna happen."

Sean sat down on the sofa and leaned back, exhausted. "Brian," he began, "we don't need to know that. We just need to know — how you met her, if there's anything she knows that she could use against you in this campaign, and if we should be aware of any other — surprises."

"As far as other women, there are none, so don't even ask about that," Brian said quickly.

"Okay," Sean said. "So how did you two meet?"

Brian did not want to talk about this now, but knew that eventually he would have no choice.

Sean got up quickly. "Actually, first I'm going to get us some water and order dinner. It's gonna be a long night."

He opened the door of Brian's office, then turned around.

"Don't worry, Brian," he said sarcastically, "It's not going to be that bad for you. In fact, this whole situation, as far as campaigns go, won't be half as bad for you as it will be for her."

Brian's face hardened as he glared at his friend, knowing that he was right.

Chapter 18

Monica sat on a comfy armchair in her office, holding a mug of tea that Nicole had brought her.

Don leaned against Monica's desk, and Nicole sat on a small sofa. They had ordered dinner, but Monica had only picked at hers. She had no appetite.

"How come you didn't tell us?" Don asked.

"I didn't think anyone would find out."

"People always find out," he said, frustration in his voice. "Oppo is everything right now! As your campaign manager, you should have told me."

"But no one knew. I didn't tell anyone."

"Guys brag about their conquests. I bet you money he bragged about being with you."

"No, he didn't." But she cringed anyway.

"How do you know he didn't?"

Because I was nothing to him, she thought. But she said, "because it was meaningless."

"So it wasn't serious?" Don asked.

"How did you meet him?" Nicole asked.

Monica ignored Don's question. Instead, she looked at Nicole, speaking slowly. "Brian used to run this PAC, in addition to his day job. I had a friend who had a friend who worked with the PAC. And my friend was invited to a fundraiser for the PAC, and she invited me to go with her." Monica felt strange talking about all this in the open, after working so hard to keep it in the dark for so long.

"You met him at the fundraiser?" Nicole prodded.

"Yes. And we talked most of the time I was there." Monica smiled weakly. "He told me that I was the first Republican to attend one of his fundraisers and I said, 'Well, there's a first time for everything.'"

She didn't relay the entire conversation to her friends, but she remembered it.

"Yes, I'm actually a libertarian and a registered Republican," she had said. "So if that's a dealbreaker for you, tell me now."

Brian had given her that smile that she now knew was so infrequent. "Well, in this town, everyone seems to have a different definition of what a 'libertarian' is. And, I'll admit, there are actually several areas in which I believe there should be less government, so —" his eyes had twinkled. "It's not a dealbreaker for me if it's not one for you."

Monica had smiled in spite of herself. "It's not a dealbreaker for me, either," she had told him. "It's just that, usually when I tell people in this town that I'm a Republican, they look at me like I have two heads, so I figured I would just get it out of the way in case you refused to associate with anyone from the dark side."

Brian had laughed then, and that had made Monica smile even more.

"So where are you from?" she had asked him.

"San Francisco," he had said.

"Oh, God," she had said, laughing and shaking her head. "I've never been."

"Yes, I'm not sure if a two-headed Republican from the dark

side would enjoy such a liberal town, but I like it."

"I guess you would."

Then he had asked her if she would go out for a drink with him the following week, so that they could talk politics, since he didn't have many Republican friends. She had had the feeling that it had been a pretense, but she hadn't cared because she had really liked him. That week, Brian had been all she could think about.

They had not been able to meet the following week, since Brian had had to travel for work. In fact, it took about a month for them to meet again. However, during that month they had talked several times. Brian had confided to her that he was not altogether happy in his relationship with Abby. And Monica had told him that she was unhappy with Christian.

When Brian was back in town, he had told her that he still wanted to meet for a drink. Monica had proposed meeting at his place. He wasn't living with Abby at the time.

When Monica went over to Brian's apartment that day after work, they had had sex right away. Monica remembered that, afterward, they had lain in bed together, Monica curled up underneath his arm, resting her head on his chest and hooking her leg over his.

"So that went on for two years?" Don asked, and she was wrenched away from her reminiscing.

"Yes, we would — see each other when we could." Which hadn't been often, she thought.

"So it was purely a sexual relationship?" Don asked.

Monica was uncomfortable talking about this with Don, but didn't want to let her discomfort show.

"Yes," she lied. Her voice was hard.

"Did anyone else know about it other than Ross?" Nicole

asked.

"Not that I know of. I never told anyone, and Brian swears that he never told anyone, either." Monica sighed. "And Ross only saw me the one time. He worked on the Hill, and was always either at work or traveling."

She went on. "One day, I went to Brian's place in the morning, before work, and I was leaving the apartment, and Ross came out of his room as I was leaving Brian's room." It was an unpleasant memory for Monica. "We were literally face to face. And I recognized him immediately. I mean, I was shocked. I had no idea who Brian's roommate was. And I prayed that he wouldn't recognize me. Then he asked me what I was doing there, and I told him that Brian was a friend of mine." She threw up her hands. "I didn't know what else to say." Monica paused, then bit a fingernail.

"He recognized you?" Nicole prodded.

Monica nodded. "He said he knew me from law school, the gunner in the front row of Contracts and Constitutional Law."

Nicole couldn't help smiling at the memory of her friend showing everyone else up in class.

"I was always petrified that he would tell someone. And, as time went by, and that didn't happen, I figured he had forgotten. I wish I knew who the hell was behind this."

"It doesn't really matter at this point." Nicole shrugged. "But we'll try to find out."

"So — how did it end?" Don continued.

Monica shrugged, trying to look as casual as she could. "Just ran its course, I guess." She looked from Don to Nicole, and from Nicole's eyes Monica could tell that her friend knew she was lying.

"I mean," Monica went on, "at the beginning it's all hormones and — craziness — and it's something new and exciting, and then — we didn't have much in common. No real connection. It just fizzled out." It hurt to pretend that it had been meaningless.

"It's difficult to make your schedules work," she continued, "and you're afraid that people will find out — I mean, at the time I was moving up in the local party, and I kept thinking about what would happen if people found out. And that's it."

"So —" Don narrowed his eyes, "did you guys leave on bad terms?"

"No," Monica shrugged again, another lie. "We just kind of left as friends." For some reason, whether due to her own embarrassment or something else, she didn't want to explain how it had really ended.

"Have you seen him since then?" Don pressed.

"Not in person, no. Just in the news." That was the truth.

Don nodded, apparently satisfied for the moment.

Nicole sighed a long sigh. "It's not the end of the world," she said, looking at Don.

Monica wanted to believe her. She closed her eyes for a moment, leaning back in her armchair. "Look, you guys," she said, opening her eyes again, "I should get home, face the music."

"What do you think he's going to do?" Don asked her directly.

"He'll probably file for divorce." She wanted to add, don't look so happy about it, Don.

"Monica, I am so sorry," Nicole told her, brows furrowed in concern.

"Don't be," Monica said. "This is all entirely of my own doing." Then she added, "I'm just really glad you guys are here."

Don smiled at her warmly, and she thought at that moment that maybe he really did care about her beyond just the campaign.

Chapter 19

Brian picked up his cell phone with dread. He had several missed calls from Abby.

But he couldn't put off calling her any longer. He had filled in Sean and Mike on his past relationship with Monica. Well, he had filled them in as much as he was going to, having told them that they had met at a fundraiser for his PAC, that they had hit it off and had started seeing each other shortly after that. He had also told them that they had seen each other off and on for about two years.

Sean was in the office with him. Brian could tell that he was still curious.

"You haven't told us how it ended," Sean said.

"I don't see how that's relevant," Brian hedged.

Sean sighed. His sleeves were rolled up and his tie was undone. He had bags under his eyes. Brian thought Sean looked as exhausted as he himself felt.

"Brian, I have to admit. I'm kind of losing my patience."

"Then quit." Brian was losing patience as well.

Sean took a deep breath and relaxed his shoulders. "Look, I get that this is difficult for you, and I can tell that —" he paused, as if choosing his words carefully, "I can tell that it wasn't just a casual thing for you."

Brian raised his eyes to look at Sean in defiance.

Sean continued quickly. "Because if it would have been casual, you wouldn't be holding back so much. Whether you're doing that to protect her or because it's so personal for you, or both, I don't know, but either way — look, just tell me whether it ended on bad terms or not."

Brian waited a long time before speaking. "It did."

"It ended on bad terms?" Sean asked to clarify.

"Yes." And I've regretted it since, he thought.

"Okay, that's helpful to know. It makes it more complicated, but it's helpful to know."

Brian remained silent.

"Women can be vindictive —"

"Monica's not like that," Brian said defensively. Indeed, after it had ended he had never heard from her again.

"Are you sure you know what she's really like?"

An image formed in Brian's mind of Monica in bed with him, with her arms around him, listening to him complain about his job, complain about having to travel so much and how it affected his relationship with Abby, and complain about his boss. She rubbed his back and told him that no one should ever criticize his or her partner for having to work, since that was their livelihood. Brian thought then that Monica had always been exactly what he needed.

"Yes, I know what she's really like," Brian said under his breath. He ran both his hands through his thick hair. "Sean, I need to call Abby."

"Okay." Sean moved to leave. "Don't worry, I'm not quitting, not yet, at least."

"I appreciate that."

When Sean was out of the office, Brian dialed Abby's number, steeling himself.

She answered in a whirlwind, almost shouting into the phone. "Brian?"

"Yes, it's me."

"What the hell?! Why haven't you called?!"

Brian imagined her on the other end of the line, eyes huge, one thin hand on a narrow hip, jaw stuck out in defiance. Physically, she could not have been more different from Monica. Abby was attractive, with straight, blond hair, but was constantly worried about her appearance. She was always impeccably made up; she constantly monitored what she ate, and complained about aging. She was only 31. She was also a long-distance runner, with the thin frame that accompanied that pastime.

Monica, on the other hand, had toned arms and legs, and an hourglass shape and womanly hips. Brian suddenly thought of his hands on those hips. He shook his head to clear it.

"I'm really sorry. I've been insanely busy here —" His tone was all business.

"I saw the interview. What the hell is Ross talking about? This is a joke, right?"

"Look, Abby —"

"Well, it's not true, right? Right?!"

There was no easy way to say this. Brian sucked in air and held his breath. "I'm sorry, Abby, but it's true."

He waited but heard only silence for several moments.

"*You cheated on me?!* But — she's so *old!*"

Age is a state of mind, Brian thought then. Monica was more youthful than Abby, and much more comfortable in her own skin. And Monica didn't care what anyone thought about her.

But Brian didn't say any of that.

"Look, I haven't seen her for about five years —"

"You cheated on me! I can't believe it!" Abby scoffed. "And

this is why you wouldn't marry me, right?"

"What are you talking about?" Brian said impatiently. "No, that's not it —"

"Please, Brian, we have been together for, like, what, eight years?! And you obviously don't want to marry me, and it's a good thing we didn't get married, isn't it?"

She became increasingly worked up, chattering on and on. Brian didn't blame her, but he was exhausted from the day's events and had a difficult time dealing with her emotional reaction.

"Abby, calm down. Let's talk —"

"No, Brian! Honestly! What the hell were you thinking?!"

"Abby —"

She continued to interrupt him. His face felt hot. She wouldn't let him get two words in.

"Abby, wait —"

"Don't talk to me like that —"

"I didn't want to marry you because I didn't know if I loved you anymore!" he exploded into the phone. "I didn't want to be tied down! And you always complained about me having to work but, honestly, what the hell did you expect me to do?! I need an income, don't I?! So we can take all those trips you want and go to happy hour every night with your friends, right?!"

"Oh, and that *woman* didn't complain about you having to work? She didn't complain that you didn't have time to fuck her enough?!"

"She *never* complained about that! In fact, she always listened to me. She understood —"

Brian realized how loud his voice had gotten when Sean entered the office.

"Is everything all right?" Sean asked.

Brian nodded, then said into the phone. "Look, I'm on my way home, and we'll talk, all ri —"

"I will not be here when you get home," Abby interrupted, her voice like ice. She hung up.

Brian looked at his cell phone, then sighed heavily.

"Well," he said to Sean, "I guess that's that."

"How'd she take it?" Sean asked.

"Not well. I'm pretty sure I just got dumped."

"Hey, I'm sorry."

"Don't be," Brian smiled weakly. "Frankly, it was a long time coming." He shook his head. "I need to get home, get some sleep. We'll regroup here tomorrow, all right?"

Sean nodded. "We'll need to talk tomorrow first thing. The Chairman called."

Brian looked at Sean questioningly.

Sean wore a resigned expression. "The local Chairman," he explained. "Actually, Chairmen, to be precise."

"Damn it," Brian cursed. Sean was talking about the Chairmen of the local Democratic Committee. The Eighth District covered parts of both Fairfax County and the city of Alexandria; and the Chairmen from both of those local parties would be here. They would want an explanation.

"Go home, Brian, and we'll deal with it tomorrow. But don't worry."

"I'm not worried about myself," Brian told his friend. Maybe it was the deliriousness from lack of sleep, or the weighing of the emotions of the day, or his conscience, but Brian let something slip. "I'm worried about Monica. They're going to come down even harder on her. I wish — I wish I could talk to her." He meant that he wished he could talk her through it.

"That's not a good idea, Brian. I strongly advise against that.

104

Besides, there's no guarantee she would even want to talk to you."

"You're right." Brian got up and made a move to leave.

About fifteen minutes later, when Brian was in the cab on the way home, he found himself still thinking about Monica.

He took out his cell phone and texted her.

Hey, are you okay?

In about a minute, he had the response.

I'll survive. How's everything over there?

He wrote back: *I could say all right, but I'd be lying. But I'll survive. Good night. Sleep well.*

Good night. You too, she answered.

Then he realized the stupidity of telling her to sleep well. He had the strong inclination that neither of them would sleep at all that night.

Brian arrived home to a dark house, and a note on the kitchen table.

I'm staying with my mother for a little while. Don't bother calling. Abby.

Brian lay down on the large bed, which was unmade, fully clothed. He closed his eyes, and all he saw was Monica reaching an arm across his bare chest and touching his face like she used to when he was upset.

Chapter 20

The cab pulled up in front of Monica's house and she sat there, staring at her front door.

"That will be $15.00, Ma'am," the cab driver said.

She was ruthlessly brought back to reality. "Uh — okay, sorry," she stammered. She fished money out of her purse and handed it to him.

"Thank you, I appreciate it," he told her.

She exited the cab, then stumbled onto the sidewalk in her high heels while she rubbed the mascara from her eyes. She walked slowly up her front steps, as if she were weighed down, and stood in front of her townhouse. It was mostly dark, except for a light on in the kitchen. Christian would be working at his computer, or maybe watching TV. Thank God David would be asleep, she thought.

Monica turned the key in the lock and opened the front door slowly. She recited the Litany Against Fear as she did so.

"And only I will remain," she finished as she shut the door.

Bandit came running up to her, wagging her tail furiously and waiting for a sign of affection. Monica bent down and scratched the dog's head.

You are probably the only one who loves me without condition, she thought, and who doesn't judge me for anything.

Resigned to her fate, Monica walked upstairs and turned into the kitchen. Christian sat at the kitchen table.

She couldn't tell from his expression how angry he was. The past couple of years, he had been increasingly difficult to read.

"*Hola*," she said by way of greeting.

He looked at her, his hand over his mouth and his elbow on the table. Monica felt horrible, as if she were the worst person in the world.

After the affair with Brian had ended, she had cried herself raw when she was alone. Finally, time had started to dull her pain, such that she had been able to think more clearly. At that time, Monica had been consumed with guilt for what she had done to her husband. She had been petrified that Christian would find out, that people would think horribly of her, and that everything would change.

And now, the worst had happened. All Monica could think about was how she had hurt her husband.

"Christian, I'm — I'm sorry." She didn't know where to begin. "You must know that things haven't been right between us for a while, for like, years —"

"I can't believe you," he said quietly. "I can't believe you let another man stick his dick in you."

Monica was shocked. "It wasn't like that —"

"Oh, so you didn't have sex with him?" Christian stood up.

She couldn't deny that. "Yes, I did, but — I wasn't —" she tried to state it as diplomatically as possible. "I wasn't only looking for sex."

"Oh?" he asked in mock amazement. "What were you looking for then?"

"Where to start?!" Monica couldn't believe that that was a serious question. "Christian, we never talk! I mean, we never talk about anything substantive!"

"Lower your voice, you're going to wake David!" Christian whispered urgently. Then he stood up and crossed his arms, and Monica realized for the first time just how angry he was. "I want to know everything! How did you meet?"

Monica's shoulders fell. "He runs a PAC, and we met at a fundraiser."

"When?"

"Like — about seven years ago."

"When did you start having sex with him?"

"Shortly after that."

"For how long?"

"I saw him maybe — once every few weeks or months for about two years."

Christian cursed in Spanish under his breath, then shook his head at her. "When would you see him, after work?"

"Sometimes," she shrugged.

"What was it like?"

Monica understood, but pretended that she didn't. "What was what like?"

"The sex — what was it like?"

Energetic, but sometimes tender, she thought. "Are you sure that you really want to hear this?"

"Absolutely."

"It was fine." When she saw that Christian wasn't satisfied with the response, she added, "you are not in the frame of mind to hear this right now."

"Oh, yes, I am," he said angrily.

"What the hell do you want me to say? It was fine, normal." We would have sex and then talk politics, she thought, and he would hold me. Remembering all that made Monica sad. She needed to change the subject. "You and I, Christian, we never talk," she repeated. "And the more success I have in my life, the more content I am with how things in my life are going, work, volunteering, politics — the happier I am, the more you resent me. You are forty-six years old and you act like you're seventy."

"Your problem is —" Christian began.

"Oh, I would *love* to hear what *my* problem is!" Monica interrupted, her voice dripping sarcasm. "*Your* problem is that all you do around here is mope. You have no initiative to do anything! You just clock in at work and clock out!"

Bandit started to bark at the noise, and Monica shushed her.

"Because you're too busy for me —"

"Too busy? You never want to do anything, so I make my own plans! I have *never* been the type of woman to sit around and wait for a man! I don't *need* a man! You knew that when you married me!"

"I want you to quit the campaign," Christian said, a bit more calmly.

"What? No." Monica couldn't believe it.

"Quit the campaign, and we'll work on it."

"Work on what?" She was skeptical.

"Work on our marriage."

Monica shook her head. "Christian, I have tried to tell you over the past few years that I wasn't happy. I have tried to ask you why you seemed so unhappy and stressed, and you would never, or could never, tell me." She paused. She had even asked him to go to counseling with her, but he had refused. She didn't mention it now. She didn't see the point. "*Francamente, a estas alturas...* if you didn't want to work on it then, I don't see why you would now."

"Just quit the campaign. Isn't your family more important?"

That was a low blow, Monica thought. "If you really knew me

109

and supported me, you would see how important this campaign is to me. But you don't."

"If you don't quit —" he left it hanging.

"Then I'll deal with it." She meant that she would deal with him leaving her. "Do *not* give me an ultimatum, Christian."

He seemed surprised. Monica continued slowly for emphasis. "If you want a wife who will be here every day when you get home, who will do what *you* want to do all the time, then you need to find someone else."

When Christian didn't respond, Monica began to turn to leave. "I'll sleep in the guest room," she said. He didn't follow her.

She dragged her feet upstairs, weary from the events of the day. The entire district, no, the entire state, no, the entire country, would know her business. The media loved a good scandal, and you could not have made this stuff up. Two newbie opponents in a congressional race had had an affair years ago, and they had both cheated on their significant others, and the age difference! The press would call her a cougar, and worse.

She dreaded reading the newspapers the next day.

Monica peeked in David's room. Ever since he was a baby, no matter how horrible her day had been, she would check on him before she went to bed, and her heart would fill with happiness, because he was hers, with her nose and her forehead, and her brown hair and large, dark eyes. He had always been affectionate as a little boy. When she had cried, he had stroked her shoulder and said, "It's okay, Mommy."

She went to the side of his bed and sat down on the edge. She pulled the covers up over him.

David opened his eyes. "Hey, Mom," he said.

Monica sighed, deflating a little. She smiled at him. "Hey, sweetheart."

"Are you okay?" he asked her.

Monica wondered how much he knew. She didn't have the guts to ask him. "Yeah," she said. "Look, it's late. Go to sleep."

Monica suddenly felt the exhaustion sweep over her like a wave. She lay down on the edge of David's queen-sized bed, fully clothed. She kicked off her heels and let them fall to the floor. She was on her side, facing her son.

Monica began to think about her parents, and what they would say to her next time they talked to her. She thought about Christian's family. She loved Christian's brothers and sisters as if they were her own siblings. She probably wouldn't have contact with them ever again. Her world was turning upside down, and it was entirely her fault.

Monica felt the tears come and couldn't find the will to try to stop them. In about a minute, her face was wet and she sobbed.

David touched her hand. "It's okay, Mom," he said.

She knew then that he knew everything, because he didn't ask her why she was crying. Whether he had seen the broadcast, or Christian had told him, he knew.

"Just tell me — tell me you don't hate me," Monica managed to say between sobs.

"I don't hate you, Mom." He swallowed. "I love you." Then he said something that reminded her how mature he was. "Remember what *abuela* always says?"

"What's that?"

"Everything is always better in the morning."

Chapter 21

It was indeed slightly better in the morning, if only for the fact that it was a clear, sunny day with low humidity for this time of year.

Monica woke up in the guest room in her underwear. The night before, she had stripped off all of her clothes and climbed into the guest bed without brushing her teeth or washing her face. She looked at her cell phone. It was 9:30am. David would have already left for school, and Christian would be at work.

She had missed calls from her parents. She hoped that Val had filled them in, so that she didn't have to. She also had several missed calls and texts from Nicole and Don. When she read their texts, she felt bad. They were already in the office, working for her, and here she was, sleeping in, feeling sorry for herself.

She called Don.

"Hey!" he answered with concern in his voice. "Are you all right?"

"Yeah, I'll live. I'm really sorry I'm late. I just got up. I'm going to check the headlines and get dressed and I'll be right there."

There was silence on the other end.

Monica got goosebumps. "What's wrong?" she asked.

"The local Chairmen are on their way over. Just get here as soon as you can."

Thank God Don was all business, Monica thought, because

she didn't think that she could take it if he started asking her questions about what she had said to Christian and if she was going to leave him.

"What do they want?" Monica asked, her heart sinking, even though she knew perfectly well what they wanted.

Don sighed, as if he were about to give her some bad news.

"They want to talk about what happened with you and Brian. I'll be honest, Monica. They don't seem too happy about being kept in the dark."

That was an understatement, she was sure. But she felt angry that the Chairmen thought that they had a right to know all about her past.

"Okay, give me twenty minutes, and please get some breakfast and coffee for me. I'm starving."

"You got it." He paused again. "You sure you're okay?"

"Yeah."

They hung up and Monica willed herself to put both feet on the floor to get up. She did so, and almost stepped on Bandit, who had been sleeping next to her bed. She should have known; Bandit always followed her around.

Monica showered and put on one of the most conservative black skirt suits that she owned. It was boring but at least no one could accuse her of dressing provocatively.

Then she carefully put on her war paint, foundation, eyeliner, eye shadow and mascara, determined to mask the circles under her eyes.

She called a taxi, and when the company called to say that the taxi was outside waiting, she grabbed her purse and briefcase and headed for the door.

As soon as she stepped outside, she was broadsided by a group of reporters. She took one look at them and turned her head away to lock the door as quickly as she could.

Jesus Christ, why didn't I think of that? she thought, angry at herself.

She pushed past them, keeping her head down. She felt relieved that she had put on makeup.

The questions came lightning-fast.

"Is it true that you had an affair with Brian Murphy?"

"What's going to happen with your marriage?"

"Are you going to withdraw from the race?"

"Why did you stop seeing Murphy?" Monica noted, with some amusement, that the last question presupposed that what Ross had said was true, and to answer it would be to admit to the affair. Not a bad ploy.

"Were you in love with Murphy?"

Monica pressed her lips together and didn't say anything. Her campaign had already indicated that they had no comment for the moment, so she shouldn't say anything else.

She got in the cab quickly and closed the door, without regard to whether any of the reporters were in the way. That was their problem, as far as she was concerned.

She shielded her face with one hand. *De Guatemala a Guatepeor*, she thought. From bad to worse.

If the cab driver knew who she was, thankfully, he didn't say anything.

As soon as she arrived at the office, she sought out Nicole and Don.

"How's everything going?" she asked them.

"Good," Nicole said, appearing to have everything under control.

At least someone does, Monica thought then.

"I had a group of journalists outside my house this morning."

Nicole sighed with exasperation. "I'm sorry. I should have warned you. I figured you would assume that."

"I *should* have assumed it," Monica replied. If I hadn't been overthinking so much, she thought.

"Hey," Don told her, "get some breakfast. You have croissants and coffee in your office. The Chairmen are on their way over. I put them off as long as I could."

"Thank you," she said, smiling weakly.

Monica went to her office and scarfed down a croissant, washing it down with coffee. Everything was happening so fast, that she didn't really have time to process anything.

She forced herself to take a deep breath. Just tackle one thing at a time, she thought.

Don entered her office after knocking once.

"The Chairmen will be here in five or ten minutes."

"Okay," Monica nodded. "What am I going to tell them?"

"As far as what you should say, just tell the truth as much as possible. But only answer the questions they ask you. Don't volunteer any information, you know, like a good lawyer."

Monica nodded.

She continued to drink her coffee and grabbed the day's copy of the local paper, which someone had placed on her desk.

There was an above-the-fold front-page article with the headline "Opponents Murphy and Orellana had an Affair." Monica scoffed and started reading the article. It basically reiterated what Ross had reported, and there was a great deal of speculation. Monica took that as a good thing, since it strongly suggested that the journalists hadn't been able to find anything else to corroborate Ross' allegations.

There was a rapid knock at her office door, and Nicole walked in. "They're here," she said.

115

A few moments later two men walked in, followed by Nicole and Don. Monica knew both of them.

Steven, the Alexandria Chairman of the GOP, was younger than Monica. He was enthusiastic and always a bundle of energy, organizing things left and right.

Conrad, the Fairfax County Chairman, was older, and had been with his local committee for much longer. He was no-nonsense and formal. He was quite tall and looked down at Monica from above his dark-rimmed glasses.

"Have a seat, gentlemen," Monica told them. "What can I do for you?"

Both men remained standing.

"Monica," Conrad began, "we were kind of unsettled by the report last night."

Monica crossed her arms and waited. She said nothing, since he hadn't asked a question.

"Is it true?" Conrad continued.

Monica looked at Don, then Nicole, in turn. She had half a mind to completely deny it. If Ross' story was all the evidence that they had, all the evidence that existed, then denying may be a better option. But Monica thought that was a risky proposition.

Don had told her to tell the truth. Plus, she was an attorney, and the Virginia State Bar ethics rules stated that attorneys couldn't lie, about anything. Never mind that she had lied to Christian when she had cheated on him.

With all that going through her mind, she answered, "yes."

"So how long did the affair go on?" Conrad pressed.

"You do realize that my campaign has not made any formal statements thus far regarding this issue, so this conversation is entirely off the record," Monica made clear.

"We understand that, and we won't share this information with anyone," Conrad assured her.

Monica exhaled. "Two years," she answered.

"And you were married at the time?"

"Yes."

"How did you meet him?"

"At a fundraiser for his PAC."

"What was the nature of the relationship?"

Monica was uncomfortable with this line of questioning. "That is none of your business."

"Monica —" Steven began.

"Steve, I don't see why the hell I should have to share personal information with you guys."

"We don't like this either, Monica," Conrad told her. "And if we had known this beforehand, it would have been easier to deal with."

"Would you have supported me if you had known?" Monica asked.

Neither man responded. Monica smirked, then shook her head, not really seeing the point in stonewalling anymore.

"It was a — physical relationship. That's all you need to know."

"When did it end?" Conrad asked.

"About five years ago."

"Have you seen or talked to him since then?"

"No."

"How did it end?"

Monica gave them the same answer that she had given Don, that the relationship had fizzled out.

"Here's the thing, Monica," Conrad said, putting his hands together. "This was always going to be a difficult race for us. And," he paused, exhaling. "Now, with this revelation —" He left it hanging.

"What are you saying exactly?" Monica hated it when people beat around the bush without getting to the point.

"Just that now it's going to be even more difficult."

"So," Monica made a hand gesture, emphasizing her point. "If I understand you correctly, I'm not going to get any support from the Committees. Is that right?"

"No, no," Steven said. "We will still go door-knocking for you, we will put up yard signs, fliers, all that. That's what we had planned to do since the beginning. We'll also help organize local events if you need."

Monica was direct. "What about any financial support from the National Committee? That was something we had initially discussed."

Conrad sighed. "Look, Monica, we don't think you can expect any help in that area."

"But we're doing well in the polls!" She was incredulous. "We have a real shot here!"

"That was before yesterday." Conrad look resigned.

"Hoffman has been here for over twenty years. For the first time, the GOP has a shot at this seat. I am well-connected in this area. People know me; they like me —"

"I know, but —" Conrad seemed at a loss for words.

"Yeah, I get it," Monica said with sarcasm. "I'm damaged goods. All the good I've done, all the people I've gotten to know over the years, it's all worth shit because I hooked up with a guy over five years ago!"

"Not just any guy," Conrad emphasized. "Your opponent."

"How the hell was I supposed to know seven years ago that he would be my opponent today?!"

"That's politics, Monica," Conrad said with a note of finality in his voice. "Look, if it's any consolation," Conrad began cautiously, "The Committee most likely wouldn't have given you much financial support anyway."

"First of all, it's not a consolation. And, second, apparently they would rather see a Democrat in office in this district than someone like me, because I don't always toe the party line. That's the truth."

Neither man said anything. They said goodbye, professing that they would be in touch and would provide campaign volunteers and election-day support as available.

After they left, Monica sat down in her armchair, with her hand supporting her forehead. She turned to Nicole and Don.

"So we're going to have hardly any money, while the Democratic machine just rips through us," she said forlornly. "Because you guys know that the DNC's still going to give Brian money."

"Not necessarily," Nicole disagreed. "Monica, this may actually work to our advantage a little bit. The DNC is going to assume that this election is a given, that Murphy'll win, so they may not give him that much money."

"But they have money to give," Don countered. "The second they think he's in trouble, the funds will come pouring in. Just like with the last governor's race. The Dems spent so much money, and the Republican candidate lost by so little. It was amazing."

Nicole still wasn't entirely convinced. "But if the funds come pouring in at the last minute, they may not do much good."

"Come on," Don said. "The public doesn't have that long of an attention span. Funds at the last minute always help."

Monica was deep in thought. "Should our campaign strategy change and, if so, how?"

"Honestly, Monica," Nicole said, looking like she was about to give her friend bad news, "we really can't answer that question until we know the political fallout from this — situation."

"You have to make a statement before Murphy does." Don's expression turned serious. "As soon as possible."

"What do I say?" Monica bit her lip. Her heart began to race. "Can I deny it?"

Nicole and Don both sighed at the same time.

Nicole spoke first. "What if you deny it and he admits to it?"

"What if I ask him to deny it, too?"

"Too risky," Don said immediately. "We can't trust anything his campaign says or does."

"Plus," Nicole added gently, "if Christian moves out, or if there's visible trouble between you two, then you would have to explain that, and people will assume that it was because of the affair."

"I already admitted it to Christian," Monica said absently.

Don looked like he was about to say something, then closed his mouth.

"You're going to have to admit to it publicly," Nicole said. "It's the only way to get past this, because every time you speak in public, or go to an event, people will be asking you about it. And, frankly, the longer you wait —"

"The more it looks like I have something to hide," Monica finished.

"That's right," Don agreed.

"What about doing a press conference?" Monica asked, although the idea of it made her feel nauseous.

"Risky," Don said, "but it also suggests you have little to hide. I like it."

"It's doable," Nicole concurred, "but we'll need to prepare. Can you —" Nicole stopped.

When she didn't continue, Monica looked at her. "Do you mean can I keep my shit together?" She chuckled. "Yes, I can." Although she appeared full of bravado, Monica doubted herself. "How soon?"

"As soon as we can," Don said.

"Tomorrow afternoon or evening?"

"That might be too late," Nicole said.

"I'm not sure I can get it together before then," Monica said honestly.

"Then let's do it whenever we can." Don seemed confident.

"But we won't announce until the last minute, right? So Murphy won't know," Nicole offered.

"Exactly," Don said excitedly. "He may issue a statement before then, but we can go ahead with the press conference, because it's bolder, and it will look like we're in better control than he is."

"Let's hope that he's too busy until then to think of making a statement," Nicole said.

Monica thought of how Brian had sounded on the phone last night, downright at a loss, when he was usually controlled and hard to read. She guessed he hadn't slept much.

"He won't make a statement today, and most likely not tomorrow," she said.

"How do you know?" Don asked, his brows furrowed.

She looked at Don. "Because I know him."

Chapter 22

If Monica wasn't a basket case the day before, she was closer to it today.

She woke up the next morning with a bad headache. She had again slept in the guest room. It was early and she could hear David and Christian downstairs.

She had stayed late at the campaign office talking with Don the night before. He had asked her what was going on with Christian. She had been honest with him, telling him that they weren't sleeping in the same room, but that, other than that, it was pretty much up in the air.

"Is he going to file for divorce?" Don had asked her.

She had been thoughtful. "I don't know. I probably would if I were him."

Then she had gone home, and Christian and David had already been asleep.

Today, Monica got up, taking care not to step on Bandit, and put on her robe. She was downstairs in time to give David a kiss goodbye.

"Bye, Mom," he said. "Hope to see you tonight."

His statement made her feel guilty. She felt that she was becoming an absentee mother. The campaign was taking over everything. It's only temporary, she told herself.

After Christian and David left, Monica looked at the news on her laptop. The story of the affair was everywhere.

What did I expect? she thought. *That the news would magically disappear?*

Monica finally began to think about the repercussions of Ross' interview. No one else was around to talk to, and since the night before last, she hadn't really had time to sit down and think about the consequences of the revelation.

It occurred to her that she would never spend vacations with Christian's family in Argentina again, that she would never hold Christian again, wrap her arms around him like she used to do when he was sleeping. She didn't see any way to hold her marriage together, and she wasn't sure that she really wanted to anyway. And how would David take it?

And after this election, would she be able to get her old job back? If not, who would hire her? Who would date her?

Monica's cell phone range, and she jumped in her chair.

"Oh, no," she said aloud when she saw who was calling.

She answered the call anyway.

"Hi, Mom," she sighed into the phone.

"Monica, *¿que está pasando?*" Her mother got directly to the point, without the usual small talk.

Monica paused. She didn't know where to start.

"Mom," she began tentatively, "did you watch the interview the night before last?"

"Yes!" Her mother sounded less than thrilled. "And I talked to your sister." She punctuated her words slowly. "Did you have an affair with that man? Is that true?"

Monica opened her mouth but no words came out.

"You did, didn't you?" her mother continued. "Why would you do that? Why?!"

"It was a long time ago. And, anyway, it's in the past. I can't

123

change it now, even if I wanted to."

"Do you know your aunts called me, and your cousins called me, from Spain? They heard the news over there."

"Oh, Goodddd," Monica said. Indeed, God only knew what they were saying about her. Some of her aunts and cousins were the worst gossips.

"Why would you put your marriage in jeopardy like that? What were you thinking?"

I wasn't thinking, Monica thought.

"It's in the past. It can't be undone. I just have to deal with it," Monica said softly.

"You've ruined everything!"

"For who? For *you*? I'm so sorry, Mom," Monica said with sarcasm. "I'm so sorry that you're embarrassed."

"I'm not embarrassed," her mother said, softening her tone.

"Bullshit." Monica was tired and upset. "I'm so sorry that not everything is perfect for you."

"So will Christian leave you? You can't blame him!" her mother exclaimed.

Never mind that he and I mentally and emotionally left each other years ago, Monica thought.

"Probably," Monica answered. "Maybe, I — I don't know."

"So what will you do?"

Good question, Monica thought. "I'll finish the campaign, first of all —"

"Wait, you're still going to run?" her mother asked as if Monica had just said the craziest thing in the world.

"Yes. What else *can* I do?"

"You can quit the race, and focus on your family," her mother said matter-of-factly.

Of course, Monica thought, my mother *would* say that. "I'm

going to finish the race, and then I'll move on."

Move on. What did that mean exactly? It means go live by myself, share custody of David, hope that Christian doesn't put too many roadblocks in my path, that the divorce doesn't get too contentious, that I come out of this financially solvent.

"Do you really think that's a good idea, in light of —"

"Mom, I am forty-four years old! *I* decide what's best for me. And right now, I'm going to run in this campaign." And I won't allow you to guilt me into anything else, she thought.

"What about David?"

Her mother had hit the real sore spot.

"David will be fine. He has two parents who love him very much, and he knows that he is loved."

"But —"

"Honestly, we're done. There is nothing else to say, is there?"

Her mother was silent, for once.

"Look, I'm sorry this is so difficult for you. I can only imagine what my aunts said to you on the phone," Monica said. "But I can't change the past. I can only deal with what I've got, all right?"

There was a pause. "All right," her mother said. "I just can't believe you did this. I never imagined you capable of —"

"I don't expect you and Dad to agree with everything that I do. Please, just offer your support, if you can. That is all I ask."

Another pause.

"All right," her mother said, and sighed dramatically.

"Believe me, I know what I'm in for here."

"Monica, I know things between you and Christian haven't been perfect. But you should have tried to work on them before —"

"I know, but we're past that now. Look, I'm sorry about all

this. I love you. We'll talk soon."

"I love you, too."

Monica said goodbye and hung up before she started to cry. She knew what was going on.

Her mother disapproved, of course, but knew that her daughter was headstrong and wouldn't listen, anyway. She also knew that her mother was worried about her. Frankly, it would just be easier to quit.

I am in way over my head, Monica thought.

She sat there, unable to move.

Her phone rang again. It was Nicole, calling to see how she was doing and when she would be in the campaign office.

"I am freaking out, Nic, I am freaking the fuck out!" Monica cried into the phone.

"Monica, the problem is that you are letting them define you. The longer you wait to respond, the more time the Dems have to control the dialogue. You're not talking, so the media is talking for you."

"It doesn't matter, anyway. If I do talk, they'll just twist all of my words around. You know how that goes —"

"Not if I can help it. I will make damn sure that doesn't happen. We will be out there all day, every day, hammering our story in the press. And you will be everywhere, campaigning. It's about the campaign, about the people of this district."

"I'm a horrible person."

"No, you are not a horrible person. You did a bad thing, but you are not a bad person, because I know you."

Monica smiled through her tears. "Thank you."

"Hey," Nicole began, then used a line that she had said to Monica several times in law school. "You are the Antonin Scalia to my Ruth Bader Ginsberg."

"You know those two were friends in real life, right?" Monica said.

"Yes, so it's a valid comparison."

Monica chuckled, then exhaled to compose herself. "I'll be at the office in thirty minutes."

Chapter 23

That afternoon, Monica swung her car around the front of David's school, swerving then stopping to wait in line behind the other cars. She hated to wait. There were so many things to do and waiting was a waste of time, but she had promised to pick David up today. He didn't always like her hanging around with him and his friends, but he still liked the fact that she sometimes picked him up from school.

Monica's press conference was scheduled for early that evening, and she had spent the entire day prepping for it with Nicole and Don.

She was finally able to bring the car around and David approached.

"Hey, Mom," he said after opening the car door and throwing his backpack in the backseat.

"Hey, sweetheart. How was the day?"

"Good."

She searched his face, knowing better than to press him for details. Once he had told his grandmother to please stop asking him questions about his school day, and that he didn't want to talk. His grandmother had told Monica that she should "fix this."

Fix what? The fact that my son is introverted and needs some space after being forced to interact with people at school all day? she had thought.

There's nothing to "fix." David, like his mother, would talk when he was ready.

"You okay, Mom?" David asked, bringing his mother out of her reminiscing.

"Yes, sweetheart," she answered as she pulled onto the main road, heading to the house.

"Crazy stuff, huh?"

"Yeah," she said, sighing. "David," she began, then stopped, questioning whether she should continue.

"What is it, Mom?"

"You know — everything that's going on — you know that it has nothing to do with you, right?"

"I know." He looked downward.

"What's going on with your father and me — I'm not sure what will happen." She stopped at a red light and looked at David. "I love you more than you know, and that will never change."

David looked up at her. "I know, Mom."

"As long as you know that. And you can tell me anything. Do you have any questions for me, about anything?"

"Yes. Are you still in the campaign?"

"Yes."

"Good."

Good? Monica was pleased but surprised at his answer.

"In fact," Monica said, "I have a press conference in just a little while. I'm going to drop you at home, then head to the conference."

"Can't I come with you?"

"You want to come with me?"

"Yes, please?"

"Are you sure?" Monica would greatly welcome her son's

presence.

"Yes." He nodded.

"David, the reporters may ask very uncomfortable questions. Do you realize this?"

"I don't care."

"They may say things about me that you don't like."

"Then I'll kick their asses."

Monica smiled at her son's bravado, but said, "Thank you for that, but you cannot commit assault and/or battery on anyone. That's the deal. Or any other illegal activity," she quickly added before her son tried to "lawyer" her.

"Okay, okay." He threw up his hands playfully.

"Okay, last chance," Monica said firmly. "Home or not?"

"I'm going with you."

Monica smiled and continued driving.

Chapter 24

"Monica's holding a press conference today at five," Sean said to Brian and Mike. "They just announced it."

"Why aren't *we* holding one?" Mike asked rhetorically. "Oh yeah, because we couldn't get our shit together."

"Brian, you're being quiet," Sean said. "What do you think about this?"

The three men sat in Brian's office. Brian had his arms crossed and stood in front of the window, thinking. His usually reserved demeanor belied his racing mind; he struggled to focus his thoughts.

He abruptly shook his head. "Honestly, I'm surprised by it."

"Seriously?" Mike said, his face red. "Did you think she'd drop out?"

"I don't know," Brian said, his voice betraying his uncertainty. "She didn't tell me about it."

"Why would she tell you?" Sean asked, confused.

Brian shrugged. Indeed, why would she?

"Well, looks like she's not gonna drop out," Sean continued. "I mean, she'll take a beating at the press conference. But man, she has balls doing it. Most people would just do a quick mea culpa statement and take no questions."

"Maybe that's what she'll end up doing," Brian said.

"Well, my contact says that it's a full-blown press conference, questions from the press corps and all," Sean said, shaking his head. "We should've been out in the front with this. We should've held one first."

"We still can," said Brian, a hand to his chin, pensive. He felt confident that he could salvage the election, and that in a few months this wrinkle would be just a memory.

"Oh, we'll have to, and the benefit will be that we can respond to what Monica says. The downside will be that she'll get her version of the story out first."

Monica's press conference was set to begin in a few minutes. She paced nervously in the small room where she had gotten ready. David and Nicole were with her.

Don opened the door to the room quickly and stuck his head in.

"Just a few minutes, Monica."

She nodded, feeling the beginnings of perspiration under her armpits.

"This will go fine," Nicole told her.

Monica looked at her friend. "Thank you."

"Are you nervous, Mom?" David asked her suddenly, his big brown eyes open wide.

She looked at her son, and instantly relaxed a bit.

"Yes, a little, but I'm fine. I'm so happy you're here."

David gave her the goofy sideways grin he had been giving her since he was a little boy, showing that he appreciated her loving words and was embarrassed by them at the same time.

When Don called Monica to the stage, she followed him immediately, before she could get cold feet and back out.

"I will face my fear," she murmured to herself.

Once on the stage, looking out at the sea of people, she froze. She was overwhelmed by the lights, the noise, and the number of journalists present.

Don't think about how this is gonna suck, she told herself. *Or the constant overstimulation. Just do it.*

Monica looked on the stage around her. A podium rested in the center.

She suddenly knew what she wanted.

"Get this podium out of the way!" she said to no one in particular.

Nicole scurried up and said, "I'll get it."

"And please get me a bottle of water," Monica said with more calm. She took off her suit jacket and handed it to Don.

A few moments later, they went live.

"Okay, thank you all for coming. We have limited time so let's begin," Monica said.

The shouting and camera-flashing began. Monica took a deep breath and tried her best to tune out the noise.

She would open with a brief statement.

"As far as Ross Goldman's statement the other night," she began, and the journalists quieted down. "Unfortunately, it is true." She forced the words to leave her lips, even if she hated it. "Mr. Murphy and I had an on-off relationship several years ago."

The noise level in the room increased considerably, and Monica held up a hand for silence. "You will get the chance to ask questions in a minute. Let me say that it happened a long time ago, and I am deeply sorry for it. I am deeply sorry to my husband and my family. They don't deserve this." She then stated the words that she had rehearsed with Nicole. "We have many things to focus on in this campaign, and this should not be one of them. I would please ask for your understanding and for privacy as my family deals with this personal matter."

Monica was done with her opening. She exhaled. "Now we'll take a few questions."

They were like vultures on fresh meat, all yelling and gesticulating at once.

Monica locked eyes with a reporter. She took another deep breath and pointed. "Yes, you."

"When did the affair begin?"

"About seven years ago."

"How long did the affair last?"

"About two years."

"So when did it end?"

"Let's see, if you do the math, about five years ago. Or did you go to journalism school to avoid doing math? Because that's why I went to law school."

There was some laughter from the press. Monica called on another journalist.

"Were you married at the time?"

"Yes."

"And he had a girlfriend?"

"As far as I know, yes."

"Do you regret it?"

Monica paused. "I completely regret the pain I caused to my loved ones, to his loved ones. If I could take that back, I would." She paused for a moment, reconsidering her words. "Yes, I absolutely regret the relationship."

"Why did it end?"

"Um, it was a mutual decision." In her mind, Monica saw a door closing, and heard loud voices and sobbing. She almost became teary but held it together. Her son was watching this, after all.

She pointed to another journalist.

"Did you love him?"

Monica leaned back, surprised. She thought for a fraction of a second that she could ignore the question, but quickly decided that that would look worse.

"No," she answered, shaking her head quickly for emphasis. She quickly moved on to another reporter.

"Will you step down from the campaign?"

"No," she said without more.

"Have there been requests that you step down?"

Monica considered the question. The GOP representatives had mentioned that they wouldn't assist her with campaign funding, but that wasn't the same.

"No, not that I'm aware of," she said, and motioned to someone else.

"What would you say to people who would say that this is not how a candidate acts? That this is not something that voters in good conscience could vote for?"

"By all means, cast the first stone. Honestly, I don't think you should judge someone just because their sins are different from yours." She paused briefly. "That is what I would say."

"Are you a victim?" another reporter blurted out, and Monica decided she would answer the question.

"No. We are all masters of our own destiny and we have free will. The best and worst thing about the human mind is that we can rationalize any decision we make. We make mistakes doing so. I made a mistake."

She answered a few more questions about the campaign, whether her strategies would shift, if this changed anything. Then she felt a tug at her sleeve, which she knew to be Nicole.

"It looks like that is all we have time for. Thank you for coming."

Monica kept her back straight as she turned and walked side-by-side with Nicole off the stage, watching her feet so that she wouldn't trip in her heels.

"You did great," Nicole whispered to her.

Monica nodded in acknowledgement. "Thank you."

"I think we should schedule some news interviews over the next few days," her friend continued. "It would be a good idea."

"Okay," Monica said nervously.

She felt a wave of embarrassment wash over her, but also felt relieved that the press conference was over.

Chapter 25

onica arrived home exhausted. After dinner, she and David watched television for a bit, then David went to his room to read. Although Christian was home, they hardly interacted.

After David went to bed, Monica checked on him. She watched him sleeping peacefully for several minutes. When she gazed at him all tucked in like that, his long lashes sweeping across perfect skin, she was always reminded of him as a baby, chubby cheeks and all.

The light was turned off in the master bedroom, and Monica assumed that Christian was asleep. She shuffled to the guest room, the dog at her heels, half-jumping, half-lunging in her playfully friendly way.

She shut the guest room door behind her and proceeded to remove her necklace, bracelet, and earrings, tossing them on the nightstand.

She sat on the edge of the bed, Bandit still underfoot, seeking her attention, and put her face in her hands. She took a deep breath and exhaled.

If I can just get through this week, she thought.

Her phone blipped.

Goddammit, she thought. Who the hell could that be?

Slowly, she moved to her briefcase and retrieved her cell

phone.

It was a text message from Brian.

Just wanted to say good night. And thank you.

In her weary state, Monica did not understand.

For what? she texted back.

For not making me look like a jackass tonight. Because we both know that is not how it ended.

Monica paused, dumbfounded at his acknowledgement of the truth.

Not knowing what else to say, she texted: *You're welcome. And good night.*

Monica switched off her phone and lay down, fully clothed, on the bed. Her thoughts drifted to several years ago.

* * *

She was at Brian's old apartment, getting her clothes back on, and he was telling her that he was moving in with his girlfriend. She did not understand why he appeared so contrite. After much back and forth, she finally understood.

"*You don't want to see me anymore,*" *she said, feeling stupid.*

"*It's just that — how can we?*" *he said.*

"*Oh, you mean — logistically.*"

"*Right.*"

"*Jesus Christ.*"

"*What?*" *Brian asked, confused.*

"*So all this was just for your own convenience.*" *At that moment, she understood everything. He didn't care who he was fucking, as long as he was fucking someone. It could have been Monica or some other woman. He never cared.*

"*That's not what I meant,*" *he said quickly.*

"Like hell it's not. Oh, I am so stupid!" She felt hurt and confused, and hated herself.

Brian tried to backtrack, tried to reason with her, tried to explain that she had meant something to him, but the damage had all been done.

* * *

Monica hadn't bought his explanations and had stormed out of his place, slamming the front door and crying tears of rage. That was the last time they had had any contact until his text to her right after the primary.

Now, alone, relegated to the guest room in her own house, Monica closed her eyes and cried, letting the hurt from the past wash over her.

Chapter 26

"We have a huge problem," Mike said, loosening his tie with his right hand; he held a newspaper in his left.

Brian and Sean looked up from the table, where they had been reviewing voter lists.

Brian straightened his back and began loosening his tie.

"Monica has booked herself on every major news show and talk show. We've called and they don't have room for us," Mike said. "Well, some of them may try to squeeze us in."

"We need to get our story out there," Sean seconded.

"And exactly what is our story?" Mike retorted, huffing in frustration. "What do we want our message to be?"

"He needs to say he's sorry."

"She has more credibility now because she's apologized first. She makes him look weak." Mike threw up his hands and began to pace.

"She's smart," Sean said, biting a nail.

"We should've been smarter. We should've seen this coming!"

"We didn't think she was going to do this."

"You underestimated her," Brian said, and his two friends looked at him. "I warned you against doing that."

"Well, we can't go back in time and change things. Let's just deal with what we've got," Sean said, always the practical one.

"It doesn't matter, anyway. This is a deep blue district. We've got this," Mike said with conviction.

Instead of being comforted by the words, Brian's gut told him that they were headed down a tough road.

"What's that?" Brian asked Mike, noticing the newspaper for the first time.

"Oh," Mike said. "Take a look at this. Remember we were wondering about Ross' motives?"

Mike threw the newspaper on the table in front of Brian.

Brian unfolded it and looked at the front page.

A below-the-fold headline read, "I wanted to tell people what Murphy's really like."

Brian skimmed the article.

"What the hell is this?" Brian asked, looking at Mike.

"You tell me." Mike crossed his arms.

Brian stood, and held in his temper. "What I'm *really* like? That sonofabitch hardly knows me. I mean, we roomed together for a while, but we weren't close or anything."

"Calm down," Sean said, without looking up from the table.

"This is bullshit," Brian said, tossing the newspaper back on the table. "Get me Ross on the phone."

"What?" Mike shrugged. "He's not gonna talk to you."

Brian considered for a few moments. "You're right." He walked over to the sofa and grabbed his blazer.

"Where are you going?" Mike asked, confused.

"I'm gonna shut this shit down," Brian said, feeling his back pocket to make sure he had his wallet. "I'm gonna go talk to him."

"Hey, I don't think that's wise," Sean said. "We can try to get to him another way."

"No, I'm sick of this." Brian headed for the door.

"We have to organize a press conference, Brian," Sean insisted. "We've got shit to do."

"You guys can do that. I'll be back in an hour, tops."

Without waiting, Brian walked out the door. Mike moved to go after him, but Sean held up a hand.

"Don't," Sean said. "Let him go; just let him get it over with. We've got work to do here."

Mike reluctantly acquiesced.

When he got to the street and pulled out his phone to get a car service, Brian realized that he didn't even know the law firm where Ross worked.

He did a quick search online and pulled up the information. Determined to get some answers, he rode to downtown DC.

Once in front of the firm's building, he thought about what he should say. Impatient, he decided to wing it.

He entered the building and took the elevator to the eleventh floor, which was entirely occupied by the firm.

Brian greeted the receptionist with a charming smile. "Hey, how are you?"

"How can I help you?" she asked, returning the smile.

Brian looked down at her from beneath long, dark lashes. "I'm here to see Ross Goldman."

"Is he expecting you?"

"Um — yes."

The receptionist appeared confused at his hesitation. "Can I have your name please?"

Brian pursed his lips. He knew Ross would never agree to see him. As he took a few seconds to ponder how he should handle the situation, he saw a black-haired man out of the corner of his eye, in the hallway to the right of the receptionist's station.

Brian looked up and saw Ross a second before he saw Brian, which gave Brian enough time to walk over to him before he could flee.

"What do you want?" Ross asked.

"What the hell do you think you're doing?" Brian said angrily. "What the fuck is your problem?"

"Sir, sir —" the receptionist tried to get a handle on the situation. Brian ignored her.

A couple other people entered the hallway to see what was happening.

"You can't just come in here," Ross said in an angry whisper.

"Well, we can do this in your office, or out here in the open so that all your coworkers can hear us," Brian said loudly, his dark eyes darting around.

Ross seemed to consider. "Fine," he sighed heavily, and motioned for Brian to follow him.

"It's okay, Allison," Ross said over his shoulder to the receptionist. "I've been expecting him."

As Brian followed Ross, he wondered whether the other people in the office recognized him. It didn't matter. This was too important for him to care about being embarrassed.

Once they were in Ross' office (a huge corner office, Brian noted), he shut the door. Brian remained standing.

"Okay, you wanna tell me why the hell you're doing this?" Brian asked.

Ross sat in the large leather chair behind his desk. "Doing what?" he asked.

Brian was incredulous. "Oh, come the fuck on, Ross! Why the hell did you have to out me like that? For what purpose?"

"Everyone thinks you're the shit, and they are *so wrong*."

Brian shook his head quickly to clear it. "What are you talking about?"

"You always get what you want, and it sickens me, an idiot like *you*, who cheats on his girlfriend and doesn't even realize what he has. While you were getting everything you wanted, the cute girlfriend, the leadership position with the nonprofit, I got laid off, and was running out of money. Then my girlfriend dumped me —"

Brian remembered Ross being out of work for a while. He also remembered when Ross' girlfriend had dumped him. Brian had taken him out for drinks to take his mind off of it. But he hadn't remembered Ross being so bitter about any of that.

"That's what this is about? Look, I'm sorry about your job and your girlfriend, but none of that was *my* fault —" Brian motioned toward his chest.

"And then, on top of all that, I knew you were messing around on Abby. I just knew. And when I found out it was with Monica — oh my God! A woman like that with *you*!"

Brian's brows furrowed.

"I remember her from law school, Brian. The sexiest woman there, with an even better brain. She smoked everyone, including me. She was *hot*. Of course, she was married, so I never got to know her like I wanted to. But that didn't stop *you*, you asshole —"

"Wait." Brian held up a hand. "All this is because you're *jealous*?"

"How can an idiot like you get all the luck, the job, the women —"

"Jesus Christ, Ross." Brian ran a hand through his thick hair. "So you just had to go and fuck everything up for me —"

Ross shrugged.

"— and for Monica?"

"Not *my* fault she was banging you. That's her problem."

"You're a fucking psychopath."

"So now everyone knows you're not the golden boy anymore," Ross smirked.

Brian saw no point in sticking around. "Go to hell," he said as he swung the office door open and raced out of the building.

Chapter 27

The host, a well-dressed, older gentleman, looked Monica square in the eye, and she tried as hard as she could not to look away.

She almost regretted, not for the first time, acquiescing to Nicole's request that she go on this news show.

"So what would you tell the constituents of the Eighth District of Virginia about the affair?" the host asked.

Monica remained composed. "Look, this election is about the issues. As for me, people make mistakes. We're fallible. We try to make amends and move on."

"But you didn't exactly come clean about what you did, at least not initially, way back when."

Well, what would you have done? Monica thought, holding her tongue. Isn't it easier just to sweep it under the rug, at least, in theory?

"I didn't at first, and I deeply regret that. Mr. Murphy and I made a horrible mistake."

"What was going through your mind when Ross Goldman was making those statements on national television?"

"I was shocked. Just — utter disbelief."

"Did you know him?"

She and Nicole had talked about how to answer that question. They had decided that the best course of action was to be truthful.

"I knew him from law school."

"So he was a friend of yours?"

"No," Monica shook her head definitively, "just an acquaintance."

"When did you find out that Ross was going to reveal the affair?"

"When everyone else did, on the news."

"Seriously?" He seemed genuinely surprised.

"Yes."

"Any idea why he would do that?"

"No."

"Does he have anything against you?"

"Not that I know of."

The host seemed confused now.

"Does he have anything against Mr. Murphy?"

"Not that I know of," Monica repeated. "You would have to ask Mr. Murphy about that."

"Well, of course we can't ask Mr. Murphy, because he's not here tonight. And frankly —" Monica held her breath, waiting for the next question. "With all due respect to Mr. Murphy, I find it interesting that you are the one with the gumption to come on this show, not him."

Monica took that statement as a win.

Chapter 28

The Fairfax County Republican Committee meeting was held monthly at rotating locations. Fairfax County covers about 406 square miles, with a population of over one million. The county's Republican Committee was the largest in the region, and candidates running for federal, state, or local offices always made appearances during committee meetings. Monica was to be no exception.

Don and Nicole had thought it a good idea to make one of Monica's first public appearances post-debacle in a relatively friendly environment. However, the team was leery of how social conservatives would take to Monica now.

Brian's team had hastily organized a press conference a couple of days ago. Brian's charm and good looks had appeared to serve him well, even if his answers appeared stilted and he seemed a bit on edge.

Monica was coming off of her high from the several television and radio appearances she had done over the past couple of days. Each time, she had felt more confident and in control. Now it was time to face her constituents.

Monica arrived with Don and Nicole in tow, protectively by her side. She cut a trim figure in a black skirt suit with a hot pink scarf. Indeed, she had lost a few pounds over the past several days. The stress diet actually works, she had sardonically thought.

I want to hide in a corner, Monica thought, or better yet, run as far away as I can get from here.

But that equated to conceding the election, and she wasn't ready to do that.

Monica made a point of standing tall, with her shoulders back. She didn't want to look meek.

Several people she knew greeted her with smiles, and her anxiety eased a bit. She engaged them in conversation and, as they formed around her, more people came up to her, shaking her hand and offering words of support.

The meeting was called to order and Monica sat at the table for her assigned district. She would address the crowd after the party business was finished.

When it was her turn to speak, she approached the microphone and the crowd immediately went silent.

She exhaled slowly. This was a friendly crowd. From here on out, almost all the crowds she faced would not be this friendly. In fact, they would largely be downright hostile.

"I know that the past few days have been challenging for my campaign," she began, looking over the crowd. "I'm here to let you know that I'm continuing to challenge the Democratic nominee, and we have a good chance of taking the Eighth District." She paused, and chanced a look at Nicole, who nodded slightly.

"We're always looking for volunteers, so if you are able to help us out, whether by door knocking, phone banking, posting signs in your yard, or any other way, we would very much appreciate that."

"Why should we help *you*?!" A man near the middle of the crowd exclaimed, standing up.

"Because we have a real chance at putting a Republican in the Eighth District," Monica said as calmly as she could.

"There's no way —" the man continued, "— that I could vote for an adulterer. Not happening!"

Several other people, emboldened by his statement, voiced their agreement.

"Now, now," the county chairman said into the microphone, "we will let Ms. Orellana speak."

"We all make mistakes, Sir," Monica said. "I'm asking for your forgiveness, and for your help."

"You'll be judged."

"I'll be judged someday, yes, by a power higher than all of us here. But I'll be judged sooner at the voting booth this November. And you know something? Like me or not, I'm all you got right now."

The man said nothing further and Monica thanked everyone for their time.

Nicole approached Monica as they left the meeting.

"I talked to the powers that be," Nicole began, sighing. "Doesn't look like they're going to give you much money from the coffers."

Monica snickered. "They weren't going to give us money anyway. Now they have an excuse. We have to hit donors, even small donors." Monica stopped and faced her friend. "I will talk to anyone I have to. Tell Don to set it up. No amount of money is too small."

"Hey, Monica," the chairman said as he approached.

He wore a poker face. Monica waited.

"Thanks for coming."

Monica nodded, hoping that his thanks were sincere.

Chapter 29

Monica sat in Don's car with Don and Nicole, heading to a Chamber of Commerce event. She had spent the last few days doing small meet and greets with locals; most had gone fairly well. Don said they were helping people see Monica as a real person.

She was still anxious; it was impossible for her not to be. She didn't know whether people would feel sorry for her or throw things at her. But she had had the chance to talk about policy issues, which made her feel slightly better.

"Look, I know this is uncomfortable," Don said from the driver's seat, "but if you don't go out and do things like this, people will think you're afraid."

Monica shifted her gaze from the window in the rear, where she sat. "What?" she asked. She had been daydreaming.

"If you don't go to things like this Chamber of Commerce thing, I mean."

"Oh, I know."

"It won't take that long," Don said, turning his head and meeting her eyes briefly.

Monica shrugged. "It's fine."

"You remember what we talked about?" Nicole asked from the front passenger seat.

"About what?" Monica asked.

"About how you'll act when you see Brian."

"Oh," Monica said, "yeah. I'll shake hands with him and say hi, then I'll turn toward you guys and we'll do the room."

"Right," Don said. "We worked hard to get a good showing for you here. There'll be plenty of volunteers in the audience, also some local Republican business people."

"You just stick with the answers that we practiced," Nicole said.

"Got it," Monica said.

"Okay, we're here," Don said. "Look sharp, everyone. There's a good amount of press here."

Monica pursed her lips as she put on her sunglasses. Under normal circumstances, there would be maybe one or two reporters with cameras here, just to do routine coverage of the local political scene. Now, however, with news of the affair, the place was crawling with press. All the journalists would vy for photos of Brian and Monica together, to later print them with salacious headlines.

Monica still hadn't decided if all the extra publicity was good or bad.

"What issues will you emphasize today, Monica?" a reporter asked her as she got out of the car.

"What did you think of Mr. Murphy's press conference?" another asked.

She hated that they got right up in her face, microphones inches from her mouth, invading her personal space. This was definitely not the gig for an introvert shut-in, yet here she was.

"We'll talk about all the issues that are affecting the everyday lives of people living in this district," she answered the first.

"Did Mr. Murphy tell the truth during his press conference?" the second reporter asked again.

"I'm sure he did," Monica answered, not pausing to stop or look in the reporter's direction.

Nicole took Monica's arm as soon as they broke free from the press crowd.

"That last comment you made sounded snarky," she said to her friend. "You can't sound like you have an axe to grind. Grind the axe with me, behind closed doors, but not here."

"It annoys the shit out of —"

"I *know*. But it's not gonna get any easier. We still have the debates ahead of us. And remember —" Nicole looked around to see if anyone was in earshot. "If you don't know what to say—"

"Don't say anything," Monica finished.

"You got it."

Monica followed Nicole's gaze and saw Brian walking toward her. She stood to her full height, which in her heels was about five feet, nine inches.

The two women noticed that a camera was following Brian.

"Hi, there," Brian said, his back ramrod straight as he extended his hand to Monica and smiled.

She took it and shook it firmly, not letting go until he did.

"Ready to speak to the crowd?" Brian asked.

"Sure, or you could just concede now," she half-smiled.

"Why should I do that?" Brian crossed his arms.

"Because you're going to lose." She noticed that his eyes never left hers.

"Says who?" He chuckled and Monica thought he appeared defensive.

"Brian," Sean said firmly.

Sean's chastising tone only emboldened Monica further.

"I see you haven't had time to get a haircut yet," she said, crossing her arms and leaning her upper body back, unconsciously puffing her chest out as much as she could.

"Why should I get a haircut?" Brian said.

Monica turned toward Sean and said, "shouldn't you guys clean him up?"

Monica felt Nicole tugging at her elbow.

"Seriously?" Now Brian leaned toward Monica.

"Can't even style your hair properly? How old are you again?"

"That's the best you've got?" Brian tried to suppress a smile.

"Hey, I'm just getting warmed up."

"Monica," Don said firmly, walking up to her, accompanied by an older dark-haired lady. "I'd like you to meet the president of the local Chamber."

As Monica turned to Don and the president, she allowed herself to feel a little victorious at Brian being thrown off guard.

Monica and Brian took their positions at their respective podiums. Monica willed herself not to look in his direction, but she felt his eyes on her.

"Thank you for coming here this evening," the Chamber president began. "We always enjoy having candidates speak about their positions with us."

Both candidates nodded in acknowledgement.

"The first question is —" the president paused, looking down at a note card, "if elected as congressperson of the Eighth District, how do you plan to help small businesses?"

Easy, Monica thought, money talks and shit walks.

"Ladies first," the lady said, gesturing toward Monica.

She isn't really doing me a favor, Monica thought, by allowing me to go first. On the contrary, Brian gets to hear my answer and has the opportunity to formulate a rebuttal.

"Thank you so much for hosting this event, and thank you for having me here," Monica began. "I would lower taxes for hardworking families in the District. For example, the Fairfax County government has been continuously increasing property taxes for the last several years, and is now contemplating establishing a meals tax. The purpose of the meals tax is ostensibly to fund schools, but those footing the burden would be the middle-class families of the County."

Instead of firehosing more money at the school district, we should do a line-by-line accounting of its expenses, Monica thought, to see where the hell the money is going. She refrained from articulating that, however, since it did not address the immediate question and would likely open up a can of worms she did not want to deal with right now.

"The city of Alexandria already imposes a restaurant tax," Monica said instead, "which puts increased burdens on residents." Monica continued quickly before the president could interrupt her. "And small business owners are residents, too, and would be affected by these tax increases. Further," Monica paused, feeling that she was beginning to speak too quickly, "burdensome licensing requirements are also affecting local businesses, constant taxes and license fees. Remember that small businesses also create jobs. Every time a small business closes, that affects the owner and employees, and their families." Monica wanted to say more, but left it there, seeing as how the president looked impatient.

"Thank you," the president said, and Monica was heartened to hear applause from people in the audience.

The president turned to Brian and smiled. "Mr. Murphy?"

"Thank you very much for inviting me here today. It's an honor to be here." Brian paused, but his pause was too long in Monica's opinion; it annoyed her. "Taxes are necessary to fund our schools, parks, firemen, and other local employees. However, they should certainly not be overly burdensome."

Get to the point, Monica thought. How will you help small businesses?

"We certainly want to streamline corporate applications," Brian continued, "to make it easier for start-ups to get launched. We'll also make sure our schools are fully funded."

Translation, thought Monica, we'll push the meals tax through.

"I would be fully committed to creating more jobs in this district, attracting more employers and keeping government contractors in the area."

Brian nodded in conclusion and applause followed.

Those questions were followed by others, such as how to deal with overcrowding in schools (indeed, how to get the money for additional schools? Monica thought), and what to do about transportation and traffic.

Luckily, there were no questions regarding the 800-pound gorilla in the room. There were no questions about the affair.

As Monica left the podium, she considered that.

Of course there were no questions about the affair. Even though the Chamber of Commerce was theoretically nonpartisan, the president herself was known to be left-of-center. No left-leaning individual or group would ask Brian any questions about the affair because they wanted him to win; and no left-leaning group would ask *her* about it because it would implicate Brian. Further, they would appear obviously biased if they didn't ask Brian similar questions. And they wouldn't ask him questions, precisely because they *were* biased.

"Monica!" a heavily accented voice called out.

Monica turned and saw a dark-skinned lady wearing a loose dress and a chador.

"Hi, Rahima! What are you doing here?"

"I came to see *you*," Rahima said, as if Monica should know that already.

"I'm so glad you came," Monica said. "How are you doing?"

Rahima had been one of Monica's pro bono clients. Rahima had been sued by a large company because she had co-signed a student loan for her son, who had never ended up graduating. Subsequently, she had been stuck with a $30,000 debt, and, being unable to pay it, hadn't known what to do.

Monica had filed motions of discovery to obtain copies of the supposed loan agreement, but the lender had come up empty-handed. Amazing, she had thought. You can't produce evidence of my client's debt? she had argued.

The Plaintiff had eventually dismissed the complaint, and, consequently, Rahima had no legal obligation to repay the debt.

Monica had always felt that Rahima was genuine; she made no pretense about who she was and who she was not. Maybe for that reason, Monica felt that she should be honest with her.

"I am really happy to see you," Monica told her, lowering her voice. "I'm having a rough time."

"Of course you are," Rahima said. "I saw the news."

Monica sighed, waiting.

"It must be hard to have your personal life out there like that."

Monica nodded. "Yes, it is."

After a pause, Rahima said, "Look. I told everyone what you did for me. Your personal life —" Rahima put her hands up, "is not my business."

"Thank you," Monica told her, touched by the statement.

"I am telling everyone I know to vote for you."

"Rahima, you have no idea how much that means to me."

"And I want you to come talk at our neighborhood meeting."

"Sure, yes," Monica nodded. "Let me know when and where, and I'll be there."

All in all, Monica decided that it had not been a bad day.

Chapter 30

The local news was on the radio in the car on the way home.

The commentator was talking about the Eighth District congressional race.

"I think that went well," Nicole said, looking at Monica, who was biting a nail.

"Yeah, it went all right," her friend agreed

"They didn't ask any questions about —"

"Yeah, I think that was a bit odd," Don chimed in.

"Odd good or odd bad?" Monica asked, pessimistic.

"I expected them to ask about how you would handle the bad press."

"They won't ask that," Monica said, pensive.

"What?" Don asked.

"I don't think they'll ask anything about that."

"Why not?"

"Brian's team expects him to cruise to victory in November. This is a blue district," Monica explained.

"Yeah?" Don asked, unsure.

"No one's going to ask him about the affair, and no one's going to ask me about it. Because if they ask me —"

"It implicates him," Nicole finished.

"Exactly," Monica agreed.

"And if they ask you and don't ask him —"

"It's bad optics; they look biased, which, of course, they are."

"The local media has to raise it at some point," Don said.

"What's there to raise?" Nicole asked. "We've both done press conferences on it."

"The national media will be all over it, though," Don said. "Because they love this kind of stuff."

"The key is, they think they're going to win this district, the Democrats, I mean. Can you imagine how bad it would look if they *lose*?" Monica said with glee. "And what reason would they give for losing? Brian's past? How could they, when his past is *my past*?"

"They sure love a good show," Nicole said, a finger to her chin.

"Goddammit, you guys," Monica said enthusiastically. "Hell, then I think we should give 'em one."

Chapter 31

The next day, after spending time at the campaign office with Nicole and Don, including fielding phone calls from reporters, Monica went home at around 4pm. Christian wasn't around, but she could tell that David was home because she saw his backpack in the foyer.

"David? Sweetheart?" Monica called.

She heard movement upstairs and David came down slowly. He seemed a bit morose, eyes downcast and head hanging a bit.

Monica sensed immediately that something was wrong.

"Sweetheart, what happened?" she asked

"There's a note for you," David said with resignation.

She and her son never hid anything from each other. He told his mother everything, eventually, even if not at first.

David retrieved his backpack from the floor and opened it, in no particular hurry. He took out a large rectangular note.

From the note and David's demeanor, Monica deduced that he had gotten in trouble at school. Her brows furrowed in confusion. It was unusual that David would get into real trouble. She remembered when he was a toddler, and even in kindergarten, he would occasionally receive warnings for failing to listen or follow directions, and also for occasional "disrespectful" behavior. Monica almost smiled remembering one time he had gotten a warning for pretending to snore when the teacher was talking.

"David, what happened?" Monica asked.

"I got in a fight, Mom," he said, handing her the note.

The note indeed indicated that he had been involved in a "physical altercation." Monica laughed inwardly about the euphimistic use of the term "altercation." As far as she knew, fights in David's private school were not a regular occurrence, although they were not completely unheard of.

"Someone hit you?" Monica asked in surprise.

David opened his mouth to speak, inhaling deeply as he did so, then paused.

"Yes, but —" Monica could see in his eyes that he was thinking, whether about whether to lie or not or how to articulate what happened, she did not know.

"Are you hurt?" Monica asked hurriedly, automatically grabbing his chin and tilting it upward to look for marks.

"No, no, Mom, I'm fine," he said, moving his head back and away from her grasp.

Monica relaxed a bit. "So what happened?"

"I just got in a fight."

"You were provoked?"

"Yes."

"Well, then you were defending yourself. I don't blame you for that." Indeed, what was he supposed to have done? Lay down and let the other guy keep hitting him?

"I'll call the school, and I'll talk to that kid's parents," Monica continued. "Who was it?"

"Mom," David said resignedly, looking at his mother in the eyes for once, "it wasn't like that."

"What are you talking about?"

"I mean, I hit a kid, yeah. I hit a junior, because he was saying

162

things about you."

Monica was incredulous. "About me?"

"Yeah."

"Wait, I don't understand —" Even as she said it, she realized what had happened. Because he was her buddy, who had gone almost everywhere with her since he was a baby, she sometimes tended to think of him as her friend, rather than her son. And then, when things like this happened, she was reminded that he was not yet an adult.

Monica walked over to the living room and sat down. David followed her and sat down next to her.

"I'm sorry, Mom."

"Why are *you* sorry?" Monica looked at him.

"For getting in a fight."

"What did he say?"

"Just — something about you, you know, what's in the news and all —"

"Oh," Monica sighed. "He said something about — the affair?"

"Yeah."

"Okay."

They sat in silence together for a couple of minutes, each looking straight ahead. They spent time like this frequently, ever since David was a young child, and Monica had first noticed his introvert tendencies. She had noticed them right away because they were her own. They had often spent quality time in the same room together, both reading different books; or in the car, her driving and listening to music while David read or gazed out the window and daydreamed.

"I'll talk to your father about this," she said at last. "But don't worry."

"Thanks, Mom." He looked at her. "Are you and Dad getting a

divorce?"

Monica had always made it her goal never to lie to her son. She looked at him. "I don't know, it's possible."

"Okay."

Monica wanted to assuage some of her son's anxiety. "If we do, I'll live here," meaning locally; she wasn't sure if she would stay in the same house or not, "and you can go to the same school." Did it help him to hear that, she thought? To have something of continuity?

"Okay," he answered.

"And if we do, it has absolutely nothing to do with you," Monica said, putting her hand on David's back.

David nodded. "I know, Mom."

"I love you," Monica told him. "And Dad loves you. And that will never change."

"I love you, too, Mom."

There was a pause. "Okay, let's order pizza later for dinner."

David smiled. "Sounds good, Mom."

Monica's conversation later that night with her husband did not go nearly as well as her conversation with her son.

After David was in bed, Christian approached his wife in her office.

"I can't handle being here in this house with you," Christian told her.

Monica wasn't sure how to respond to his statement. She put her mug of tea on her desk.

"What do you want to do?" she asked him.

"I don't want to be around while this campaign is going on."

Monica nodded. "Okay."

"I talked to my boss. I can work remotely for a while, for the next few weeks."

"All right."

"David will be in school."

Monica still wasn't sure where he was going with this.

"I think the best thing to do would be for me to stay with my parents in Florida for a while."

Monica inhaled deeply. "If that's what you want."

"It's not what I want," Christian said angrily, instinctively leaning toward her.

Monica jumped anxiously.

"But since you want this marriage to be over, it's what I'll do."

Monica said nothing. She knew that nothing she could say would make him less angry. This was his way of being.

She merely nodded.

"I'll pack and leave in a couple of days," Christian said.

"Okay." She felt shitty, but relieved at the same time. She looked forward to having alone time with her son, and was already thinking about how the atmosphere in the house would be more relaxed with her husband gone.

Chapter 32

L ater that week, after Christian had left for Florida, and David was asleep upstairs, Monica sat in her home office, looking at spreadsheets that Don had sent her. She tried to be as busy as possible to avoid thinking about the demise of her marriage.

It was late, but Monica wasn't tired. The overstimulation of the day made her wired and jittery, and she knew she wouldn't be able to sleep even if she tried.

The spreadsheets reflected polling data in different areas of the Eighth District over the past few years. Monica considered them as she kept in mind how many areas she would need to carry the vote in November.

How many of these registered Democrat votes can I reasonably get? she thought.

The old adage taught her by a couple of senior congresspeople was, if people get to know you, they will vote for you, despite party affiliation. Most everyday citizens, in the end, are not partisan.

That was difficult for most people in the DC area to fathom, given that here everyone seemed to be partisan. How could you *not* have a position on everything?

But Monica was quickly learning that it was true. Most people she met "in the field" responded to her when she talked about issues that concerned them, despite the R after her name.

Her team would have to schedule more meet and greets. Her feeling was that Republicans who had been unsuccessful in the past in historically blue areas had not done enough of that. Showing up at a parade was one thing, but how many people did you actually connect with that way?

As she chewed a nail, thinking, her cell phone blipped.

She looked at it, expecting it to be Don. Incredibly, it was Brian.

How was your day? he asked.

What could she possibly say about that?

Probably about as good as yours, she texted back.

That bad, huh?

Monica became annoyed at the interruption.

What can I do for you? she responded.

Just wanted to see how you were.

I'm all right, thanks for asking.

You going to be up late?

Why does he want to know that? she thought.

She texted back.

Look, you know most of us Gen X'ers don't like to have long, convoluted convos via text. If you have something to say, say it.

Monica's cell phone rang. She looked and saw Brian's number.

"Goddammit," she said under her breath.

"Yes?" she answered.

"Hey, there," came the response. "What's up?"

"Not much. What's going on?"

"I was wondering —" He paused.

"Dude, what? It's late, and I have stuff to do, you know, make a liberal candidate suffer, all that stuff."

He chuckled.

"Would you like to meet for a drink — or a cup of coffee?"

Monica froze, startled. "I can't tonight."

"Oh, I didn't mean tonight. I know it's late already. Maybe another night?"

She thought for a few seconds, suspicious but also intrigued.

"Okay, depending on the place," she said.

"Tomorrow?"

"I have to check the schedule. Text me tomorrow afternoon," she said, seriously doubting that he would.

"Sounds good. Talk to you tomorrow."

"Okay, bye." She hung up, wondering what the hell just happened.

Chapter 33

The following afternoon, Monica was at her office reviewing the weekly calendar with Don.

"We're doing what you suggested," Don said to her, "and organizing meet and greets with local Hispanic groups."

"Okay, keep the size of the groups small when we do the meets," Monica said. "That way, everyone gets a chance to ask questions and make comments."

"Will do. Also, the neighborhoods we're thinking of, they don't typically vote Republican."

"I figured. We'll need to practice my talking points."

"For sure."

"I'll prep my answers to questions I know they're going to ask, even if they're super uncomfortable." She gave Don a sly smile, and he gazed at her like a lovestruck teenager.

God knows why this guy is into me, Monica thought, if that is indeed the case and not my overactive imagination.

Monica's phone vibrated.

She looked at it and saw a text from Brian.

Are we on for tonight?

She thought for a few seconds, then answered: *Yes.*

What time is good for you?

Around 8pm.

Okay, see you then. I'll pick a place and let me know if it's convenient for you.

Okay, Monica texted back.

Monica considered that this could be some kind of trap, but what would be the motive?

Or is he going to try to get some information out of me? That's not going to happen. And the limited polling we've done so far doesn't reflect that I'm in a significant lead, or any lead that his team would be concerned about.

Monica's curiosity had gotten the better of her.

The bar Brian had chosen was in Adams Morgan, way up in northwest DC. She figured he had chosen it to avoid them being spotted together.

She pushed the bar door open and entered. The place was empty, which she preferred. Crowds overwhelmed her.

Brian sat alone at a booth, looking at his phone, with a beer in front of him.

She approached him and sat down quickly, opposite him.

"Hey," he said as he looked up. He immediately put his phone in his suit jacket pocket and clasped his hands together on the table.

His face was lined. Monica wondered if he was sleeping all right.

"Hey," Monica answered. A few seconds passed.

"What can I get you?" he finally asked.

"Umm —" she looked around. Monica was mostly a wine drinker, and only sporadically, but this place looked like more of a beer place. The decor was somewhere between Halloween ghouls and rustic kitsch. She noticed a painted clown statue on one side of the long wooden bar, and bare light bulbs of different colors surrounding the mirror behind the bar.

"I know, this place is a bit weird," Brian said, noticing how she gazed around.

"It's — interesting."

"I have good memories from here." He apparently felt the need to explain further. "After college, when I started working here in DC, some friends and I used to hang out here a lot, because one of them was doing a Master's at American University, and this place was close by. We used to meet here late, around this time, during the week, because it was less crowded." He took a swig of beer.

Monica nodded. "I never pegged you as not liking crowds."

"Hmm?" Brian seemed not to understand.

"I mean, you appear to be very comfortable in crowds, even — you seem to like being the center of attention." Monica paused. "I mean, you seem very extroverted."

"Oh, I don't know about *that*." He tilted his chin and raised an eyebrow.

Monica considered him in silence. Then, "Well, you seem to have a lot of friends."

"I know a lot of people," Brian said. "But that doesn't mean I have a lot of *friends*." He rubbed his chin and met Monica's eyes.

A server approached them. "What can I get ya?" she asked Monica. The server was waiflike and appeared to be barely twenty years old. She wore her hair short and spiked, and dyed a deep purple.

"Um, I'll have — I'll have a Corona," Monica decided on the spur of the moment.

The server left.

"I didn't peg you as liking Corona," Brian smiled slyly.

Monica shook her head. "You didn't peg me as a lot of things."

"Can't argue with that." Brian took another swig of beer. "So what's going on?" he asked then.

"What's the purpose of this meeting?" Monica asked in response, folding her hands and leaning across the table.

Brian instinctively leaned back in response to her leaning forward, then quickly regained his composure.

"Does every meeting have to have a purpose?" he asked rhetorically.

"Come on," Monica tsked and looked away for a second. "This is — highly irregular, to put it lightly." She looked at him.

She continued to stare, and finally Brian sighed. "I just wanted to talk."

"About what?"

"I talked to Ross."

Monica's eyes widened. "You did?"

"Yeah, I kind of barged into his office."

Monica half-smiled. "What did he say? Did he say why the hell he's doing this?"

"Yeah." Brian looked at his beer bottle, then back at Monica. "Apparently, he hates my guts and he had the hots for you."

"There's gotta be more motive than that," Monica shook her head.

"There isn't," Brian said. "Revenge. One of the oldest motives there is. He's jealous of me and wanted to make me suffer, and I'm really sorry that you're a casualty too."

Monica looked away and sighed. Honestly, at this point his motive didn't even matter.

"I mean, you could've told me that on the phone."

Brian's eyes met hers. "I wanted to talk to you, too."

Monica shrugged. "About what? What else, I mean?"

"Just talk. About nothing in particular."

Monica's brows furrowed in suspicion. She pursed her lips.

"You don't have anyone else to talk to?"

"Abby left," he said suddenly.

"Jesus, I'm sorry."

The server showed up with Monica's Corona. She pushed the piece of lime inside the bottle and drank a long swig.

"Well," Brian continued, "she said — she said she was going to stay with her mother for a while. Her mother lives in Centreville, way out in Fairfax County, you know, but Abby travels and can work at home sometimes, so the commute's not always bad."

Monica nodded. She couldn't think of anything to say.

"She made it sound like she wanted to split."

"Can't blame her," Monica couldn't help saying. She couldn't blame Christian either.

"Yeah, well, I don't blame her either." Brian ran his finger up and down his beer bottle, his eyes intent on the label.

"I'm sorry."

Brian shrugged, then straightened his back. "I honestly think it's for the best. We didn't always get along."

"Sorry to hear that," Monica said honestly.

Brian continued, and Monica wondered why he felt the need to tell her all this. "Abby always wanted the relationship to appear perfect. The relationship, the relationship — pfft. She was always like, what's wrong with our relationship? You know, because everything wasn't perfect all the time."

"She expected it to be perfect all the time?"

"Pretty much."

"Did she expect you to be happy all the time?"

"Yes!" Brian said emphatically. He picked up his beer bottle and slammed it back on the table for emphasis.

"But you wanted the freedom to be in a bad mood once in a while."

"Yes, exactly! How did you know that?"

"Good guess, that's all."

When Brian remained silent, Monica explained carefully, "you see, people, especially women, I think, tend to think of a relationship as a thing of itself, as either good or bad. They evaluate the relationship at every moment. Is it good or bad right now?" She tilted her head back and forth.

Brian's eyes met hers and she paused for a moment before looking at her Corona bottle.

"But really, a relationship is a series of moments." Monica put her thumb and first finger together and drew an imaginary horizontal line. "A smile, a laugh at a dumb joke, when your partner rubs your feet, or tells you how beautiful you are when you think you look terrible. Or, my personal favorite, when your partner does a chore for you without you asking him to." Monica looked back at Brian.

"A relationship is made up of countless moments like that," she continued, "and if the moments are mostly positive, you'll want to be with the other person because being with them makes you feel good. Nothing is perfect all the time."

Brian nodded, pensive. "She could never relax. I don't know why."

"Maybe she liked the *idea* of a relationship more than the relationship itself. Anyway, on a basic level, people seek pleasure and avoid pain. If your partner nags you constantly, you feel bad. And, in that case, is it any wonder that you question your relationship?"

Brian nodded. "Yes," he said after a moment. "Why couldn't she just leave me alone?"

Monica drank her beer. "Most people, as far as I can tell, are not self-reflective. They usually don't consider how their

174

actions affect other people. For instance —" She put her beer down. "I hear from my single friends all the time, that men can be too pushy, trying to get them to date them or get them into bed. So let me ask you. If someone pressures you into doing something when you don't want to, does that make you feel good or bad?"

"Bad, obviously."

"Exactly. So, don't people see that pressure is a huge turn-off? And likewise, you shouldn't pressure someone to be in a relationship. Why aren't we exclusive? Blah, blah, blah. But they don't realize that anyone who makes a decision based only on pressure, that's not a conscious decision. That's not a real commitment." Monica leaned back.

"Abby kept pressuring me to get married."

"Good thing you didn't. Because if you split up now, there's no issue regarding dividing up your assets. Sorry if that's blunt, but it's the truth."

"No, you're fine." Brian looked curiously at Monica and crossed his arms. "How do you know all this stuff?"

"What stuff?"

"About relationships."

Monica shrugged. "I saw a therapist for a couple of years. It was helpful, for my own edification. Don't think it helped my marriage, obviously."

"Why didn't it help?"

Monica looked away, thinking. "I think he and I had both checked out by then."

"I'm sorry."

There was silence for a moment, then Brian motioned towards Monica's left hand, where she still wore her wedding band. "Are you guys still together?"

She hesitated, wondering how much to reveal.

"Technically, yes." She didn't feel the need to share with Brian that Christian had decided to visit his parents in Florida, and had gotten permission from his employer to work remotely.

Brian said nothing, so Monica continued.

"Both people have to work at a relationship. I mean, you both have to make an effort. If only one of you is doing the rowing, you become exhausted and resentful." Monica took the last swig of her beer and stood up. "And resentment, my friend, is a relationship killer. Take it from me."

She retrieved her purse and opened it, looking for cash. "I gotta go," she said. "It's a long ride back to Old Town."

"No, no," Brian said, putting his hand out toward her, "I got this."

Monica locked eyes with him. "Thank you."

"Thanks for coming out with me. And thanks for the talk."

Monica nodded. "No problem."

She left the bar and whipped out her phone to summon a ride, all the while pondering their conversation.

Chapter 34

Nicole and Monica stood in Nicole's narrow kitchen in her tiny Georgetown apartment.

Monica had left David at home studying that evening, and the two women were taking a little time for themselves while prepping for the upcoming campaign debates.

Monica thought about the fact that Nicole had taken time off from her day job with the DNC to work in Monica's campaign. She felt a pang of guilt about that. It made her more resolved to win, for Nicole and for Don. Their professional reputations were at stake.

Nicole poured two glasses of red wine. Monica leaned against the kitchen door frame.

The two women were reviewing Monica's answers to possible questions in the upcoming debates.

As usual, Nicole acted as Monica's foil, challenging her answers.

"I don't understand the issue that some people have with *Lochner v. New York*," Monica said. "Individuals have the right to freely enter into contracts for employment, and if they want to work twelve hours or more a day, then so be it. Economic rights have been ignored in this country for too long."

"But the Constitution doesn't specifically protect the *right* to contract," Nicole responded.

"Contracts are specifically mentioned in the Constitution. The Contract Clause is in Article 1." Monica repeated the constitutional text. "No state shall enter into a law impairing the Obligation of Contracts."

"True, but it doesn't mention a right to contract."

"Oh, come on. The Supreme Court has found many rights that are not articulated in the Constitution. The Constitution doesn't specifically protect the right to have an abortion, but the Court found there is such a right."

"Well, the Court found the right under the Fourteenth Amendment."

"Yes, but the Court provided no rationale for that finding. Anyway, I want the government out of my wallet and out of my bedroom. I don't need the government to tell me how to organize my life. I can do that on my own. Period. The end."

"Well, we can agree on that, at least," Nicole retorted, holding out her wine glass. The two women made a toast.

"Don said that your numbers look pretty good," Nicole said with satisfaction, "and he thinks they'll go up." She smiled.

Nicole's comment was heartening, but Monica knew she couldn't fully relax. She refused to be complacent.

"And next week we have some events in some friendly locations, and the meet and greets. I really think we have a shot at pulling ahead of Brian."

At his name, Monica's mind started to wander.

"Why so pensive?"

"Hmm?" Monica looked up.

"You're deep in thought about *something*," Nicole said.

"He used to kiss my forehead," Monica said, staring at her friend.

Nicole stopped talking and shook her head as if to clear it.

"What?"

Monica crossed her arms and sighed. "Brian. He used to — when we were — sometimes I would lean toward him and he would — he would kiss my forehead." At that moment, Monica could feel the touch of his lips. She put a finger to her forehead involuntarily.

Nicole sighed a long sigh.

"This whole time," Monica continued, "I feel like I've kind of been playing the victim, but it takes two, right? It wasn't like he was a horrible person. He could be very sweet."

Nicole moved closer to her friend. "You can't think about that now."

"Oh, believe me, I don't want to be thinking about it," Monica said. "And I had boxed all that stuff up, to the point that I didn't remember anymore. But a few weeks ago, before everyone found out about us, I ran into him, just randomly, walking alone at night, and he took my hands, and he put them on his face." Monica mimicked the gesture. "And all of a sudden, everything came back. And I hated him for it. I was so angry."

"What a jackass," Nicole said with exasperation.

"I don't think he did it to be a jackass —"

"Oh, please, Monica, don't defend him now."

"Hey," Monica said defensively, touching her chest with one hand, "it's not like I was forced into this. It was all of my own doing."

"I know, I know. But whatever issues you have, you can work them out after this campaign."

"Yeah," Monica agreed, sighing.

"Okay, then, forget about him for the moment, and let's focus on next week."

But for the rest of the night, Monica couldn't stop thinking about how Brian used to kiss her forehead, and hold her hand. Sleep did not come easy.

Chapter 35

The next morning, Monica and Don were in Monica's small office at her campaign headquarters, poring over lists of names.

"These are the people who are going to be at the Spanish meet and greet planned for tomorrow afternoon," Don said. "I'm trying to get some info on them. Some are self-employed, some are stay-at-home moms, others work construction, some have desk jobs."

"Got it."

"Just helpful to have the info."

"I appreciate that."

"Here's a partial list of people who'll be at the meet and greet the day after tomorrow. Now, they're mostly Middle Eastern and Ethiopian."

"Okay."

"Some are Christians, but not all."

"Gotcha."

"Only reason I say that is because Christian Ethiopians, some at least, may tend to vote for us."

"It's a tough call, Don. Many Christians vote Dem."

"True."

"We'll listen to them, see what's important to them."

"That's the right attitude," Don agreed

181

"Well, that's the right thing to do," Monica said. "That's what I believe we *should* do, listen to the constituents." And if I didn't believe that, why would I even be in this campaign? she thought.

Don nodded. "What's your schedule like tonight?"

"You know my schedule," Monica shrugged one shoulder.

"No, I mean, not your campaign schedule."

Monica stopped in her tracks and looked at Don. "Why?" She could hear the suspicion in her own voice.

"You've been through a lot, Monica. I wanted to take you out to dinner."

Monica didn't ask, but sensed that he meant just the two of them.

"Don, that is very kind. Another time, for sure. Tonight I promised David I would be home early to have dinner with him. I'm heading home right after the meet and greet."

"Oh, gotcha," Don nodded.

"If anything urgent comes up, just text me," Monica said, and went back to the lists in front of her.

The meet went well. Monica spoke in Spanish the entire time, and everyone seemed pleased to meet her. No one brought up the affair, thank goodness. What else could possibly be said about it, anyway?

As Monica walked home from the campaign office, long-past thoughts invaded her mind. During the first week after she and Brian had stopped seeing each other, she had felt like a zombie, a husk of herself. He was always there, inside her head. Then he was merely in the back of her mind. Later, as time had worn on, she had merely thought about him once in a while.

In the beginning, the pain made her want to hide in a corner; she hadn't wanted to deal with anything. But the sensation had gone from a knife in the chest to a dull ache, and, at that point, she had been better able to deal with it. She would immediately busy herself with something to occupy her mind. Monica's incredibly stressful day job had come in handy at that time. She was so busy that she hardly had had time to be sad.

Then, weeks later, when David had asked her why she was so sad all the time, she knew that she was wasting her life not doing much of anything except for work. Monica had mentally and emotionally run away for months. She had volunteered for cases that took her far away from DC, to places like Tulsa and Pensacola. She had felt the tiniest bit better being away from the scene of it all. It was also liberating that she didn't have to pretend to be happy. She could hole herself up in a hotel room at night and cry, replaying the time she had spent with Brian over and over in her head.

But she had also learned from that experience. She knew that she had been incredibly stupid.

What possessed me to do that? she thought. Of course Brian had treated her as less than she was, because *she had behaved* as less than she was. He hadn't valued her or considered her worthy of his attention.

It only took me a couple of years of therapy to figure that out, Monica thought.

Monica then thought of Don. She didn't know what he wanted from her, if indeed he wanted anything at all. It made her feel good to have attention from him, but getting involved with him now would be political suicide. It would throw the campaign off balance. She had to keep everything with him strictly business. After the campaign, who knew?

Chapter 36

The next night, Monica had agreed to meet Brian at a quaint bar somewhere in Georgetown, which was not metro-accessible. She had not yet figured out why she had agreed to meet him again, but she had enjoyed their last conversation. She had been able to drop her guard a bit and be herself.

She felt as if she was never able to be herself. Things at home with Christian had been stiff and overly formal for years. They usually only talked about David and his activities or extremely mundane areas of life, such as who would take out the garbage and whose family they would visit for the holidays.

At work, everything was about the campaign; Monica had to deal with people all day long, with short breaks alone in her office to recharge her batteries as best she could. It was good to leave all that behind, even if only briefly.

She arrived at the appointed bar. It was one of those pseudo-trying-to-be-European places, and was near-empty. Monica found Brian in a booth near the back. She purposely arrived a little late, because she hated to wait uncomfortably for people. Brian could wait uncomfortably for her.

"Hey," Brian said as she sat down. He ran both his hands over his face; he looked tired, but Monica refrained from saying that.

"What's going on?" she asked instead.

"Same old. It's only September and I'm beat."

"Well, just concede and it'll all be done," Monica deadpanned, opening a menu.

"Ha *ha*," Brian said slowly, his dark eyes twinkling. Then, noticing her perusing the menu, "are you hungry?"

"Yeah, I haven't eaten dinner and it's almost 8."

"Actually, that sounds like a good idea. I haven't had dinner either."

A waiter, dressed in a tuxedo shirt and black bowtie, stopped by their table to take their drink orders.

To Monica's surprise, Brian asked her, "would you like your usual?"

"Yes," she answered, without more.

Brian addressed their waiter. "She'll have a glass of red wine." He looked at Monica. "Which kind would you like?"

She gave him a look that told him he should already know the answer to that question.

Brian smiled. "Malbec then?"

"Sounds good. Thanks."

"Would you like to order food as well?" the waiter asked them.

"Yes, we'll need a few minutes to decide," Brian said, and the waiter walked away.

"I don't think they have Corona here," Brian told Monica with an impish grin.

"Then this place has no class," she answered, shaking her head in mock derision.

The waiter brought their drinks and they ordered dinner.

"This is good," Brian said after tasting his drink. "Want to try this?"

"Sure," Monica answered. She took a cautious sip; her tolerance wasn't what it used to be.

You know what that reminds me of?" she said. "Reminds me of my trip to Scotland; I did a lot of whiskey tasting there."

"Oh, my God," Brian said then. "Woman, that is *scotch* you're talking about. Not whiskey! You're drinking whiskey right now, not *scotch*!" He emphasized the term derisively.

Monica didn't bat an eye. "Dude, I was just testing you."

"Yeah, I'm sure. Good save, by the way. Think on your feet. I like that." He took another sip, shaking his head.

"Dammit, Murphy. You're too young to drink whiskey. I don't drink whiskey and I have ten years on you!"

"Well, I feel like I'm sixty years old," he retorted.

They sat in silence for a few moments, Monica enjoying just being. She noticed that Brian wore no tie and his shirt collar was open. She saw a small tuft of dark chest hair.

She looked down and drank her wine, then held the bottom of the stemmed glass with both hands.

"Do you think Fairfax County taxes are too high?"

Brian looked at her, surprise registering on his face.

"Why do you ask?" he asked as he leaned toward her.

"Just asking." She shrugged.

He seemed to be weighing whether or not to answer. It occurred to Monica that he might think she was fishing for his own words to use against him in the campaign. He would be right.

"Taxes fund necessary things, like —"

"Like roads?" Monica asked derisively.

"Yes."

"Jesus Christ," Monica shook her head. "At some point, the tax burden becomes too much for the middle class to bear. Don't you see that? Then, people figure that not working and receiving public assistance is more advantageous than working their asses off to pay taxes."

Brian opened his mouth, to which Monica said, "I swear, if the next thing that comes out of your mouth is 'tax the rich,' I'm outta here."

Brian closed his mouth, looked away, and took a drink. "Yes," he said after a few seconds. "I'll concede that there can be such a thing as paying too much in taxes."

"Well, thank God for that."

"Man, I could cut the sarcasm in here with a knife," Brian chuckled.

Monica willed herself to refrain from responding to his comment.

Brian looked at her and suppressed a smile.

"What?" Monica asked, confused.

"I've never seen you so passionate before."

"You've never paid attention before." She sipped her wine, then moved her glass and hands out of the way as their waiter brought dinner.

As Monica attacked her grilled salmon, she noticed that Brian hadn't begun eating. She considered asking him why not, but decided that she didn't care.

"See," he began, shaking his finger, "that's the thing with you liberty Republicans."

"What's that?"

"You think the free market solves everything."

"It *does* solve everything, at least, economically." Monica rolled her eyes, annoyed, and drank more wine.

Brian shook his head and raised his chin. "You Adam Smith people."

"It stopped working when the government found out how to milk people for money. Oh, you need a license to fish, get married, operate a business, be a hairdresser —"

Brian shook his head.

Monica ignored him and continued. "— you have federal income tax, state income tax and, in some localities, county income tax, state car tax in Virginia." Monica stopped and took a breath. "Do you realize how asinine that is? You pay sales tax when you buy a car, and then you pay an annual tax just to own a car. Fucking ridiculous."

Monica stabbed her salmon and Brian sat in shock.

"I've never heard you drop an F bomb before."

"We've never talked about anything this serious before," Monica countered.

"But taxes fund —"

"Taxation," Monica sat up suddenly and raised her hands, "is theftification."

Brian laughed out loud, the lines around his eyes crinkling. Monica was glad to have eased the argumentative turn the conversation was taking.

"Gen X neocon," Brian said, smiling and shaking his head.

"Left-wing Millennial," Monica retorted.

Brian finally began eating, and Monica noted how rare it was to see him laugh.

After a couple of minutes of eating in silence, Monica asked, "what's your greatest fear?"

"Loneliness," Brian answered immediately. "What's yours?"

"Boredom."

"Those kind of go hand-in-hand."

"Not really. I'm never bored when I'm alone. I'm usually bored when I'm around other people."

"Sorry if I'm boring you now."

Monica shook her head. "You're not." She stole a glance at

Brian as he continued to eat. "By 'loneliness,' do you mean being alone? Because you can be in a relationship and be lonely."

"Yes, that's true." He looked away, thinking. His long lashes framed his dark eyes, making them stand out even more. "I guess, I mean, not having anyone to talk to."

"You mean having someone who just listens to you, with no judgment?"

Brian stopped and considered, then looked at her. "Yes." He nodded. "I don't know that I've ever thought of it like that before, but that is exactly it. Abby would question everything I would say to her. She didn't like the colors I picked out for the walls. She criticized the restaurants I wanted to go to."

"Makes you want to just not say anything, right? Because it's easier?"

"Exactly. How did you know that?"

"It's something I learned from parenting books. If your child talks to you, opens up, and you criticize or freak out, then they will stop telling you things to avoid the emotional outbursts. It's just easier not to say anything. Then later you have parents who say, why won't my kid talk to me? Sometimes, I wonder what the hell people are thinking, you know?"

Brian nodded. "You're really —" He searched for the words. "You try to think of the other person's perspective."

"I try. I don't always understand, though. I don't always understand why people act the way they do."

"Oh, me neither." He raised his eyebrows.

Monica suddenly felt a connection with him, and she didn't like it. She wasn't sure if the connection was only on her end. It made her skittish.

Although she hadn't finished her plate, she abruptly got her coat and took out some cash, leaving it on the table.

"I gotta go," she said. "Gotta get some sleep."

Brian put his utensils down. "I hear ya."

As she prepared to leave, Brian said, "Monica." His voice had gone down an octave.

She looked at him. "Yeah?"

"I'm sorry," Brian said unexpectedly.

"Sorry for what?"

"I'm just sorry."

She nodded. "Thank you for saying that, but it's ancient history." She left without more.

Chapter 37

"This place is closer to your house, so I figured it may be more convenient for you," Brian said when Monica met him during the evening at a gloomy bar in Old Town Alexandria a few days later.

"Sure, but it's also kinda risky, isn't it? People may spot us."

"Oh, no one comes here. The food's terrible and the drink prices aren't much better."

Monica laughed. "Sounds fantastic."

"Plus, it's Monday night. People are still recovering from the weekend."

They sat down upstairs, and it was indeed deserted.

"You know, I've been in Old Town a long time, and I've never noticed this place," Monica said.

"I told ya," Brian said, "no one comes here."

"Must be a front for money launderers or something."

Brian chuckled, then went to get their drinks at the bar, before returning to sit beside Monica.

"So how did it go as a state delegate?" he asked without preamble.

Monica looked up at him. "It went all right. Challenging to do together with my day job, but I managed."

"Seems like you were really popular."

Monica shrugged. "Don't know if 'popular' is the right word."

"I can see why they voted you as candidate for this race, since you won the delegate race here."

"Yeah, a lot of people didn't think I could do it," Monica said, hoping that would underscore her potential in the current election.

"How did you get so involved in politics?" Brian asked.

"Don't you know?"

"Well, you volunteered in campaigns, right?"

"Because of you."

When Brian looked at her, she said, "you inspired me. Or, I was inspired because of you. Maybe that's the better way to put it."

"Really?" Brian asked in amazement.

"Yeah, well, I was always kind of involved. Then, after, I mean — a few years ago — afterward, I needed to be busy. Like, insanely busy. So I started to get more involved, volunteer for more campaigns, talk to more people, and learn from others who had already held office for a while."

"Wow. So I created a Republican giant. Fantastic."

Monica laughed. "Yes, you did. Thank you." She did a mock half-bow from her seat.

"What about you?" she asked Brian. "Why so eager to run for office?" She didn't harp on the fact that Brian had had no prior public office experience. It wasn't unheard of, anyway, for someone to run for a seat in Congress with no prior experience.

"I don't know. I — I came to DC to see what I could do. I was excited. To be out here, and to be so young and to *get* to be out here. I worked for non-profits for a while, but the truth is that it's grueling. The non-profit world can be an old boys' network. And no one listened to me because they thought I was too young. Like I was too young to have an opinion."

"And that bothered you?"

"Well, just because someone is young doesn't mean they haven't had life experience —"

"And it doesn't mean they can't have an opinion on things."

"Right. So I didn't know what else to do — I started working on campaigns, but the thing with that is, well, you know what the work environment is like. You have no life for a few months. Then, if your candidate doesn't win, you're scrambling around for another job. If your candidate *does* win, then you can get a great gig if you were high up in the campaign, but if not, you're slogging it out, battling for face time with a bunch of other people. And then it's like, for what?"

"So you decided to run for office?"

"Why not?"

"Well, you've never held public office before." She couldn't help bringing it up now.

"So? Sean and Mike told me —" he looked at Monica and stopped abruptly. Monica knew why.

"They told you that winning the Eighth District would be easy." She took a sip of her drink.

"Not exactly."

"Yeah, they did," Monica said, nodding. "Look, that doesn't bother me, that they told you that. They're most likely correct. So if *I* lose, I'll have an excuse. Not the scandal stuff. I mean, a Republican hasn't held this district in forever. It wasn't going to happen. That I was only running to get my name out there —"

"*Are* you only running to get your name out there?"

Monica smirked behind her glass. "Wouldn't you like to know?"

Brian drank and there was silence for a few moments.

Then Monica continued. "But if *you* lose..." she said without finishing.

He understood immediately. "Yeah," he said, draining his glass.

Chapter 38

Monica was reviewing donor lists and maps of the Eighth District with Nicole and Don at her campaign headquarters.

"So where should we focus the door knocking?" Monica asked Don.

"Here, and — here," he said, pointing to the map. "Don't know if we have enough volunteers to cover the entire district, but we'll start with these areas."

Don leaned closely toward Monica, and it heightened her senses. She then noticed that neither she nor Don were moving.

"When will we have the results?" she asked to break the silence.

"From door knocking?"

"Yes."

"Folks will send in the results immediately, and it'll take a bit for me to go over them." He turned his face toward her.

Monica backed up, then noticed that Don was looking at her. When he didn't say anything, she said, "what?" and shrugged.

"Nothing," he said, but Monica wasn't convinced.

Monica and Brian had made plans to go out and play pool.

Monica wondered whether they should even play pool together. Men bonded through competition, she knew. Not only that, they would be walking near each other and maybe touching each other. She would have to lean down, exposing some skin. And when she leaned over to shoot, her butt would be visible in all its ample glory. It all made her nervous.

The seedy bar where they met was deserted. The slot on the pool table to insert money to play was jammed. They had to call the one server in the place to come over and fix it.

Once that was done, Monica selected a pool cue that was the right size.

Brian gestured at her to shoot first.

As they moved around the pool table, Monica sinking more balls than Brian, a song came on from Monica's youth.

"You know this song?" she asked Brian.

He listened for a second. "No," he shook his head.

"It's Madonna."

"Really?"

"Yeah, *Crazy for You.*"

He looked at her intently, his eyes wide.

"It's the name of the song. God, you're full of yourself!"

Monica mouthed the words of the song as it played.

"Yes!" she said under her breath as she sunk another ball.

"What, no way!" Brian said then. "That's impossible. I think you moved the ball with your cue first."

"Did not, you're just a sore loser!" They both came around the pool table at the same time and met at one of the short ends, face to face, mock arguing.

"You're cheating!"

"Can't stand that I'm beating you at pool, can you?" Monica said as she backed up.

They finished the round, which Monica won. "We're playing again," she said. "Whoever loses buys the next round of drinks."

"Done." Brian pointed a finger at her. "You're on."

Monica used the chalk. "You're going down, *again.*"

"I'll even let you go first again," Brian said, mock bowing.

"As you should, West Coaster."

Monica made a clean break, scattering the balls and sinking one.

"I'm stripes," she said.

A man entered the room and sat in front of the TV. Monica looked at him and they both inclined their heads in greeting.

The man changed the channels to watch a basketball game. As he was flipping through channels, Monica saw a quick scene from her all-time favorite show.

"Let's find out if we're going to continue talking," Monica said to Brian.

When he raised his head to look at her, she said, "do you like *X-Files* or not?"

"I want to believe," Brian answered with a half-smile.

"Good enough. We can still be friends." Monica caught herself. "I mean — we can still be acquaintances."

"Oh, come on, we're more than acquaintances."

"Yeah, you're right. We can still be opponents."

Brian laughed heartily. "Don't you ever quit?"

"No." Monica shot and sank two more balls.

"*Goddammit,*" Brian muttered, sinking his head and chuckling.

He positioned himself to shoot. Monica leaned across from him, puffing out her chest and squeezing her breasts together with her arms.

"Stop that!" Brian laughed. "You're distracting me."

"Oh, what?" She pretended not to know what he was talking about. "Oh, sorry."

Brian sunk one ball.

"So what are we talking about tonight?" Monica asked.

"Whatever you want?" He asked it as a question.

"*Whatever* I want? Okay, then — what do you think about the state corporate income tax rate?"

"It's pretty competitive. It's only six percent."

"Oh, for sure. Especially considering the federal corporate income tax rate is 21%." Monica turned her attention to the TV screen, where two basketball teams she didn't care about duked it out.

She could feel Brian's eyes on her. "You trying to get me to say the Virginia rate should be raised?" he asked.

"Should it?"

When Brian remained silent, she looked at him. He studied her curiously, then ended up smiling.

Brian didn't have a chance to answer. All of a sudden, the tempo of the music changed.

Monica knew the song, and smiled. She figured a change in the direction of the conversation was in order.

"My son's middle name is Angus," she said then, to no one in particular.

"What?" Brian looked at her, apparently irritated at having missed his shot.

"My son, his middle name is Angus."

"Seriously?"

"Yeah," she said, pointing upward.

"Ah, this song." Brian finally understood.

"Yes."

"Wait, you named him Angus after — ?"

"Yes," she nodded decisively, "after Angus Young."

Brian shook his head slowly. "That's crazy."

Monica only had two balls left on the table, whereas Brian had four.

After Brian sunk one more, he said, "this song, though. It's kind of how you have my campaign team right now."

"How's that?" Monica asked, raising her chin and furrowing her brow.

Brian stopped and leaned on his cue. "Thunderstruck."

"Is that right?"

"Yep."

"I think you're full of shit, Brian."

"Hey, you don't have to believe me." He positioned himself over the table. "So how are you doing it?"

"Doing what? Maintaining my own in the polls?"

He nodded.

"Just showing up. Showing up gets you halfway there." Monica wondered whether he was interested in spending time with her in particular, whether he was lonely, or whether he was fishing for inside information to assist him in the campaign. She would assume it was the latter, and would keep her guard up.

"Gotta be more to it than that," he said.

"There isn't." Monica considered that Brian and his campaign team thought that all they had to do was secure the Democratic nomination for that race, and that it would be a lock. She further considered that he and his team probably thought that they didn't have to show up to events other than the big ones like debates, and that they could merely coast through to the election.

And now his team was starting to think it wouldn't be a lock, after all.

"You nervous?" Monica asked, approaching Brian from one end of the pool table.

"About what?" he asked. He didn't move as she approached him. Normally, people automatically stepped away when

199

you approached them, she thought, invading their American personal space. But he didn't move.

Monica stopped when she was a few inches from him. She raised her heels so that she stood on her tiptoes and looked up toward his face.

"You nervous about this race?" she said coyly.

"Naaahh," he answered under his breath.

"I think you are."

"You're cute when you're trying to be all tough."

"Dude, I'm cute all the time."

"Yes, you are."

Monica froze abruptly. Neither one of them moved or spoke. She put her heels back down on the ground, and Brian stayed where he was.

Then, Monica was horrified when his face moved toward hers, and she could feel his breath.

Shit, I need to move.

His lips were right in front of her. She breathed in the scent of him, remembering.

Move! She shouted silently to herself.

Monica backed away so quickly she almost tripped.

"Are you okay?" Brian asked.

"Sorry," she said quickly.

"No, *I'm* sorry," he said, reaching out for her.

Monica struggled to regain composure. "What the hell is going on?"

"I'm sorry, I didn't mean to."

Monica bit her bottom lip, then shook her head slowly.

She exhaled loudly, and sank her remaining two balls with precision.

"You owe me drinks next time," she said, pointing at Brian.

"But not tonight. I need to go."

"Okay," he said, his face screwed up.

"Bye," she said, grabbing her coat and walking out. She didn't wait for him to say anything else.

Chapter 39

A few days later, and multiple campaign events later, Brian had asked Monica to go out with him again. Logically, she knew she shouldn't, not with things starting to turn her way in the campaign, but her intuition told her to go.

They met at a bar in DC, but it was filling up fast and was way more crowded than either of them had expected.

"Oh, damn," Brian said.

"What?" Monica followed Brian's gaze to look.

"I know that guy."

Monica wasted no time. "Let's go."

They left together, crossing the street to walk on the other side, which was darker and less crowded. "Maybe if we dyed our hair, dressed like bums," Monica mused.

"What's that?" Brian seemed distracted.

"Or wore wigs. When we go out. So that we're not recognized."

"I could dye my hair blond," Brian said. "I always wondered what I'd look like blond. Maybe dirty blond."

"Well, you *are* dirty."

He shook his head in mock disagreement.

Monica fixed her gaze at the street ahead, and slowed down her pace. She noticed that Brian walked considerably more slowly than usual.

"So what now?" she asked.

Brian slowed down even more and seemed to be deep in thought.

"Maybe I'll call it a night —" Monica began, then grew frustrated at Brian's excruciating pace. Turning toward him, she barked "why in the name of God are you walking like that?!"

Brian hobbled along in a wide-leg position.

"Have you been horseback riding?" she asked.

"Yes, during my spare few minutes a day, I ride a horse through the city. Jesus —"

"Damn, you're pissy."

"It hurts."

"What hurts? Men are such wimps."

"You don't understand. I went biking yesterday."

"You're right, I don't understand," Monica deadpanned, turning and continuing to walk.

"And I didn't have the right shorts."

"What, they weren't hipster enough? Not the right color?"

Brian chuckled. "No! I mean—slow down! You're walking too fast."

Monica stopped and turned, looking at him. "Okay, what's your problem?"

"I didn't have the right shorts for biking. And I didn't have any lotion —"

"TMI," Monica said, holding up a hand.

"You don't get it. I have a —" Brian gestured his hands toward his general groin area. "I have a *scorched earth situation*."

Monica looked down at his legs, then back at his face, understanding, and erupted into laughter, doubling over.

"Scorched earth! Oh, my God!"

"Well, I'm delighted that you find it so amusing."

"No, no, I mean, I get it. In the summertime, when women wear dresses without tights, they chafe, too."

"Glad to know we're not alone."

Monica's laughter finally died down and she wiped tears from her eyes.

"Scorched earth," she repeated. "That's brilliant." Then she looked at Brian, who was calm once again, smirking at her. "Well, I'm sorry that's the case."

They turned and continued to walk.

"Want to come over and have coffee?" Brian asked without preamble.

"To your place?"

"Yeah."

Monica stopped, her guard up, and Brian stopped with her.

"By 'coffee,' do you mean sex?"

"Jesus Christ. *No.*" His overemphasis of the word "no" automatically made Monica suspicious.

"Good," she said, "because that would be highly inappropriate at best and horribly disastrous at worst."

Brian half-smiled, but it didn't touch his eyes.

"Okay, let's go," Monica said.

They arrived at Brian's house, and he held the door for her. Had he always done that? Monica didn't remember.

"Sorry, it's a mess," he apologized. "I'm kind of busy lately. There's this congressional candidate, and she's really giving me a run for my money."

"BS," Monica said in response. "Seriously, I don't care how messy someone's place is."

Monica sat down on the living room sofa and looked around.

She could definitely tell that the townhouse had a woman's touch. She didn't like to be reminded of Abby; in some way she still saw her as the reason for her breakup with Brian, even though consciously she knew that wasn't the case at all.

Monica leaned back against the sofa and exhaled.

"Stressful day?" Brian asked.

She opened her eyes and saw Brian standing in front of her. He held out a beer for her.

"Sorry, don't have any Corona," he said with a sideways grin.

Monica rolled her eyes. "That is not the only beer I drink."

"Thank God," Brian chuckled and sat down.

They sat in silence for a few moments, then Monica said, "to answer your question, yes, it was a stressful day."

"What happened?"

"People happened. Any day I have to deal with people is a stressful day."

"Isn't that every day?"

"Yeah, pretty much," Monica shrugged.

"You don't like people?"

Monica gazed ahead and yawned. "It takes me a tremendous amount of energy to deal with people all day long. The small talk, *uuuuggggghhh*." She put her head in her hands, and her chestnut locks cascaded forward.

"Oh yeah, I know what you mean about that."

"Just the — the pretending to be interested in everything all the time. Small talk is worthless. It's — devoid of any meaning."

"Then you're living in the wrong town for that."

"Don't I know it."

"That's not normal for a Latin woman to be so introverted," he mused.

"Hey, I never said I was normal."

205

"*Touché*," Brian inclined his head. Then, "you must not be enjoying this campaign then."

Monica stiffened. She suddenly felt as if she had revealed too much about herself. Her opponent was sitting next to her, not a friend. *Definitely* not a friend.

So why was she here?

"Why am I here?" she asked out loud, turning to look at Brian.

Brian opened his mouth but no words came out. He furrowed his brows, thinking.

"Exactly." Monica drank from her beer bottle.

"I don't have anyone to talk to," Brian said then.

"And," Monica began carefully, using a method of questioning she had learned from her shrink, "that makes you feel — how, exactly?"

"I feel lonely, I feel —" he trailed off, but Monica didn't say anything, allowing him to finish.

"I feel lonely," he repeated. "And alone, and — dammit, I feel like no one gets me." He looked away.

"What do you think it is that people don't get about you?"

"You sound like a shrink," he smiled, looking at her.

"Sorry," Monica said, looking down.

"No, no, I didn't mean it in a bad way."

Monica looked back at Brian. "I have no skin in this game. I mean, you can talk or not talk. I don't care. Don't feel pressured to talk," she said nervously.

"I don't."

"Good. I don't care either way. It's your business."

They sat in silence again for a bit.

"So," Monica began, "if I remember correctly, you said a while ago that loneliness is what you're most afraid of."

Brian nodded without speaking.

"You consider yourself an extrovert?"

"I don't know. I like being by myself, but —" Brian shrugged.

"When you're in a relationship, you expect not to ever have to do anything alone again, something like that?"

He nodded. "Maybe."

"Or is loneliness for you not knowing where you fit in? What your purpose is?"

"Well, that, too." Then he smiled. "What do you know about fitting in anyway?"

Monica laughed. "Oh, nothing. I don't need to fit in."

"I always admired that about you," Brian said. His statement surprised her.

"Oh yeah?" Monica kept her voice even.

"Yeah. You never conform. Even with this election, we — everyone expects you to toe the party line, you know?"

Monica had noticed that he had said "we," presumably meaning *he* had thought that as well.

"I always do my own thing."

"I know."

"Maybe you're trying to psych me out now, get me to act all crazy so I'll lose."

Brian shook his head slowly. "Hey, you don't need anyone to get you to act crazy."

"Oh, thanks, so I'm crazy."

"You'd have to be, to run in this election, in this town, in this district. But I mean crazy in a good way."

"What do you think your team would say if they knew you were hanging out with me?" Monica asked, a sly smile playing at the corners of her mouth.

"Oh, some of them would probably quit."

"Wow. So why meet with me then?"

They looked at each other. "I can't stop," he said.

Monica nodded slowly. "Hmm," she said, as if she were pondering a philosophical question.

After several moments of silence, Monica asked, "are you really an atheist?"

"Yes, well — kind of."

"'Kind of?' What does that even mean?"

"I'm kind of undecided."

"Is that so?"

Brian nodded noncommitally.

"In any case," Monica continued, "at the end of the day, if you don't have faith that things will work out, you got nothin'." She sounded more positive than she felt, but for her own sanity, she had to think positive. She held out her beer bottle toward him, and he did the same.

"My mother had this toast while we were growing up; she still says it."

"Oh yeah? What is it?"

"*Salud, amor, y dinero. Y no necesariamente en esa orden.*" She explained to him what it meant.

Brian laughed, then clinked her glass with his in a toast. His fingers touched hers as he did so.

Monica stood up. "Thanks for the beer — and the company."

"Anytime." Brian smiled wistfully.

She looked at him one last time, his dark eyes drawing her toward him. She resisted, not without effort.

V

OCTOBER

Chapter 40

"How do you want your pizza?" Brian asked, while calling on his cell phone.

"Edible," Monica answered.

Brian looked at her as if she were crazy.

"Anything's fine but *not Hawaiian*."

"Okay, okay." He put up a hand.

Brian had invited Monica over for dinner that evening. David had wanted to spend the night at a friend's house, so Monica had felt less guilty about being away from home.

Brian hung up and went to the kitchen, where Monica nursed a glass of wine. She looked at him expectantly, lips pursed.

"Pizza'll be here in about twenty minutes," he said.

"Awesome."

Brian suppressed a smile.

"What now?" Monica asked with mild annoyance.

"I heard you on the radio today."

"Oh, yeah?" She had done a radio interview with a local station.

"You said that you agree with legalizing marijuana," Brian said, with the tone of a parent who was about to lecture a child.

The issue had come up at one of Monica's campaign events. She had discussed the subject endlessly with Nicole and Don, and, despite Don's protests, she had insisted on being honest about the fact that she thought marijuana use in Virginia should be legal. She had felt obliged to answer the question and it was the topic of much discussion in the media at the moment.

"Yeah, did you know that in states where it's legal, marijuana use actually declined after it was legalized? Use rates didn't skyrocket, like some people were afraid of." Monica stood up straight and drew her wine glass to her lips.

"Don't the Virginia Republicans come down hard on it?" Brian asked.

"Some of them do, yeah. So?" She shrugged.

"*So?*" Brian was amazed. "You're breaking away from the party."

"From *some* of the party. It's a big party. Just like you guys, we have our differences. See —" Monica set her wine glass on the counter. "The war on drugs has ultimately been a failure."

"Oh, I agree."

"So, why not legalize marijuana and have it more controlled, I mean — have it out in the open — you could still get a DUI for driving under the influence of marijuana just like you could for driving under the influence of alcohol or narcotic painkillers. Plus," she clicked her tongue, "it could be taxed. More revenue for the government."

"Of course."

"Oh, I knew you'd like that last point," Monica said.

"Makes sense."

"See?" She smiled. "We agree on something."

Brian chuckled. "Wanna watch a movie?"

"Sure, may not finish it, though. May get too late."

They sat on the sofa next to each other and Brian cruised through Netflix.

"Oh!" Monica sat up suddenly, excited.

"What?" Brian seemed amused.

"*Say Anything*, let's watch that."

"Anything you say," Brian said coyly.

"It has John Cusack in it, not that you know who he is; the movie's before your time."

"I know who John Cusack is," Brian met her sarcasm and raised it a notch. "Even *Millennials* know who he is. Well, they should, anyway."

"Damn straight they should."

They started watching the movie.

"Oh, my God, I love this scene," Monica said, then, paraphrasing, voiced aloud, "He's just a regular guy. No, don't be a *guy*. Be a *man*."

Brian nodded, then said, "women are hard to read."

"Yeah, you're probably right about that," Monica conceded. "Most of them don't always say what's on their mind."

"Why not?" Brian looked at her, his eyes sharp and laser focused.

Monica shrugged. "Most of them are afraid."

"Of what?"

"Of what a man will say, how he'll respond. What if he doesn't like me back? What if he doesn't want to go out with me? What if, what if?" Monica seemed annoyed.

"Men are afraid of that, too," Brian said.

"Could be," Monica said.

They sat in silence for a few moments. "What most women don't realize," Monica said, "is that men want their women to be happy."

Brian turned to look at her, apparently very interested now.

"A man wants his woman to be happy," Monica said. "If she's unhappy, and he can't make her happy, he's not happy."

"His *woman*," Brian chuckled at the term.

"What? You know, in Spanish, that's the term for 'wife.' *Mujer* is the term for 'wife.' And *mujer* means —"

"Woman," Brian finished.

"Right."

"I don't think Abby would have liked me calling her my 'woman.'"

"Why? She is — was — whatever, your *woman*, and you were her man."

"Well, you know, she's all progressive and shit."

Monica laughed. "Progressive *and shit*? Oh, that's priceless!"

"Well, being progressive isn't always a *bad* thing."

"God, bring me my vomit bucket," Monica said, screwing up her face.

Brian pursed his lips. "That is totally unacceptable," he said.

"Jesus, you're so sensitive. I didn't mean —"

"It is totally unacceptable that you don't know where your vomit bucket is at all times."

Monica pressed her lips together to stifle a laugh, but couldn't contain in. She laughed until she coughed, them composed herself and turned her attention back to the movie.

"I love how the female protagonist is close with her father, even if he ends up being a crook," she said.

"Eh," Brian shrugged, taking a swig of beer.

"What?" Monica asked, confused.

"I'm not really close to my family. Probably something I should work on."

"Is there a reason for that? I mean, that you're not close with them?"

"Not really. They're just far away."

"Yeah, men don't usually talk to their parents as much as

women do." She sighed. "Anyway, to give you some unsolicited advice —"

"Yes?" He turned to her and swept his dark lashes upward. Monica became on edge with his face closer to hers.

"I strongly suggest that you cultivate a good relationship with your family, if possible. Because, let me tell you, when the chips are down, and everyone's against you, your family are likely the only people that are going to be there for you."

"You make a good point." He smiled.

Brian had Monica on his mind long after she left. When they were watching the movie, he had gazed at her surreptitiously. Her light brown hair had been pulled back into a messy bun. He had admired the curve of her neck, following it with his eyes down to her collarbone.

Then he had chanced a glimpse at her chest through her white blouse, and had remembered her large, shapely breasts crushed against his bare chest.

He had also daydreamed of taking one of her hard nipples in his mouth, running his tongue over it until she threw her head back and placed her hand on the back of his head, pressing him against her.

Brian didn't fall asleep until 3 a.m.

Chapter 41

T he next night, as Monica was brushing her teeth, her phone chimed.

"God, who the hell is that now?" she said aloud, irritated with herself for not turning off her phone earlier.

She looked and saw a text from Brian.

Hope you had a good day. Sleep well.

She texted back: *The day was all right. Long. Thanks. You too.*

She was suddenly seized by a crazy idea. She typed: *I'm going to sleep, but before I do I have an important question for you. And I need an honest answer.*

She took silent delight in the confusion that her question would cause him.

Of course, he responded.

I need you to be completely honest, she texted.

I will be, Brian wrote. She imagined him holding his breath while he waited.

Monica wrote, *if a tree falls in a forest, and lands on a mime, and no one's around, does anyone care?*

She expected him to be sorely irritated with her, and she didn't give a shit.

Instead, she received an unanticipated response.

Pffffth.

Monica was silent, waiting.

Then Brian's text appeared: *obviously, the undertaker.*
Monica laughed in surprise. She had not been expecting that.
I am literally laughing out loud right now! she texted.
Brian wrote back, *then my job here is clearly done. Good night :)*
Good night, Monica texted.

Chapter 42

Monica and Brian had taken to meeting at Brian's house for the occasional quiet dinner and drink, instead of in public. Their conversations often involved arguing over politics, and tonight was no exception.

"You have to go back to the Constitution, and you have to respect the separation of powers inherent in the Constitution. The President cannot do things unilaterally. The legislative and judicial branches are meant to be checks on his power."

"Yes, yes, I know."

"Do you have any idea how many times the federal government has tried to overstep its bounds? In cases like *Youngstown*, for example, where President Truman wanted to take over the steel industry?"

"Sorry, I'm not a lawyer," Brian said flippantly and drained his beer. They sat together on the sofa.

"I know. That is painfully obvious. And, anyway, I'm all for national security and defense, but that doesn't mean I approve of laws like the PATRIOT Act, that run counter to the Fourth Amendment."

"And that's why I like you," Brian said, grinning. "You don't always toe the mainstream party line."

Monica rolled her eyes at his comment about liking her, and barreled on. "Everything must be done according to the methods the Constitution provides. The Founders were very wise in that."

"I don't remember you being this argumentative," Brian said suddenly.

"Of course you don't," Monica countered. "I was trying to get you to sleep with me."

"Come one, you didn't have to try very hard."

"Jesus. Well, okay then."

"No, no, I meant —"

"You'll sleep with anybody?"

"No. I mean —" Brian appeared to be at an uncharacteristic loss for words.

Monica crossed her arms, waiting.

"I was really into you. It's not like you had to convince me."

Monica's guard came back up.

"Whatever," she said. "Seeing as how I will never sleep with you again, now I just don't care."

"Oh, is that so?" Brian asked, raising an eyebrow.

"Yes, you self-centered narcissist."

"Damn!" His eyes widened in pretend shock at her comment.

"Well, of course, in your dreams. I mean, I have no control over that."

Brian shook his head, chuckling.

Monica raised her wine glass to her lips. As she did so, Brian touched his hand to her left, and met her eyes.

"What?" Monica asked, her gaze following his to her left hand.

"You're not wearing your ring."

Monica put her wine glass on the kitchen counter.

"Yeah."

"He left?"

Monica wasn't sure what to say, especially since her team

hadn't made an official announcement about it.

She nodded without comment, then shrugged as nonchalantly as she could.

"I'm sorry," Brian said, his dark brows drawn together.

"Was bound to happen. I don't blame him."

"I'm still sorry."

"Look, let's talk about something else."

"Come here." Brian reached for her and Monica allowed him to pull her gently into his arms. It felt so good to be held, but the irony of the situation was not lost on her.

She lay her head against his chest and breathed in the scent of his aftershave, which contained a hint of eucalyptus. She felt his heart beating underneath his dress shirt. It felt so good.

Brian enveloped her in a warm embrace. Monica felt co-cooned and comfortable. He kissed the top of her head and his lips lingered there.

Then, before she thought about it, she nestled her face into his shoulder. He drew her closer against him and her lips pressed against his neck. She breathed him in, inhaling deeply.

Brian brushed her thick hair away from her face and kissed her temple, his hand resting on her cheek.

Monica pulled her head back gently so that she could look at him. His hand still on her cheek, she held onto his wrist, eager to maintain the connection.

"You're adorable right now," Brian told her.

She chuckled. "Whatever."

Brian smiled warmly, the lines around his eyes deepening. He moved toward Monica slowly, deliberately, his eyes fixed on hers.

Her mouth went dry and she felt her pulse quicken. Her lips parted and she tried to remember to breathe.

Brian's forehead touched hers, and she noted that his breathing rate had increased. She was impatient but allowed him to seek her lips slowly, as if they had all the time in the world.

He brushed his lips against hers, and she pressed her mouth against his. She felt the heat of his body and reached a hand around his head to grasp his hair.

Brian placed his arm around her waist and pulled her into him, pressing her body against his. Then he opened his mouth and sought out her tongue.

Monica melted against him and felt a sensation of merging at being wrapped up with him.

Doubt suddenly surged in Monica's mind about what was happening, and she wondered about the sincerity of Brian's words and gestures. It made her upset that she felt compelled to wonder about it.

She stopped kissing him and leaned back, pulling away from him and placing her hand against his chest.

"Wait, wait," she said.

"You okay?"

"We can't do this."

"What do you mean?"

It annoyed her that he thought only with the lower half of his body. Did she really need to enumerate the reasons why sleeping together was a horrible idea?

Instead, she said, "this means something different for you than it does for me."

Brian shook his head. "No."

"Look, Brian, this is painful enough, spending time with you —"

"— it's not like before —"

"I can't do this, not when I used to love you." The words just slipped out.

Brian's eyes widened.

"Didn't you know?" Monica asked. "I loved you then. That's why I took it so hard."

Brian opened his mouth but didn't say anything.

"Doesn't matter," Monica shrugged. "'Love' only means a surge of brain chemicals, anyway. Doesn't mean anything."

"Like hell it doesn't."

Monica remained silent and watched Brian, wondering about his thoughts.

Shouldn't have come here, she thought. Bad idea. Mistake.

Monica let herself feel the aching feelings and raw emotions that had been bubbling up for the past several weeks.

She unwound her right leg from around him and sat beside him on the sofa.

"This isn't fair. It isn't fair to me. Fool me once, shame on you. But fool me twice —" She left the phrase hanging.

"No, you don't understand," he said, leaning toward her slightly but maintaining the space that she had created.

Monica pursed her lips in anger.

"Don't give me that shit," she said. "This is about you thinking that after you threw me away, that I was just going to hole up in a corner and wither away. Well, get the fuck over yourself. You're not all that."

"No, no!" Brian insisted. "It wasn't like that."

"What was it like then?"

"I liked you."

"You *liked* me? You like *everyone*." Monica turned away from him, then felt the need to unload, even to him.

"You can't just say you're sorry and magically make everything all right. You have no idea how much it sucked for me, the realization that it was meaningless for you."

"It wasn't meaningless," he said, but his insisting only made her angrier.

"It was meaningless to *you*. And by the way, words mean nothing to me. Words from a man mean *nothing* to me. I was nothing to you. And, looking back, I would've realized that much sooner if I hadn't let my feelings for you cloud my judgment. I can't believe how stupid I was, letting you lead me on like that."

"I didn't mean to," he said firmly.

"It doesn't matter anyway. I was an idiot, shouldn't have done it, and now I'm paying the price."

"I'm sorry."

"You cannot imagine how sad I was."

Brian sighed deeply. "I know. I was sad, too," he said slowly.

Monica didn't believe him but didn't protest; she didn't think it was worth it.

"I guess I should thank you. I had forgotten what it was like to be nothing to someone."

Brian looked pained.

"We never had a real chance, Brian. We shouldn't have had one, anyway, not under the past circumstances." That was sugar coating it, she thought.

"I'm sorry," was all he could say. "I would've wanted that."

Monica ignored him because she didn't believe him.

She sighed in exasperation. "You know, for a long time, after it ended, you were all I could think about, *all* the time. But then you start to live your life again, and you start to forget. Well, you don't really forget. You just push everything away, try to keep yourself busy. And now, all I can think about is getting this entire election over with, so that I can go back to doing whatever, so that I can forget you again. Because that's what I want. I just want to forget you again."

Brian sat silently staring at her, his face stone.

Monica shook her head, annoyed at his apparent indifference. "But please don't try to start anything with me. You're a guy. You need to get laid. I get it. But it's incredibly unfair to me. Do you understand?"

When Brian didn't respond, she repeated more emphatically, "*do you understand?*"

Brian nodded; his breathing was heavy.

Monica stood and walked away from him, facing the front door. She took a deep breath, composing herself.

"One thing," Brian said.

Monica said nothing but stood where she was.

"I'd give anything to roll the dice just one more time."

Monica shook her head. "You're crazy," she said without turning around, then added, "not to mention, completely full of shit." She hastily grabbed her purse and hurried out, slamming the front door.

Chapter 43

Mike paced the small pavilion where Brian's campaign team had set up shop, right before walking in a local parade. Sean was deep in thought. They had just received the latest poll numbers for the race, and the results were not as solid as they had expected.

"You're the one who used to consult political candidates, how is she ahead of you in the polls?" Mike demanded in a loud whisper, making sure that no one else heard.

Brian shrugged. He didn't have the patience to deal with Mike today. "We have plenty of time."

Mike pointed to the list on the table in front of him. "How's she beating you in this poll?" he asked, like a rabid dog.

"It's only one poll," Sean said. "And it's not by much."

"She shouldn't be beating him in *any* polls." Mike looked at Brian. "*You're* the one with the campaign experience, she's just a corporate attorney! How come she's doing so well?"

"*Lay off*," Brian said through gritted teeth.

Just a corporate attorney, Brian thought, scoffing to himself. That's why she's so articulate, especially in explaining her position on issues.

"*You're* the one who used to sleep with her. Tell us how she thinks, what's going through her mind!"

"Is that really necessary?" Sean asked, annoyed.

"Well, it's true," Mike scoffed.

"It's not helpful," Sean countered.

"Fuck off, Mike," Brian said. Then, "I'm going to walk around and shake hands."

The truth was, Brian thought, Monica had always kept her feelings close to the vest, and he doubted that had changed. He remembered all the times she had shared her thoughts and feelings with him, since they had been so few.

Brian suddenly remembered being with her in bed, as she argued vociferously about economics.

* * *

"Soon there's gonna be a new day," Monica insisted, the bed sheets barely covering her generous breasts. "The old political guard will have to give way to the rise of the Ubertarians."

Brian chuckled as he moved her hair out of her face. "Ubertarians? What's that?"

"The Millennials are already figuring out that the free market is a good thing. Over-regulate and kowtow to groups like the taxi unions in DC, and you lose lower-cost services like Uber. Don't you use Uber?"

"Sure."

"So don't you think then, that competition is a good thing?"

"Of course." He listened to her speaking while he kissed her neck.

"So government artificially inflating prices, or otherwise meddling in private business, hurts consumer —"

"Hmmm," Brian said, nibbling on her earlobe.

"Don't tell me protectionism is necessary. If someone's working in an industry that's not competitive, then they better offer some kind of added value —"

"Oh yes, added value." Brian chuckled and moved on top of her, grabbing her hair with one hand while she dug her nails into his back.

* * *

While Brian was reminiscing and chatting with members of the public, Monica and Nicole approached his campaign tent looking for him.

"Like you have a shot here," Mike said to Monica.

"Well, hello to you, too," Nicole said, crossing her arms. "We just stopped by to say hi."

That was only partially true. They had really stopped by (with Monica's campaign photographer) to get a photo opp of the candidates talking nicely. Nicole hoped that it would make Monica look good.

Without saying anything, Mike waved a hand at the women, as if shooing them away.

"This is all posturing," Nicole whispered in Monica's ear.

Monica knew that her friend was right. If Brian were indeed clearly in the lead, then his team wouldn't feel the need to make aggressive comments. They were scared, which brought a smile to Monica's lips.

"It was great seeing you guys," Monica said sweetly, in reply to Mike's gesture.

Without more, she turned around and walked away to shake hands with members of the public, followed by Nicole.

"Come on, Mike," Sean said, "keep it together."

"Can't believe that slut's beating him."

"Shut up!" Sean whispered fiercely. Then his eyes were drawn to something over Mike's shoulder.

Sean's eyes fell on a young man wearing a Republican elephant pin and a Monica Orellana sticker on his lapel.

The man was holding a cell phone, shaking his head slightly.

"You done *fucked up*," the young man said.

"Listen to this," Nicole said, placing her iPhone on the table in front of Monica.

Monica raised her head. "What's this about?"

"Just listen."

Nicole pressed a button on the iPhone, then they heard the following: "Can't believe that slut's beating him."

Nicole smiled. "That's Mike."

"What? Who recorded that?"

"One of your campaign interns. He was standing just behind Sean and Mike after we left."

"He was recording them?"

"He told me he had a hunch, and that he put his cell phone on record just in case."

"Damn. That's amazing," Monica said, stunned.

"What do you want to do?"

"First, send that intern in here. He's gonna get a promotion."

"Yes, Ma'am."

"And I'm thinking of sending that recording to the press."

"I'm thinking you're right." Nicole winked at her friend.

"Do it, before I change my mind."

"Oh, it shall be done." Nicole smiled and nodded.

Nicole and Monica watched the news later that night in Monica's office.

The press had a field day with the recording.

"In an embarrassing moment for Brian Murphy's congres-

228

sional campaign in Virginia, his campaign director was heard calling Murphy's female opponent a slut," the announcer said.

The media then replayed the recording. It was being played over several TV and news channels. The conservative-leaning media were especially publicizing the story, since it without question made Murphy look bad.

Now the pundits came on the television program.

"How will this affect the Murphy campaign?"

"Well, that's the question, isn't it? He's leading in the heavily Democratic Eighth District, but not leading by as much as we would expect. That district has not had a Republican congressman for at least a quarter century. And this can certainly hurt his lead."

"The thing is," another pundit jumped in, "I mean, the irony of the situation is that *his* team is calling *her* a slut when *he's* the one she had the affair with. So if he calls her a slut, he's calling himself a slut."

"This is probably the first time, at least in an election of this magnitude, that this situation has happened, where if either side criticizes the other, then that reflects on the other side."

"Exactly," the host emphasized.

Don burst into the room. "Initial polling not looking bad." He smiled. "Not bad at all."

Monica shook her head slowly. "Honestly, I don't think that this will have much of an effect on the outcome of this election."

"I don't know," Nicole said slowly. "If he pisses enough women off…"

"Well, there are probably enough women who agree with him," Monica said. "I don't want to be overconfident."

"Hey, we still have time," Don said.

"I'll tell you one thing," Monica said, holding up a finger.

"I would love to know what's going on at Murphy campaign headquarters right now."

Brian paced the room, irate.

"I leave you assholes alone for two minutes, and this is what happens!"

"Brian," Sean attempted to calm down his friend, "we're really sorry."

"I told you before, saying this type of shit will hurt us!" He wheeled around and faced Mike. "I'm seriously thinking about firing you right now."

"Hey, I brought you all those donors! Where would you be without them!?"

"Like we needed all that," Brian said derisively. His throat suddenly felt constricted and he loosened his tie.

"Okay, okay." Sean stood up and stepped between the two men. "Yes, it was an extremely dumb thing to say, especially in public." He looked at Mike, then back at Brian. "Let's just move on, and focus on the next goal. We're still ahead in the polls. Women make up a big voting bloc in this district, and they'll likely still vote for the candidate with the D after his name."

"If he does anything else this stupid, he's gone," Brian said to Sean, as if Mike weren't in the room.

"He *won't*," Sean said. "I'll make sure of it."

"Well, you didn't stop him earlier." Brian pointed a finger at Sean.

"Look, man, I'm sorry —" Mike began.

"You realize, Mike," Sean said, "that you can't criticize Monica without it coming back on Brian. Whatever you say about her is about him, too. You call her a slut, then you're calling him one, too."

"Yeah," Mike said in response, sighing.

"Whatever," Brian said, frustrated. "We have the first debate next week. Let's spend most of our time prepping for that. And let's lay low for a bit."

Neither Mike nor Sean challenged him.

Brian sighed with exhaustion. "I'm going home. I need a break from this shit." He got up and walked straight out the door.

Chapter 44

The crowd at the first debate was larger than Monica had expected. Of course, she thought cynically. Everyone loves a good show.

Looking out at the crowd, she became instantly nervous. She remembered reading in some book about introverts that the human reaction to crowds was explained via biology. When a person sees a large horde of people, it is biologically a sign of danger, as if being confronted by a hostile army, and the body reacts accordingly. You sweat, your palms become clammy, your throat dry. In other words, a physical reaction to a perceived biological threat.

But today she had to pretend to be an extrovert.

"We'll be live in just a couple of minutes," Don said in her ear, immediately moving off to the side.

Monica was left alone, standing behind her podium. The only other person on stage was Brian; she turned slightly to look at him.

His tie was slightly askew, and he had a few strands of dark hair out of place. Other than that, he was impeccably put together.

Without thinking about it, Monica rushed over to him.

He turned to her and she stood in front of him, putting her thumb in her mouth, then smoothing the strands of his hair back in place.

"Honestly, who does your hair?" she asked.

"I do," he answered with a sideways grin.

"Damn, you're usually so meticulous," Monica chuckled.

"Twenty seconds!" someone called.

Monica straightened his tie, yanking from the neck. "You don't mind me doing this, do you? Fixing this?" Her eyes were all challenge.

"No, of course not."

"Oh, are we friends now?" Monica asked with mock incredulity.

"Ten seconds!"

Brian pretended to consider the question. "Friends with potential."

Monica laughed, recognizing his reference to the movie *Say Anything*.

Brian brought his hand up, touching Monica's with his own.

Monica froze, her hands on his tie, looking up at him.

"I miss you," he told her, half-closing his eyes.

"Five, four —"

"Thank you," he mouthed, his eyes tender.

"Three, two —"

Monica broke out of her trance, and slid over to her spot behind the podium just as time was called.

"We are live!"

Watching the candidates from the control room behind the stage, Don groaned. "What was all *that* about?" he said to no one in particular.

"I don't know," Nicole shook her head. "So odd."

"And who put her in red?!"

"It's her color," Nicole said, shrugging.

"But it makes it that much more noticeable when she blushes!"

The debate started to go well, although Monica became increasingly nervous. She took deep breaths, while trying to make it look like she wasn't taking deep breaths.

She thought she was handling the questions decently.

When asked a question about gay marriage, she answered, "I have no problem with gay marriage. In fact, the government should stay out of marriage, should stay out of our private business. If you are going to vote for the other guy because of that, then I promise you that he will be much more liberal with spending your money. He will support putting the government in every aspect of your lives. Ask yourselves, do you want that?"

And when asked a question about whether she supported immigration, she stated, "how can I be against immigration? I'm a child of immigrants, grateful for the opportunities that this country has provided."

When the debate was over, Monica felt Brian's eyes on her. It was impossible to determine how her performance went with the audience. Usually, the Republicans felt that their candidate performed better while the Democrats thought the same of their candidate. But, would she win over anyone on the fence? That was yet to be seen.

Brian took two long strides and was at her side. "Thanks again," he said, fingering his tie.

Monica nodded and started to say something, but Don and Nicole appeared and whisked her away. The hard look Don gave Brian wasn't lost on her.

She chanced a look back at Brian as Don led her off the stage. He was still looking at her.

As she turned her head around to head offstage, she heard

Mike ask Brian, "does she still have a thing for you?"

Brian ignored Mike, but thought, God I hope so.

The three men left and filed into Mike's car, headed to get something to eat.

"What was all that about, Brian?" Sean asked.

"What was *what* about?" Brian asked.

"She was *fixing your tie.*"

Brian challenged Sean with a stare. "And?" he shrugged.

"*And?*" Sean's eyes widened. "What did she say to you?"

"Something about my tie being crooked." Brian crossed his arms, annoyed at the intrusive questioning.

"All right, Brian. I'm done being nice," Sean said, visibly upset. "You were touching her hand, and you were talking."

Brian gave Sean a hard look, but said nothing.

"What were you talking about?"

"Nothing important."

"Look, I know she means something to you —"

"That's enough," Brian said with an edge to his voice.

"But we're in the home stretch here —"

"*Stop.*" Brian's voice was ice. "Just do your damn job."

Sean stopped mid-sentence, staring at his friend.

"Oh my God," Mike said from the driver's seat, as if something had just occurred to him. "He's fucking her."

"*No*, I am not," Brian said adamantly.

"Brian, were you alone with her?" Mike continued, looking into the rearview mirror to meet Brian's gaze.

"No."

"You're lying."

"Accuse me of lying one more time, asshole," Brian challenged.

"Do not have any more contact with that woman, Brian," Sean

said, his hand slicing the air. "No talking. No physical contact of any kind."

"Dammit, Brian, we're so close to the end here," Mike seconded. "Don't fuck this up for us."

Us, Brian thought with derision. At the end of the day, these two only care about themselves.

Chapter 45

Monica had been looking forward all week to tonight. David was staying with his grandparents since Monica wasn't sure what time she would be home. While her son was certainly old enough to be at home by himself, she had felt bad leaving him alone so late.

It was Nicole's idea to have a campaign event at a bar in Old Town Alexandria. She had chosen an Irish restaurant known for its nice bar area and occasional live music. It was Monica's idea to have an open bar for the first hour, which she used her own money to pay for. That way, she surmised, people would be drawn to the event early and would be drunk enough — um, she meant happy enough — to stick around after the open bar ended.

The event started at 8pm, after the traditional DC-area happy hour had ended. Monica's team had taken a gamble with the time. Would people show up? It so happened that people did, in fact, come at around 8 and partook greatly of the free drinks and hors d'oeuvres.

Don had already judged the event a success when Val showed up at 9pm.

"My little sister!" Monica exclaimed. She had already had a couple of drinks, enough to feel warm but not enough to do anything dumb.

Monica promptly introduced her sister to everyone around her. She was thrilled that Val was able to join them since she had the next day off from work.

"How you doin'?" Val said, hugging her sister tightly.

"Doin' great," Monica answered. Then she marveled at the fact that since she had been having such a good time, she had hardly thought of Brian at all.

The drinks continued to flow, the crowd continued to grow, and the lips continued to loosen.

Val pulled her sister aside to have a private word.

"Seriously, how are you doing?" she shouted in Monica's ear.

"Doing well. Our polls are looking good."

Val gave a thumbs' up. "You're gonna beat him, aren't you?"

Monica didn't want to seem overconfident. In her mind, such bravado always led to disaster.

"We're staying positive," she said instead, although, in reality, she was overjoyed that the polling was turning in her direction. "It looks good, but we have a ways to go. Anything can happen, you know?" She shrugged.

"Yeah, I know. October surprise and all."

"You got it," Monica agreed, although the biggest "surprise," i.e. the affair, was already out in the open. Thinking of that led Monica to ponder what other embarrassing things Brian's team could possibly leak about her. But Monica didn't want to start overanalyzing things now; she wanted to enjoy tonight.

"How you doin' with the younger voters?" Val asked, breaking Monica out of her thoughts.

Monica was surprised at the question. "Pretty well, I think. Why?"

"Well, maybe if you loosened up a bit." Val shrugged, giving her sister her infamous shit-eating grin.

"Oh, don't you give me the shit-eating grin!" Monica said, laughing.

"I'll give you the SEG whenever I feel like it," Val countered, moving her shoulders with her best devil-may-care attitude.

Monica took another sip of her drink, consciously trying to drink slowly so that the alcohol wouldn't go straight to her head.

"Come on!" Val said suddenly, inclining her head towards the bar.

"What?" Monica asked, not understanding.

"Let's dance!"

"Let's go to the dance floor, then!" Monica was confused.

"No, dude! I mean there!" She again motioned toward the bar. "Let's go dance on top of the bar!"

Monica's eyes widened. She hadn't danced on top of anything since college.

"I'll distract those guys!" Val lifted her beer toward a burly dude standing next to the left side of the bar. He looked as if he would rather be anywhere than at this place.

"You're crazy!" Monica shook her head.

"Whatever," Val smirked. She downed the rest of her beer and sauntered over to the burly dude. Val's hips swayed in tight-fitting jeans as she walked, and Monica mused that the bouncer didn't stand a chance as soon as Val turned on the charm.

Monica watched her sister cock her head to the side and stand up as straight as she could, all five feet ten inches of her frame, in front of the dude, blocking his view. Monica could only imagine what was coming out of her sister's mouth.

After almost a minute, Val turned slightly, and the burly dude turned with her, so that his back faced the bar. Without looking away from the bouncer, Val motioned her right hand toward the bar, obviously meaning for her sister to get on top of it.

Monica looked around the place. Everyone was having a good time. Nicole and Don were talking to different people, and both looked as if they were out with good friends, not at a campaign event. The atmosphere of the event was celebratory, and everything seemed to be flowing naturally.

A Latin dance tune started to play then. Suddenly seized with the feeling that this felt fated, Monica walked to the bar, turned around, and waited a second. Nothing happened and no one, including the bouncer, appeared to have noticed her. Monica pulled her rear end up using her triceps so that she was sitting on the bar, then swung her skirted legs up, scrambling to her feet. As she did so, the thought occurred to her that dancing on top of the bar was not appropriate in a skirt, but she was in too deep to go back now.

In no time flat Val, much more flexible and limber than her older sister, was up there. When people in the crowd noticed that Monica had gotten up on the bar, they started hooting and hollering.

Monica recognized a couple of her campaign staffers. They probably thought that this stunt was planned, and started roaring.

"Wooooohooooo!"

Nicole and Don are gonna have a shit fit, Monica thought, which made her break into a wide grin.

As the audience cheered, Monica and Val began to dance. They didn't have to dance well for the crowd to appreciate the sight; they just had to dance. Monica saw the burly bouncer dude become lost in a sea of crushing gawkers. It occurred to Monica that it was stupid to think that one guy could control a crowd. Then again, she thought, who knew a crowd of Old Town Republicans could get so rowdy?

Out on the floor, Nicole turned in the direction of the crowd. When she realized what was happening, she exclaimed, "what?!"

Then Don was at her side.

"Why weren't you watching her?!" she shouted, indignant.

"I didn't know she would need watching!" Don countered.

"Jesus! I'm gonna get her off of there!" Nicole shouted, moving toward the bar.

Don looked around for a second, then held Nicole's shoulder, stopping her.

"Wait!" he yelled into her ear. "Look around!"

As they did so, they noticed that the crowd appeared to be electrified. Don's instinct was apparently to let the performance continue.

"Why would you want to get her off of there, when it seems to be going great!"

"Well, she could fall off and hurt herself!"

Ever the attorney, Nicole saw the headline, "GOP candidate falls off bar while dancing" in her mind.

"Give her a minute!" Don shouted to Nicole over the crowd. "Just wait!"

"I don't know," Nicole said.

Don laid a hand on Nicole's arm. "Look around, looks like everyone's having a good time."

Nicole turned her head from side to side, taking everything in. "Oh, my God, they love it."

"They do," Don said. "I think this is a good thing. Just leave it for now."

Nicole looked around the crowded room with Don. People were laughing, shouting, and encouraging Monica and Val on. But they weren't mean-spirited. In fact, they looked impressed.

The song ended, and the crowd roared, the volume increasing such that Monica thought her eardrums would explode. Her extroverted sister soaked up the approval, waving both arms toward Monica, as if showcasing her.

Monica pumped both her hands downward to get the crowd to mellow a bit.

One of her staffers produced a microphone, and the candidate raised it to her lips.

"Thanks for coming out tonight. By the way, we're not done yet. And —" she hesitated. "Let no one say that Republicans don't know how to party!"

Val raised both her arms to the sky, and the crowd's roar grew wilder, deafening Monica's thoughts.

In the car on the way home, Monica was half-deaf. She could still hear the cheers of the crowd, and her ears rang.

Val sat next to her sister, grinning from ear to ear.

Monica chanced a look at Don, who was her touchstone for these sorts of campaign-related happenings. Nicole had already gone home. She continued to look at him until he turned to face her. When he smiled, she knew he wasn't mad. When she saw the sparks in his eyes, she knew that he was pleased with how the event had turned out.

"I think that went pretty well," he said.

"Really?" Monica half-shouted back, still practically unable to hear her own voice. Ugh, she had to remember that she wasn't a twenty-something anymore. Places such as that bar completely overstimulated her.

"The crowd ate it up. What made you do that?"

Monica resisted the urge to look at Val, who had been the instigator.

"It felt right, I don't know, it felt as if people wanted a show like that."

Don nodded. "Well, they definitely got one. I think they responded well to it."

Don dropped Val off at her apartment and continued to Monica's house to drop her off.

"We don't have much longer until November," Monica mused.

"Don't worry, we'll get there," Don said reassuringly.

"I'm surprised to hear that coming from *your* mouth," Monica said, smirking.

"What do you mean?"

"You're usually the practical one, even pessimistic, bringing us all down to earth."

Don smiled, and Monica didn't miss the twinkle in his eyes. "Well, let's just say that I'm cautiously optimistic now."

"I'd say that's a good sign."

"Just don't get too complacent." He playfully punched Monica on the shoulder.

By the time they arrived at Monica's house, she was yawning.

She unlocked the front door and felt relieved to be home at last. She was looking forward to relishing a few moments of quiet before falling down in bed.

Bandit came up to her, wiggling her rear and tail. Monica never got tired of seeing that sight.

She turned to Don. "Thanks for driving me home."

"No problem. You're good?"

Monica paused, not understanding the question. "Yeah," she said.

Don stood there for a moment longer.

"Can — can I get you anything?" Monica asked, as a way of trying to get him to leave. Why was he hanging around?

"No, no, I'm good."

All of a sudden, Monica became anxious. The mood seemed to have changed a bit.

"You were great tonight," Don said, his eyes intently locked on Monica's face.

"Thanks," Monica replied, shrugging. "It was my sister who really — made that happen."

"I think it only helped."

Another moment passed in silence.

"Okay, see you tomorrow, then," Monica asked.

He sighed before responding. Monica wondered how much he had had to drink. Not much, probably. He tended not to drink a lot when they were doing campaign events. He liked to be in control of every situation.

"Monica —" he began, with the conviction of a man who was about to take a huge risk.

WIthout more, he stepped forward, closing the distance between them.

Suddenly, his lips were on Monica's; his breath tasted of mint. The close contact made her pulse quicken, and her face suddenly felt overheated.

"Woah, woah, woah," Monica said, pushing his chest so that he was forced to take a couple of steps away from her. She was sorely irritated; his kiss, on top of the loud noise of the evening, had made her jittery and overstimulated. She needed alone time, stat.

"This is *not* a good idea." She took a step backward to put more distance between them. "Well, that's actually an understatement."

"Monica, come on. You know how I feel about you."

This was a horny, tipsy kid talking, she thought, not a

professional campaign director, but she knew she had to be more diplomatic than that.

"We cannot do this during the campaign. *You* work for *me*, remember, and I'm still married."

"In name only."

"Wait," she said, her tone harsher. "Maybe my husband and I will work it out, you don't know that." She knew it wasn't the case, but tried to reason with him.

He seemed about to say something, but apparently thought better of it. Instead, he said, "Well, I'm sorry."

"Look, tomorrow when you wake up, during the day, after the effects of the drinks have worn off, you will understand that this is a bad idea and you will regret it. Got it?"

He stuck his hands in his pockets, considered, then nodded.

"Don, you are great at what you do. I need you to keep a level head here, okay?"

He nodded again. "Campaign'll be over soon anyway." He grinned.

Monica understood his meaning, but didn't want to get into an argument this late. You mean, we can screw after that, she thought. Dumb idea. If she won, Don would get a place in her administration. And if she didn't win — well, she was determined to win. She wouldn't even consider losing this late in the game.

"We'll talk about that later," she said instead, and overemphasized her next words so that Don did not misunderstand them. "Thank you for driving me home. I've got to get some sleep. See you tomorrow."

Without worrying about appearances, she walked to the front door and held it open for him.

"See you tomorrow," Don said on his way out, without meeting

Monica's stare.

He either took it well, or was seething inwardly, Monica thought. Don was hard to read much of the time; he kept his most private thoughts close to the vest. This characteristic was valuable during a pressure-induced situation such as a political campaign. However, currently it did not help her.

Monica locked the door and sat down heavily on the living room sofa. When her dog approached her, she scratched her behind her ears, and wondered how things could possibly be more screwed up right now.

Chapter 46

"Doctor, could we get some help over here?!"

The nurse sounded desperate. Val spun around, curious. She was almost done with her nighttime shift at the hospital, and was on her way to write up her last notes before heading home to sleep. Now this. She pursed her lips in annoyance, and stepped into the hospital room.

Two nurses struggled with a large man, trying to get him to lie down on his hospital bed.

"What happened?" Val asked tightly.

"He was admitted for chest pains," one of the nurses said, as she held the man's right arm, trying to force it down. "We tried to give him nitro, but he refused."

Val addressed the patient. "Sir, please calm down. We need to give you some medicine and run some tests to make sure nothing is wrong with your heart. You may be having a heart attack."

"Get off me, bitch!" the patient yelled at one of the nurses.

Val wasted no time and stepped just outside the room. "We need security in here now! Also need a Haldol and Ativan combo, 5 mg Haldol, 2 mg Ativan, now!" She quickly looked around, and pointed to a nearby nurse. "Now, please!" The nurse scurried off.

Val had a second thought, and turned back toward the two

nurses struggling with the patient. "Does he have any allergies?"

"We don't know, he refused to give us any info during intake."

"Well, I guess we'll find out," Val murmured, mostly to herself.

When the other nurse came in with the syringe, Val told her, "also get me a syringe of .3 milligrams of epinephrine, just in case. We don't know if he's allergic."

The nurse rushed off again.

"Whose patient is this?" Val asked, rolling up her sleeves.

"Dr. Anderson's, but he got held up."

God, Anderson owes me big time, Val thought. Maybe I can parlay a date out of this. She smirked. Anderson was good-looking and single, and had no lack of suitors.

A burly security guard entered the room, hitching up his pants as he approached the patient.

"We need help here," Val said to him while motioning towards the patient.

"Got it," he answered.

The security guard held the patient down by his arms as Val approached the hospital bed, holding the syringe nonchalantly in her right hand, which was lowered by her waist.

"Okay, Sir, we're going to give you something to make you relax a little, and then we'll do some tests, an X-ray and maybe an MRI —"

"Get away from me, bitch!" he yelled.

Val got close enough to look at his eyes, but he wouldn't let her get close enough to lift his lids to see his pupils.

"Looks like he may be high," she said under her breath to the nurses.

"Yeah, intake said that, too, even though he refused a physical exam," one of the nurses replied.

Val sighed, but knew she didn't have much time. The patient

resisted and the guard was getting fatigued. For a second, she considered letting the man leave, but was fairly certain he would refuse to sign an AMA, a form allowing him to leave against medical advice, which would hopefully absolve the hospital of liability for letting him leave. If he refused to sign the AMA form, Val and her colleagues could be liable for negligence, something Val did not want responsibility for.

Another nurse entered the room briskly, holding a syringe.

"For the epi," she told Val, who nodded in response.

"Okay, Sir," Val said as calmly as she could, moving toward the patient. "We're just going to give you something to help you relax a little."

As Val lifted the syringe, the patient became even more agitated.

"Get that shit away from me!" he yelled, throwing the guard backward. The guard hit the wall and fell down.

Val knew she had only a few seconds to do this. She rushed forward, trying to get a grip on the patient's left arm. He seemed to have a sudden surge of strength, and brought his right arm up to grab Val's left arm. She couldn't get her right hand on his arm where it needed to be for the shot.

As tall and lean as Val was, she did not have the strength to match the patient's. He sat up, falling off and on top of Val. She struggled and, in doing so, dropped the syringe on the floor.

"Fuck!" she screamed. Her head hit the floor.

As Val tried without success to push the patient off of her, he put his hands around her throat. Val panicked, clutching at his fingers. She saw the nurses pulling at the man's shoulders and shouting. Then, in a haze, she saw the uniformed security guard.

Val gasped for air and started to see spots. Holy fuck, she

thought. Of all the ways to go. Familiar but long-ago scenes ran through her mind, of her and her sister playing outside, her first car, her first day as an undergraduate, her first boyfriend.

All of a sudden, the hands fell away from her throat. She opened her mouth and gasped, raggedly drawing in a long breath. As her breathing returned to normal, she saw a man in a white coat standing over the patient's passed-out body, depressing the rest of the contents of a syringe into the man's shoulder.

"You all right?" the man said worriedly, bending down.

Val nodded. "Fuck you, Anderson," she rasped. "You owe me big time."

Chapter 47

Monica heard her cell phone ringing as soon as she walked into her campaign office at 7:30am. She had wanted to get an early start that day.

She opened her purse and searched it furiously, silently cursing herself for carrying such a voluminous handbag.

She ignored Don as he approached her, still pissed off from the moves he had made on her the other day.

Monica found her phone. She stared at it for a second before answering, not recognizing the number. But people from all over the place were calling her during the campaign.

"Hello?" she said.

"Hi, Monica?"

"Yes, this is Monica. Who's this?"

"Hi, sorry to bother you. This is Dr. Chris Anderson. I work with your sister."

Monica's chest immediately tightened. "What happened?"

"Well, there was an incident here."

Monica's full maternal instinct kicked in. "My sister! Is she okay?!"

"Well, she was treating a patient of mine —"

"Dammit! Is she okay?!" she raised her voice into the phone.

Dr. Anderson seemed surprised at Monica's tone. "Yes, yes, she's okay," he said quickly.

Monica relaxed a bit, exhaling. "Okay, so what happened?"

"She was assaulted by a patient, but she's all right. We treated her and she's going home. She asked if you could come pick her up."

"She's at the hospital?"

"Yes."

"I'll be right there."

Monica hung up and faced Don, who had been listening.

"Is everything okay?" he asked.

"I don't know. I think so. I have to go."

"You have an event at lunchtime."

"I'll make it. I'll text you."

Monica was not prepared for the bruises around her sister's neck. She gasped when she saw Val in the hospital bed.

"What happened?"

Val started to cry. Monica immediately went to her sister and hugged her.

"It's okay, it's okay. You don't have to say anything."

A man in a white coat entered the room. "Are you Monica?" he asked.

"Yes," she answered. "Doctor, I presume?"

"Yes, I'm Dr. Chris Anderson. Can I talk to you out here for a second?"

Monica turned toward her sister. "Val, don't worry. I'll be right outside."

Monica stepped outside the room and Dr. Anderson explained to her what had happened.

While Val had no cracked bones in her neck, there would be bruising. She needed to rest and had been given prescriptions for pain medication, anti-anxiety medication, and a sleep aid.

"She doesn't want to go home. I mean, she doesn't want to go to *her* house," Dr. Anderson said. "She wants to go home with you but doesn't want to be alone."

"Okay," Monica said, nodding. "I'll take her home with me."

"She also needs to see a psychiatrist, because of —"

"Yeah, I got it."

"I'll give you the name of the one I'm referring her to. He's here in the medical building next to the hospital."

"Thank you."

Dr. Anderson paused and Monica sighed.

"I know it's a lot," he said. "Call me anytime if you need anything."

Monica nodded.

After Val was discharged, both sisters went to Monica's house. After getting Val settled in, Monica started to make preparations to leave for her lunchtime campaign event, but Val insisted that she didn't want to be alone.

Monica called Don and explained the situation.

"Monica, that's terrible what happened to your sister, but you need to be here," Don said.

Monica had known she wouldn't get any slack from him.

"I can't leave her alone, Don."

"This is a luncheon with Hispanic community leaders. We moved a lot of things around to make this happen. You *have* to be here —"

"I hear you," Monica said impatiently.

"It will look horrible if you're not here. What do you want me to tell them?"

"That I had a family emergency."

"That sounds like you're blowing them off."

"Well, what do you want me to do?" Monica threw one hand up in the air in frustration.

"Can't you get someone to watch her?"

Monica pondered. David was in school; otherwise, he could have stayed with his aunt.

"Put Nicole on the phone," she said tightly.

"Nicole needs to be at the luncheon to run things and make introductions."

"Either Nicole's there without me, or I'm there without her. Take your pick."

Don hesitated. "Fine, I'll put Nicole on. She can go while you're here."

"Thank you." Monica tried hard to keep the sarcasm out of her voice.

Chapter 48

A couple of hours later, Monica stumbled through her front door, exhausted.

Nicole emerged from the kitchen.

"How'd she do?" Monica asked her friend.

"She's fine," Nicole said. "She ate a little and took her sleeping pill."

Monica exhaled, dropping her purse on the floor.

"She's sleeping now?"

"Yeah," Nicole answered. "I just checked on her a couple of minutes ago. How was the event?"

"Good, I think," Monica said. "I did a ton of networking. I'm just — peopled out."

"I'm sorry. I can certainly understand that."

Monica plopped down on the sofa in the living room.

"Got to shed my Spanish chops, though," she smiled.

Nicole chuckled. "Awesome."

Monica leaned her head back against the plush cushions of the sofa. "Thanks for being here, Nic."

"Hey, anytime. You know that."

"OK, I'm taking the rest of the day off. David will be home from school soon."

"What do you want me to tell the women's group? We had said you may stop by this evening at their monthly meeting."

"Tell them I had a family emergency and am taking care of a sick relative. I mean, it's the truth."

"You got it. Is there anything else I can do?"

"No, I'm good. Thank you."

Nicole hugged her friend, then left.

Monica went upstairs and checked on her sister, who was sleeping soundly. She shook her head, thinking about how Val's circadian rhythms must be screwed up after working night shifts.

After David came home, Monica explained the situation to him and ordered something for dinner.

"I'm going to go upstairs and read for awhile, Mom," David said after dinner.

"Sounds great, sweetheart. Did you finish your homework for tomorrow?"

"Sure did!"

Monica gave her son a hug, and he walked upstairs, closing his bedroom door gently behind him.

Monica went to the kitchen to pour a glass of wine, marveling at how the universe had been so kind to her in giving her a son who was exactly like her, whom she could easily understand.

Monica stopped when she heard a sound, then realized it was someone knocking softly on the front door.

Always a bit suspicious, especially now, she moved slowly to check, squinting to see through the peephole.

"What the —" she said under her breath.

Monica opened the door and saw Brian standing on her front porch.

"Hey," he said softly.

"Hey," Monica sighed, dropping her shoulders all at once.

"Is everything okay?" he asked, his brows furrowed.

"Yeah — why?" Monica asked, still trying to process that he was here in the flesh.

"I'm sorry for showing up like this. I tried to call you —"

"I haven't checked my phone for a while," Monica said by way of explanation.

"I just — I don't know, I was worried. I heard you canceled all your events for the rest of the day."

Wow, word gets around fast, Monica thought. She couldn't think of anything to say in response.

"But I can go," Brian said quickly. He half-turned around. Uncharacteristically, his tie was askew and his shirt collar rumpled.

"No, no, it's all right," Monica said. "I mean —" she suddenly couldn't find the words. "I've had kind of a rough day." And with that, she put her face in her hands and cried. She had felt the urge to cry all day, but hadn't been able to in front of so many people.

"Come here," Brian said gently, moving inside and shutting the front door. "Let's sit down."

Monica let him guide her to the sofa. They sat and Brian put his arm around her while her shoulders heaved.

"What's going on?" he asked carefully. "Is everything okay?"

"More or less," Monica said between sobs. She noticed that the front of Brian's shirt was wet from her tears.

"Do you want to talk about it?" Brian asked.

Monica raised her head and wiped her eyes.

"Brian, why are you here?"

He shrugged.

He doesn't even know himself, Monica thought.

"I don't know, I — I missed seeing you. And when I heard you weren't doing any events today, I was kind of worried. It's not like you to say you're gonna do something, then not show up."

Monica sat listening.

"Sorry for coming over unannounced. Is there anything I can do?"

Monica hesitated. "Could you please put on some tea?"

"Of course."

Brian found the kettle and set it on the stove, then returned to sit beside Monica, handing her a tissue.

"Thank you." She dabbed at her eyes and pushed her thick hair out of her face and behind her ears.

"What did you do that your clothes are so rumpled?" she asked Brian, gesturing to his shirt collar.

A smile tugged at her lips, and Brian smiled back.

"Oh, I slept in them, you know, on the sofa at the campaign office. Gotta be ready to go at a moment's notice." He grinned and his eyes twinkled.

Monica met his gaze.

"My sister's asleep upstairs," she said then.

"Is she okay?"

Monica told Brian what had happened at the hospital.

"Goddamn," he said in response. "That's awful."

"I don't know when she can go back to work. And my Mom's been calling me. I haven't called her back, I don't know what to tell her. She's gonna freak out."

"Hey, it's all good. I'm sure your sister just needs some time to rest, and she'll be okay."

"And it's October already! Only a month until the —" she then realized who she was talking to.

"Jesus, don't worry about that. You're doing terrific in the polls." Brian hadn't been able to keep the amazement out of his voice.

The irony of the situation made Monica laugh lightly. Her opponent was telling her that she was doing well in the race.

"What do you have planned for the October surprise?" She looked directly at Brian, tear-streaked face and all.

Brian froze, apparently caught off guard.

"Nothing," he answered.

Monica nodded.

"There's not always an October surprise, you know," he said, attempting a charming smile. "Sometimes the opponent is perfect."

Monica pursed her lips. "Yeah, whatever."

"Why?" Brian asked, suddenly anxious. "What do *you* have planned for the October surprise?"

Monica laughed. "You'll have to wait and see, I guess," she bluffed.

"Come on," Brian said. "We're friends, right?"

Monica raised an eyebrow. "Oh, we are?"

"Of course," Brian smiled. "I told you before. Friends with potential."

Monica laughed.

They locked eyes, and Monica felt comfortable.

"Have you had dinner?" she asked.

"No." Brian shook his head.

"We got Chinese takeout. There's plenty left over if you want."

"Oh, my God, yes," Brian said gratefully. "Thank you." He made a mock bow from the waist.

Monica heard movement upstairs, then footsteps. She knew that David was on his way downstairs.

"Hey, Mom, who are you talking to?" David asked as he appeared on the staircase.

"Uh — a friend of mine."

David looked at Brian and back at his mother.

Monica introduced the two of them, and noticed the look of suspicion in her son's eyes. As always, she refused to lie to him.

"This is Brian Murphy," she said.

"Isn't he —" David began with hesitation.

"Yes, he's the guy I'm running against." Then she added quickly, "he heard I took the afternoon off and was concerned so he stopped by. He's gonna have some dinner, then he'll be leaving."

David nodded and descended the stairs.

"Nice to meet you," he said, shaking Brian's hand.

"Nice to meet you, too." Brian smiled.

"Okay, I'll be upstairs then," he told his mother, and returned slowly to his room.

Brian dug into the Chinese food and Monica flipped channels while they sat on the living room sofa.

"Crap, crap, crap, crap," Monica said to herself as she continuously pushed the remote button.

"It's all crap," Brian said. "I mean, what's the point of cable anymore, anyway?"

"Yeah, really," Monica shrugged, then yawned with abandon. She lay her head back against the sofa cushions and was too exhausted to remember anything else.

Monica woke up gradually. The lights were low and the television was on but she couldn't hear it. She squinted to focus.

Her head was on the sofa, and she had a blanket over her.

God, that was the best sleep I've had in a long time, she thought.

She heard noises coming from the kitchen and turned her head around to look for Brian.

He emerged from the kitchen and saw that she was awake.

"Oh, I just put the dishes in the sink and was gonna head out."

"It's all right. What time is it?" she asked.

"It's about ten-thirty," he answered, smiling.

"What?" Monica couldn't believe it.

"Yes, sleepyhead."

"I've gotta check on my sister," Monica said, sitting up quickly.

"David already did. He said she's doing fine. Still sleeping."

"Okay, good."

"And he told me not to wake you, that you've hard a rough week."

Monica smiled. "Yeah, he's protective of me."

"I can tell."

Monica rubbed her eyes, then caught Brian gazing at her.

"What?" she said.

Brian shook his head slowly. "Nothing. It's just — you look gorgeous right now."

"Whatever," Monica said with incredulity. "I'm a scrub."

"No, you're not," Brian countered.

They remained in comfortable silence for a few moments.

"I'm gonna head out," Brian said.

"Okay, I need to go to bed and get some rest —"

"To beat this random candidate you're running against?" Brian asked, his dark eyes sparkling in the low light.

"Something like that," Monica said, smiling. "Brian, thanks for coming. I really appreciate it."

"Anytime," he said.

"Sorry I haven't responded to your texts lately."

Brian shrugged. "It's okay. I understand."

"I just —" Monica decided to be completely honest. "I needed to protect myself."

"It's okay," Brian repeated softly.

Monica rose from the sofa and escorted him to the front door.

Once at the door, they were unsure how to say goodbye. Both kept their distance.

"I'll see you later," Brian said. "You can text or call anytime."

"Okay." Monica nodded and shut the door behind him.

After checking on both Val and David, Monica stripped off her clothes and let them fall on the bedroom floor in disarray. She fell on her bed and swore that she could still smell Brian on her hair.

"Goddammit," she said aloud.

Chapter 49

"*This* is our October surprise," Mike said triumphantly, raising his fist in the air.

"I don't know, Mike," Sean mused as he rubbed his chin. "It's risky."

"She has anorexia," Mike insisted.

"*Had*," Sean corrected. "And, according to your source, it happened over twenty years ago."

"That type of thing never goes away entirely," Mike countered.

"Anyway, your source is a former high school classmate of hers." Sean shook his head.

"Who also happened to be a friend of the family, who spent time at Monica's house."

"When she was in high school!" Brian raised his voice. "It's *ridiculous*." Brian emphasized his point by pointing his finger at Mike.

"It's emblematic of something else," Mike went on. "I talked to a shrink about this."

"God —" Brian rubbed his face with a hand.

"The shrink said that it could be reflective of other mental illness —"

"Then almost every girl I went to college with had it," Brian said.

"It's an obsession about control," Mike said.

"I don't know about that," Brian said pointedly.

"You need to do this, Brian," Mike said, pointing towards his boss' chest.

Brian shook his head, and gave Mike a hard look.

"I will say this," Sean began, "it could go either way. There's a chance it could reflect poorly on Monica, and there's a chance it could backfire, and the feminists would hang us out to dry."

Mike scoffed. "No way the feminists will care about this. They'll back us up because the woman here happens to be a Republican, and the women who call themselves feminists in this area all vote Dem. We know this."

"But we'd be revealing something so personal," Sean countered. "This isn't like a DUI or a drug charge. Arguably, the public has the right to know those things —"

"Doesn't matter," Mike shook his head vigorously. "The public also has a right to know personal information about a candidate running for public office."

"I gotta tell ya," Sean said. "I'm on the fence here. I don't like it, and under normal circumstances I wouldn't go with it, but it may be our last shot to pull ahead in the polls. I'm not crazy about how thin the margin is."

Brian thought of Monica's comment a while ago, when she told him that she didn't mind losing the election, but if he lost, that would be horrible optics not only for him, but also for the party.

Brian looked past the other two men and shook his head.

"We gotta do it," Mike insisted. "Your rep's at stake."

"It's your call, boss," Sean said evenly.

Brian felt awful. He cared less and less about the election and more about Monica.

Chapter 50

Monica's eyes trailed Don as he left her office, watching him as he brushed a hand through his chestnut hair, and lingered on his rear end as he walked away.

Nicole shut the office door in one speedy motion. "Enjoying yourself?" she said to her friend.

"Huh?" Monica started, ripped away from her daydream.

"Your campaign manager. *Really?*"

Monica looked at Nicole, who stood with her hands on her hips, her dark eyes wide.

"What?" Monica asked, confused.

"I strongly suggest," Nicole began slowly, "that you do *not* do it."

"Do what?" Monica feigned ignorance.

"Uuuugggghhhhhh," Nicole sighed, throwing her hands up in the air. "Girl, do you know how much that will screw things up, especially now? We're almost at the end, and you're doing so well!"

Monica felt her face redden.

"Look, I know you like him," Nicole continued. "But think before you act. And I know he likes you. He would jump in bed with you in a second."

"I don't know about that," Monica countered, but she remembered his kiss from the other day.

"Monica, you are vulnerable, and maybe a bit needy right now. I get that. After this election, you can date all you want. Date properly, that is."

Monica scoffed, wondering what it meant to "date properly." "Date? Me? Please." She waved a hand dismissively.

"Even if you two start something now, how do you think it would end? Remember, my friend, you've promised him a top job in your administration if you win. And, not to get our hopes up, but that is looking more and more likely."

"Don't worry."

"I mean it." Nicole pointed a finger in her friend's direction. "Believe me. I know how hot he is, but it would only complicate things. Keep your head in the game. We've got the final debate coming up. Just don't screw it up and we'll have a serious chance."

Monica saluted. "Yes, Ma'am."

Chapter 51

T he venue for the final debate was larger than that of the previous one. Upon seeing its size, Monica's heart began to thump in her chest.

"How many people are we expecting?" she asked Don.

He paused before speaking, which made Monica think that he knew she wouldn't like his answer.

"We're expecting more people than last time," he hedged.

"How many more?"

Don stopped walking and faced Monica. Their eyes met, and she froze.

Don smirked a bit. "Since last time, when the debate began with your hand on his chest, many more people apparently became interested. They want to know what's going on, see for themselves."

If Don was irritated, Monica couldn't tell. "I was just straightening his tie," she said defensively.

Don sighed. "Don't do anything like that this time, please." He wouldn't press the issue because they had already gone over it. "Don't touch him, don't go near him. You can briefly glance at him, you know, to make your point and stuff. I mean, we certainly don't want the audience to think that you're afraid of him."

"Gotcha."

"I mean it, Monica. Please."

"Okay," she agreed.

"Let's go check out the stage." Don continued walking and Monica followed.

They walked on the stage and Monica was instantly seized by anxiety upon seeing the bright lights and near-empty seats where the audience would be shortly. She took deep breaths to calm herself.

"You'll be here, same setup as last time," Don explained.

Monica looked, nodding to show him that she understood.

"Just do like you did last time. You were calm, you explained your answers well."

"Okay, thanks."

Don apparently noticed the pained look on her face.

"Hey," he said as he put his hands lightly on her elbows. "Everything will be fine."

"I know," she replied, still taking in slow breaths.

"All right, let's get you something light to eat and some water."

"It's game time," Don said as he stuck his head inside the small room where Monica was getting ready.

"Okay," Monica said. The anticipation was always killer. Once she was in the middle of the debate, she would be all right.

She stood up and put the finishing touches on her makeup, making sure to cover up any imperfections and blot out all shininess from her face.

"Are you good to go?" Nicole asked.

"I guess," Monica said. "No turning back now."

"You got this."

Monica patted her hair one more time to tame a few loose strands, then turned toward her friend.

"Let's go," she sighed.

The candidates arrived onstage at the same time, and walked to their respective podiums with a precision that appeared to be coordinated, but in reality was just good luck.

Monica felt Brian looking at her but willed herself to stare straight ahead toward the audience. No doubt he was half-mesmerized by her emerald green sheath dress. It hugged her curves, and the low boat neckline revealed just enough collarbone to be intriguing but not suggestive. The outfit was completed by black stockings and low black heels.

Monica looked out just beyond the audience to avoid being blinded by the stage lights. She thought of David, and her mood automatically changed from anxious to content. Feeling more centered, she glanced at the debate moderator and smiled, nodding in acknowledgement.

As someone counted down, Monica said the Litany Against Fear under her breath.

"And only I will remain," she finished.

"We're live in three — two — one!"

Monica took the last second to inhale deeply and exhale slowly. She plastered a semi-smile on her face, making sure she appeared upbeat, and looked straight ahead.

"We're here for the final debate in the Eighth District congressional race," the female moderator announced, and named the candidates.

"Since Ms. Orellana was asked the first question in the previous debate," the moderator continued, "it's only fair that we let Mr. Murphy go first now."

Good, Monica thought. Let's see what the tone is tonight.

"Mr. Murphy," the moderator said, turning to Brian, "the most recent poll shows you and your opponent in a statistical dead heat. Given the election history of this district —"

Read: given that this district always votes Democrat, thought Monica.

"— what do you think accounts for that trend?"

Damn, Monica thought.

Monica looked at Brian in what she hoped was a neutral way. He wore a dark suit with a cerulean tie; the color complemented his dark eyes.

"This has indeed been a challenging race," he began. His voice sounded even deeper than it usually was. "First, I'd like to point out that polls are rarely 100% accurate; they are of course meant to be a sample of the population at large, but it's extremely difficult to get an accurate representation of the entire population."

Bullshit, Monica thought. If the polls showed him in the lead, he would be all over them, screaming that they *are* 100% accurate.

"That being said," Brian continued, "there is no doubt that what the polls show is partly a result of the excellent campaign that Ms. Orellana is managing."

Is that backhanded criticism? Monica thought suspiciously.

"She has generally been doing very well," the moderator agreed, then turned toward Monica.

"Ms. Orellana, I'll now ask you the same question. In your opinion, what accounts for the current polls?"

Monica instinctively stood up a bit more straight. "Well, I agree with my opponent that it has certainly been a challenging campaign. As for the polls, I think the fact that I've been doing better than expected —" Take that, Monica thought, "— is a reflection of the fact that the population of this district is ready for positive change, including lower taxes, better-managed educational resources, and increased job growth. The people of this district are tired of the same old policies."

She was tempted to mention Mike's faux pas in calling her a "slut," but was afraid that it would appear too low of a blow. Brian's tone tonight had been pretty positive so far, and Monica felt determined to match it; if his tone darkened, then hers would, too.

The debate went on for a while in that same vein, with Monica and Brian both respectful of the other, with neither of them raising the issue of the affair, which hung over everyone's heads like the proverbial thousand-pound elephant in the room.

Then things got interesting.

The moderator paused before asking the next question, which made Monica freak out internally.

This can't be good, she thought.

"In the upcoming election, there will be a question for taxpayers about whether they are in favor of Fairfax County spending additional money on schools. What are your opinions on that?"

Brian gave what Monica considered a pat answer about how it was essential to provide adequate funding to the public school system.

Then it was Monica's turn to speak.

"What I want the constituents to understand," she began, "is that the question that will be posed on the ballot is not, 'should we spend money that is already in the budget?' It is also not 'should we divert money that has been allocated to another area to education?' The question on the ballot will be 'should the county acquire additional debt to give money to public schools?' Now, no one thinks that we should *not* fund our schools. But do you want the constituents to be burdened with additional debt in order to do so? I think that, before we do that, we should closely study the budget to determine whether taxpayer money is being wisely spent."

"So you would vote no on the bond question?" the moderator asked Monica pointedly.

"I would vote no, because to vote yes means that the taxpayers of the County would incur additional debt, and how would that be paid for? Likely by raising taxes. I don't want the taxpayers to take on additional debt before we determine whether the local government is spending their money wisely."

Monica punctuated her last sentence with a decisive nod, and hoped that she made her point clearly without sounding like she was anti-education, since, in her mind, that was invariably how the opposition would spin it.

Surprisingly, the moderator then turned to Brian for a rebuttal.

"Mr. Murphy, Ms. Orellana has raised the issue of how to pay for the extra debt the County would incur if the bond issue passes —"

If, Monica thought, laughing to herself. The bond questions always pass because most people don't realize they involve taking on additional debt to fund the issue of the day.

"Well, that would be an issue for the local government to decide," he dodged.

"Well, would you support an increase in taxes to fund programs that are partially funded by the state, such as Medicaid?"

The moderator didn't defer to Brian as much as Monica had thought she would.

"Well, we would have to look at the issue, and decide how important it is."

Monica pursed her lips, then noticed that it appeared that the moderator had no follow-up questions for Brian, since she was preparing to speak to Monica.

"Wait," Monica interjected, holding up her hand. "So the audience can understand my opponent's political doublespeak here, his answer was yes, he would support a tax increase in this district to fund federal programs —"

"I didn't say —" Brian started.

"Well, you didn't give a yes or no answer," Monica interrupted, facing Brian directly.

"It's not a yes or no question," he said, raising his chin.

His apparent smugness annoyed her. Not a yes or no question? she thought. Are you kidding me?

A calm came over her as she looked at Brian curiously. "Would you support a tax increase to fund partially state-funded programs such as Medicaid, yes or no?" she parroted the moderator's question.

"It depends," he said.

"It depends on — what program we're funding?" Monica prompted.

"Yes, among other things, such as the current tax rates," Brian said.

Monica nodded, and hoped that Brian came across as weaselly to the audience as he did to her.

When the debate ended, Monica breathed a sigh of relief and clamped her lips shut to stop talking; she felt as if she could go on all night. She was then surprised to hear heavy applause from the crowd. Don had promised to get as many of her supporters there as possible, and she wondered whether the applause was for Brian or for her.

"Thank you, Ms. Orellana," the moderator said in response,

and turned to Brian to thank him.

She stood at her podium until she noticed Brian walking toward her with purpose. She would have to shake hands with him. She walked toward him and met him near the middle of the stage.

Monica was hot from the stage lamps, and felt her cheeks redden.

Brian's eyes searched her face as she took a deep breath and extended her hand to him.

He took Monica's hand and shook it.

"You did great," he said.

She smiled perfunctorily. "Thanks." Then, "you did all right." She smirked.

Brian chuckled and shook his head slightly. His eyes held hers, sharp and laser-focused.

"How's everything?" he asked under his breath.

"Good," she answered.

They shook hands once, twice, then remained standing, hands clasped.

"Is your sister all right?" Brian's eyes were still locked with hers.

"Yeah, she's much better. Thanks for asking."

Brian still held onto her hand.

"I've been thinking about you —" he began.

But Brian didn't get the chance to finish his sentence.

In a matter of seconds, a swarm of people had descended on the stage. Nicole and Don were at Monica's side and Nicole gently pulled Monica's arm away from Brian's grasp, linking it through her own.

"What the hell was that about?" Nicole whispered to her friend.

"I don't know," Monica said quickly. She noticed Don giving Brian a look of death.

Before Brian could open his mouth to speak, Sean and Mike had him by the arms and were speaking to him. He looked annoyed.

When the three men exited, Nicole asked her friend, "are you all right?"

"Yeah," Monica chuckled in disbelief. "I don't know. He looked like he was going to —"

"Yeah, I know," Nicole interrupted.

"Goddammit, what the hell was he doing?" Don cursed under his breath.

"Tell me that wasn't live, at least," Monica said hopefully. How could she explain their reluctance to let each other's hands go?

"Wish I could," Nicole said.

Monica met her friend's gaze. "Well, damn," she sighed heavily.

"As if this campaign couldn't get any hotter," Nicole said, shaking her head.

"Where'd Brian go?" Monica asked.

"I think he's around," Don replied. "Why?"

"What happened up there was awkward, but I'm not going to let him chase us out," Monica said. "Let's shake hands, then I need a drink."

Don smiled. "That's my girl."

For the rest of the night, Brian and Monica traded furtive glances across the room.

VI

NOVEMBER

Chapter 52

The Friday night before the election, Monica had wanted to stay home and go to sleep early, to recharge her introvert brain after a stressful, overstimulating week. Don and Nicole had talked her into going out.

"Come on!" Nicole had said. "It'll be fun! We'll go out dancing, just like old times!"

Monica had relented after getting the okay from David, who would keep Val company. Even though he was fourteen and not far from legally being an adult, she still felt guilty leaving him. Val was doing much better and her therapist had told her that she could go back to work when she felt ready.

Monica felt uncomfortable around Don since he had kissed her, but she had had a hard time saying no to Nicole.

Nicole had taken them to some high-end dance club/bar in downtown DC. Thankfully, it wasn't as noisy or crowded as Monica had expected.

That's likely because it's still early, Monica thought. All the Millennials will be out after midnight.

They got drinks and sat down, waiting for the dance floor to fill up a little.

"So this is it!" Nicole said, as she handed Monica her glass of wine.

Monica shrugged dramatically. "We'll see what happens."

Don smiled at her. "You have the best chance of winning this seat of any Republican I have ever seen."

Monica took his comment as empty flattery. *He just wants me in bed*, she thought.

She thanked him anyway. No sense in annoying her campaign manager at this point.

"Jesus, is that Brian Murphy?!" Nicole said.

Don and Monica whipped their heads around. Brian was accompanied by Sean.

"Goddammit," Don muttered.

Monica sighed.

"Let's go," Nicole said.

"No," Monica said automatically. "Why should *we* leave? Looks like we were here first. *He* can leave if he's uncomfortable." She looked at both Don and Nicole in turn.

Don shrugged. "Fine with me." He drained his beer.

Brian and Sean eventually made their way over to Monica's table. She instinctively leaned back as he approached.

"Well, well, of all the clubs in all the alleys in this town," Brian said, smoothing out his tie, "you just had to walk into mine."

"Excuse me," Monica said, "I think *you* walked into *mine*."

Brian smiled, and Monica couldn't help smiling back.

"Okay, you've said your piece. Now get outta here," Nicole said, shooing both men away with her hand.

"Can I buy you a drink?" Sean asked Nicole.

"I already have one," she answered, one eyebrow raised.

Dammit if he doesn't like her, Monica thought.

"Get her another one," Monica told Sean. "She needs it. She's drinking rum and coke, by the way."

Nicole looked at her friend quizzically.

"What?" Monica shrugged. "We'll be here awhile anyway."

"Okay, but no dancing on the bar this time."

Monica laughed.

"We can dance now," Monica said to Nicole. "Dance floor's not empty and not too crowded either."

The two ladies left the table to move to the dance floor.

Don watched Brian's gaze follow Monica, and it angered him. He locked eyes with Brian as he rose from the table.

"Keep dreamin'," he couldn't resist saying to the candidate as he brushed past him on his way to the bar.

Brian scoffed but didn't reply.

About an hour later, the place had filled up, and the music had gotten faster. Brian and Sean had been talking in a corner most of the time.

"So what's it look like, in your opinion?" he asked Sean.

"How does the election look?"

What else would I be talking about? Brian thought.

"Or how does Monica look?" Sean quickly added.

Brian stared at his friend. "What?"

"Come on man, you've been making eyes at her since we got here."

Brian looked at the ceiling but didn't deny it.

"That ship's sailed, Brian, if it was ever in the harbor. And your extended handholding at the debate certainly didn't help us."

Sean and Mike had both hit the roof after that exchange. They had told Brian that anyone watching could see how he had been gazing at Monica, as if he had wanted to devour her.

"You gotta be cool," Sean said now.

The comment annoyed Brian, who wasn't used to following orders. He didn't answer. He was too busy watching Don

281

approach Monica at the bar.

"I'm gonna hit the head," Sean said then.

"All right. I'll be here." However, Brian had no intention of being there when Sean returned.

He set his beer bottle on the table in front of him and walked to the bar.

Don stared at him as he approached but Brian couldn't care less. He gingerly touched Monica's elbow as he said, "hey, there," in her ear.

Monica turned her head and guardedly pressed her elbow against her side. When she saw who it was, she relaxed a bit.

"Hey," she said back.

"What do you want?" Don asked.

Brian was tired of Don's attitude, and ignored him.

"How do you feel about dancing?" he asked Monica.

"Oh, you know I like to dance," she said cryptically.

Brian shook his head at her dodge and smiled. "I mean, would you like to dance — with me?"

"Oh, I suppose I should reward this brazen attempt at bravado with an affirmative response."

"I'll take that as a yes, then."

"You would be correct in your deduction."

Brian took Monica's hand and led her to the dance floor, despite Don's protests. He was pleased to see Monica wave Don off.

They put several people between them and the bar, so that Don couldn't keep track of them.

Monica knew what would happen that night as soon as she put her arm on Brian's shoulder and started dancing.

She tried not to think about it and rested her forehead against

Brian's cheek. He leaned into her.

"I have to confess something," Brian said in her ear.

"What's that?" Monica asked, intrigued.

"I kind of knew you were here tonight."

Monica looked up at him, surprised. "Is that so?"

"Yeah. One of my staffers was here earlier; he saw you."

"Were you keeping tabs on me?" she asked, confused.

"No, no. He texted me to let me know. He just figured I might want to know, you know, to know what the opponent is up to and all that."

Monica nodded slowly. She wasn't sure what to believe.

They continued to dance and didn't speak for a while. Monica expected Nicole and Don to come get her anytime, but that didn't happen.

Doesn't matter, she thought. It's so dark in here, no one will know who we are anyway.

Monica was enjoying herself. She ran her hand over Brian's muscular shoulder and he instinctively pulled her closer against him.

"I'm sorry I haven't returned any of your texts," she half-shouted in his ear over the music. "I mean, since —" she left the sentence hanging, but they both knew she meant since the debate.

"It's okay," he said. "I'm sorry about that."

"Don't be," she said, and laughed lightly.

"I mean, it shouldn't have been like that," he said. "I shouldn't have looked at you like that, in front of everyone —"

"On live TV," Monica finished.

"Yes," he said, chuckling. "I'm sorry."

The sparks Monica felt emboldened her. "It should have been more private."

"I agree," Brian said. "I should've picked a more private space, you know, in the dark, where no one would notice —"

"That would've been better," Monica agreed.

Brian pulled away gently and looked into her eyes. She smiled warmly at him.

He leaned toward her and kissed her lightly.

The gentle touch of his lips on hers sent a rush of desire through Monica's entire body. Their current state of physical contact suddenly wasn't enough for her.

She crushed her lips against his, then parted her mouth, in search of his tongue. He pulled her against his chest, his hands pressed tightly against her.

Then Monica put a hand on Brian's neck, and pulled him down and closer to her face. She teased him a bit by pulling her mouth away and he smiled and leaned toward her.

She locked eyes with him, and time seemed to freeze at that moment.

"You wanna get outta here?" he asked.

She rapidly glanced from side to side, and saw Nicole and Sean at the edge of the dance floor.

"Aw, shit," she said as soon as she saw Nicole point at her.

"What?" Brian asked.

She had made her decision.

Monica nodded, shifting her gaze back to Brian. "Yes, let's get outta here."

Brian drew her toward him and, in one swift movement, put his arm around her and hurriedly led her toward the exit.

Monica heard shouting from behind, but wasn't sure whether Nicole was yelling at her or whether it was merely the noise from the club. Either way, it didn't matter. She had already made up her mind.

Once they emerged outside, as if from a claustrophic underground bunker into freedom, the chill November air hit her face and instantly revived her. She felt certain; there was no turning back now.

Brian pulled her with him, dodging people along the way.

They saw a taxi and grabbed the chance, hailing it immediately.

Brian held the door open for Monica, and she got in the cab. As she waited for Brian to get in behind her, she chanced a look and saw Nicole and Sean coming out on the street. She wasn't sure whether or not they saw her, but she had no intention of backing out of her decision.

The taxi took off right away with some motivation from Brian in the form of a $20 bill. Monica snuggled up against him; he put his arm around her, and kissed her forehead.

Brian gave the driver his home address, and he and Monica sat in silence for most of the ride there, only speaking when Brian asked her if she was all right.

Chapter 53

When they arrived at his house, Brian was struck by the calm tranquility of the neighborhood as contrasted to the noisy scene at the club they had just left.

He unlocked and opened the front door and held it open for Monica. Once inside, he was overcome by a wave of shyness, as if he were a teenager alone for the first time with his high-school crush.

"Can I get you anything?" he asked Monica.

"Just some water, please." She smiled and automatically looked ten years younger. He noticed her dark eyeliner for the first time that night, and how it emphasized her hazel eyes, which now appeared green under the light.

Brian went to the kitchen and filled two glasses of water, handing one to Monica. He suddenly realized how incredibly thirsty he was.

He drained his glass and set it on the kitchen counter. He noticed Monica looking around the kitchen and living room at the mismatched furniture and bare walls. He admired the feminine curve of her neck and shoulder as she turned her head.

She noticed him staring.

"Sorry," she said quickly, "I just noticed that your artwork's gone."

"Yeah, Abby took most of the stuff." He sighed.

"I'm sorry —"

He gently put up a hand. "It's okay. It's been officially over for a while."

Brian looked at her, noticing how her wavy hair was matted against her temple from sweat.

He stepped forward and brushed a few strands away from her forehead and behind her ear. Compelled, he leaned forward and brushed his face against hers. Next, he put his lips lightly against her cheek. They remained like that for a few moments.

"I never thought I'd get the chance to be with you like this again," he breathed.

"I'm here," she whispered in response. She kissed him on his cheek, then traced her mouth to his, lifting up her heels to reach him.

Brian bent down slightly and brushed Monica's lips with his. Their contact was so restrained that it drove him crazy, but he controlled himself. He didn't want to screw this up, or make her think that all he wanted was to get laid.

Brian stood as still as a statue, taking in Monica's minty breath and the sweet scent of ginger that he would always associate with her.

While their lips were still locked, Monica reached her hands up to Brian's shoulders, then underneath his blazer. She lightly squeezed and made a move to get rid of his jacket.

When Brian realized what her intention was, he straightened and dropped his arms so that his blazer fell to the floor at their feet.

Monica now pressed her lips against his a bit more and opened her mouth. The feel of her tongue against his made his pulse race, but he steeled himself.

When Brian put his arms around her waist to draw her closer to him, she took a half-step back. Her hands went to his neck and found his tie. She slowly began undoing it, then smiled against his lips.

"Woman, you are driving me absolutely crazy," he breathed.

"I know," she said through a chuckle.

Monica pulled his tie from around his neck and cracked it like a whip before tossing it on the floor.

Brian exhaled a sigh of longing. He had never wanted anything as badly as he wanted Monica right now.

She began unbuttoning his shirt, kissing his neck as she did so.

Once his shirt was unbuttoned, he shrugged it off and hurriedly threw it on the floor.

"Oooo, someone is in a rush," Monica said playfully against his neck.

"Someone is hot as hell for you," he grunted, then reached one arm around her waist and aggressively pulled her against him.

He backed her against the kitchen counter, lifted her sheer black blouse up and over her arms, and tossed it over the counter.

"God!" he said when he noticed her large, round breasts about to pop out of her red lace bra. He fumbled with the clasp at her back, then in his extreme haste gave up and pushed her bra down. He fondled her breasts, then bent down and took a nipple in his mouth.

Monica leaned her head back and put a hand in his thick, dark hair. She grabbed a handful and yanked his head back.

"Looks like you still need a haircut," she teased.

"Enough of this torment," he growled and pushed her black skirt up around her waist.

Brian grabbed Monica just above her hips and forcibly thrust her on top of the counter. The sight of her sitting semi-nude, legs open, with her black tights was almost enough to drive him over the edge. He considered ripping her tights off her, but had just enough control left to reach underneath her skirt and hurriedly roll them down her legs, leaving them on the kitchen floor.

Monica reached out and pulled on his tee shirt, bringing him closer to her. Using both hands, she brought the shirt up and through his arms. She kissed his chest, then wrapped her arms and legs around him.

As she clawed his back, Brian undid his belt and shoved his pants down. He grunted as he placed his hands on her shapely thighs, pushing them further apart. He pulled Monica to the edge of the counter, reveling in the feel of her hot, sweaty skin against his.

"God!" she practically screamed in pleasure.

Brian had little patience left; he was about to let loose. He leaned into her and reached a hand underneath her skirt. She was incredibly wet. He smiled and shoved his tongue inside her mouth. He pressed his dick against her thigh and she reached down and grabbed it, pumping it with her hand.

He shoved her hand aside, because if she continued to do that for a few seconds more, he would lose it and he refused to do that before she did.

He had no patience to take her underwear off. Instead, he thrust aside her thong panties and shoved his dick inside her.

"Yes!" she grunted, and Brian smiled with satisfaction. He reached an arm around her to support her, pressing and shoving as deep inside of her as he could get. With his other hand, he rubbed her gently.

About thirty seconds later she grunted and yelled, her entire body convulsing with spasms of pleasure around him, taking him with her as they orgasmed as one.

Chapter 54

Monica woke up when Brian embraced her from behind and nuzzled her neck. They were both completely naked, their clothes in an abandoned, messy pile on his bedroom floor.

"Hmm, what do *you* want?" she asked in a teasing voice, her voice sleepy. She nestled further into the comfortable mattress and pillows.

"I think you know," he breathed into her ear. The sultriness in his voice made Monica tremble.

She turned around to face him and, in the moonlight streaming from the bedroom window, saw that look. That look that told her he hadn't even begun to take care of her.

She immediately became wet.

Brian half-rose to get on top of her, but she pushed him down roughly on the center of the bed and straddled him, rocking back and forth while her breasts swung up and down. Brian squeezed her ass and held her steady while he thrust upward.

"You know I like to fuck you hard from the bottom," he said.

"Oh, I guess we should take care of you," she whispered.

"I'm gonna take care of you first," he said.

Monica got off of him to lay down and turn over on her back.

But Brian apparently had other ideas. He grabbed her shoulder and turned her over so that she was on her stomach.

"I know you like this," he said into her ear.

Monica laughed, knowing what was coming next.

Brian fondled her curvaceous ass before grabbing it, hard. Almost unable to control himself, he carefully guided his dick inside her.

He lay on top of her, pinning her down, while he thrust in and out. The feel of him against her back and her ass made her crazy hot.

She loved being held down, and loved it even more when he grabbed her hair to hold her there.

"Open your legs," he commanded.

She did so, and rubbed herself against the sheets, while Brian reached a hand around her body to stroke her.

Brian was crushed against her back. He put his mouth against her ear and she heard him say, "I love you."

Monica had no time to mentally process his words. She came within seconds, then almost immediately Brian pulled out and came all over her back, while he gripped the backs of her thighs and grunted in release.

Monica woke up groggily to bright light streaming through the bedroom window. She and Brian apparently heard the muffled noise at the same time, because they both turned around and looked at each other in bed.

Monica's brows furrowed. "You hear that?"

"Yeah," Brian answered with sleep in his voice.

He half rose and listened in earnest.

"Someone's knocking on the door," he said.

More like pounding, thought Monica.

Brian pulled on a pair of sweatpants. "Stay right there," he told her, and got up to walk to the front door.

A few moments later, Monica heard him say, "Oh, shit."

Monica heard the front door open and then heard the unmistakable voices of Nicole and Sean.

"Where is she?!" Monica heard Nicole's demand through the half-open bedroom door.

"She's okay," Brian assured Nicole.

Nicole suddenly appeared in the bedroom doorway. Monica held the bedsheets up to her chin and tried not to look too sheepish.

"*Goddammit!*" Nicole said with frustration. "What were you thinking?!"

Monica started to shrug, then stopped herself.

"Get dressed and get out here. We've gotta talk! I'll wait in the living room." Nicole left the bedroom.

Monica reluctantly got dressed in the clothes she had worn the previous night. As she was doing so, Brian entered the bedroom.

"I'm sorry about all this," he said, sitting on the edge of the bed next to her.

Monica shook her head. "Don't be sorry. This was my choice." She pulled her boots on.

Brian brushed her hair off her face and kissed her softly on the mouth. "We'll figure this out."

Figure what out? Monica thought. We're competing against each other and next Tuesday one of us will be the loser.

Both of them reluctantly left the bedroom.

Nicole and Sean waited in the living area of the townhouse, and neither looked happy. Monica mentally prepared for the oncoming onslaught.

Nicole turned toward her friend.

"Do you know how many favors I had to call in so my

journalist friend who saw you at the club last night wouldn't print a story about you two?"

Monica formed the word slowly, her mind still groggy from having just woken up mid-morning. "W-what?"

"That's right," Nicole nodded furiously. "You are *damn* lucky that his cell phone was stolen last night, so he couldn't get any photos of you two. If he had, the story of the two candidates ending up in bed together would be all over the place right now!"

When Monica said nothing, Nicole continued. "Even so, I had to promise him a sit-down interview with both of you after the election."

"You did?"

"Yes! Otherwise he would've printed the story, even without the photos! We're all lucky that he owes me a huge favor; that's why he'll wait until after the election to do the interview."

Monica reeled at the thought of having to do a sit-down interview with Brian.

When Nicole saw her friend's expression, she said quickly, "oh, you'll do that interview, like it or not."

Monica glanced at Sean, who so far had said nothing. Whereas Nicole seemed angry, Sean seemed tired and exasperated.

"Mike doesn't know," he said. "I think the best thing to do right now is to keep it from him. He'll be pissed, for sure."

Brian nodded slowly.

How differently the men communicate, thought Monica.

Sean shook his head and said tiredly, "if you guys could've only waited a few more days."

Monica pursed her lips, feeling guilty but not guilty enough to have regretted it.

"Okay, shower and get dressed," Sean said to Brian. "We have campaign events today and we're running late for the lunch thing." Monica thought he appeared to have an air of merely going through the motions.

Brian looked at Monica.

"What?" she asked him.

He seemed about to say something. "I —" he gave up, sighing. "See you later."

"Sean's right, Brian," Monica said. "You've got a campaign to finish." She looked at him, trying to muster what she hoped was a stern look.

Brian looked crestfallen.

What did he expect me to say? Monica thought. That we'd both abandon the campaign, just days away?

"Come on." Nicole's demeanor had softened. She grabbed Monica's purse and gently led her friend toward the door.

Monica chanced a glance back at Brian, who looked at her with longing and what seemed like regret.

Great, so he tells me he loves me then immediately regrets it? she thought angrily.

As Nicole escorted her friend to her car, she said, "I'm sorry, Monica, but you are on total lockdown until Wednesday morning."

Monica looked down sheepishly.

"Yeah, that's right. Make eyes with the floor. I can't believe you two. Like a couple of goddamn hormonal teenagers!"

"It wasn't like that," Monica protested weakly.

"Like hell it wasn't! Don't make me monitor your phone until then."

Monica scoffed.

ELECTION DAY

"Polls close in just over an hour!" Don announced to the room. "We're not done yet!"

Monica had to admire his enthusiasm. He was great at rallying the troops.

Brian had texted her once since last Friday night. On Sunday morning he had texted:

Thinking about you. How's it going?

She hadn't responded. There was too much going on for her to wonder about what that night had meant, if indeed it had meant anything at all.

But she couldn't stop thinking about what it had been like to feel his skin against hers, to breathe him in, and have her hands in his hair.

"What are the returns showing?" Monica asked Don to distract herself. Val and David were with her in her campaign office, watching the news.

"Turnout's pretty high," he asked with a neutral expression.

"Is that good, Mom?" David asked. Monica smiled at his question. She refused to look disappointed in front of him.

Traditionally, high turnout in this district was bad for Republicans. But Monica refused to give up. She and her team had spent the entire day knocking on doors, calling voters, and giving interviews. She would be damned if she would throw in the towel after busting her ass, especially if it meant losing to Brian.

Seized with an idea, Monica got up and called Nicole into her office.

"What's going on?" Nicole asked.

"Okay, we have a little time left. Let's get on the phones. Nicole, call the registered Democrats. Don, call the registered Republicans. Give me the list of independents. Let's call ourselves, so the voters know the higher-ups are calling them, not volunteers."

"I like it. Let's do it," Don agreed.

A staffer came in then and called Don out of the office.

"I'll get right on it," Nicole said.

Monica thanked her.

Don popped his head back in the office. Monica looked at him expectantly.

"Monica, I have — what I think may be bad news," he said.

"What?" Monica wasn't sure whether she wanted to know.

"The Beatley Library precinct, on Duke Street, our volunteer there said a bus just showed up."

"Okaaay."

Don sighed. "They appear to be Muslim-Americans."

"How do you know?"

"The headscarves."

"So?" Monica shrugged.

"They're almost certainly not voting for you. And we could really use that precinct."

"How do you know they're not voting for her?" Nicole asked.

Don gave Nicole an incredulous look. "Come on, you're not serious."

"Well, a lot of Muslim-Americans do vote Democrat but not

always."

"Well, I'm on the phone now with our volunteer there. Hold on, I'll ask him." He whipped out his cell phone. "You still there?" he said into the phone.

The two women waited impatiently.

"This could be bad," Monica said, her heart sinking.

"Yeah, I want to know where they're from," Don said. Then, into his phone, "who organized the bus?"

All three waited for the answer.

Don suddenly furrowed his brows in confusion and looked at Monica. "Do you know someone called Rahima?"

Monica put her hands in her face and cried tears of gratitude.

"Okay, everyone, this is it!" Don called from the center of the room. "Polls are closed and we need to start tallying results!"

Don spoke to several volunteers individually to give them their tasks.

Monica waited in her office with Nicole, Val, and David.

"Exit polls are looking all right," Nicole said. "But we don't poll every voter, so . . . ."

"Yeah," Monica said absentmindedly, chewing a fingernail.

The results came in slowly at first. Monica had volunteered at polling stations before, and knew the long, arduous day that volunteers had already had. They had shown up at the polling stations around 5am, assisted voters, looked up names and addresses, requested ID, argued with voters who didn't have the necessary paperwork, and grabbed food and coffee when they could.

Now, they had to count up the votes, resolve any discrepancies (and there frequently were some), and call in the results. It was painstaking and tedious.

Don entered the room then and began making calls.

Monica sat with Val and David on the sofa and watched the TV, which was tuned to one of the cable news channels. Their election was getting plenty of coverage.

As the night dragged on, the news from the polls went from nebulous to surprising to downright unbelievable. Monica was holding her own and they were a few precincts away from the result. The newscasters were going nuts.

Monica stood watching the TV with Val and David.

"Oh, my God, you rock!" Val exclaimed. "You're gonna win this!"

Monica shook her head slowly. "Not over 'til it's over."

"Your Honorable Congresswoman or whatever the title is," Val continued, smiling.

Monica couldn't help laughing. She was glad to see her sister start to become herself again.

"Don't say that! You'll jinx it!" Monica said.

The newscasters continued calling in the results.

"How the hell can this be happening?!" Mike shouted; it was obvious he didn't expect an actual response.

Brian sat on a sofa while Mike continued his tantrum.

"How can a young, good-looking Democrat lose in this election?! This is a blue district. *Solidly* blue!"

"Things change sometimes," Sean said calmly. "Anyway, it's not over yet."

"Well, it's not looking good!" He turned his gaze to Brian. "We should've done the October surprise. I told you! We should've taken her down!"

Brian gave Mike a hard look. "It would've made us look worse, guaranteed." His tone brooked no argument.

"No, you're only worried about how you look in *her* eyes. That's what all this is about."

Brian stood up and went nose-to-nose with Mike. "You're full of shit."

"Am I?" Mike challenged his boss.

Brian took a step forward, and Mike instinctively backed up. "Shut your mouth," Brian said.

"Okay, okay, guys," Sean attempted to calm them down. "We're all worked up. Mike, go get the most recent numbers. Brian, go get some coffee. It's gonna be a long night."

Outside, in the general mayhem of the main room of Monica's campaign headquarters, Don called the shots like a pro.

"We're waiting on like two precincts!" he shouted to no one in particular.

"There's a call for you," an assistant said, handing him a cell phone.

"What's going on?" Don said into the phone without knowing who it was.

It was one of their observer volunteers at a local precinct, letting him know that the results were almost in.

"I think it's gonna be close," the volunteer told him.

"Wait, which precinct is that again?" Don asked, rifling through some papers on a nearby desk.

He looked at the size of the precinct and said into the phone, "if she wins this one, the election's hers. Make sure everything's legit."

"They're almost done counting now."

"Okay, I'll hold. Let me know when they call it in."

"Will do."

Don waited for what seemed to him to be an eternity. As he stood in the center of campaign headquarters, with his cell phone glued to his ear, he observed the hustle and bustle of the campaign office, marveling at how they had done so well after the ups and downs of this campaign.

"Don?" the volunteer said over the phone.

"I'm here."

"You're not gonna believe this."

Don listened carefully, then, adrenaline pumping, held the phone in his hand while he stalked over to Monica's office. Staffers jumped out of his way immediately; it was obvious he was on a mission.

Inside her office, Monica held David's and Val's hands.

"Ouch, Mom, not so tight," David complained.

"I'm sorry, sweetheart. I'm just nervous."

"I know. It's okay."

"I checked and you only need a couple of precincts," Nicole said as if she were in a trance. "This is unbelievable."

"It's not over yet," Monica corrected.

The door swung open with such force that Monica jumped, her heart in her throat.

Don stuck his head inside the room and grinned crookedly.

"It's over," he said.

Chapter 56

Monica sat, stunned, holding a cup of tea between her hands. She allowed herself to melt a bit, dropping her shoulders and her head. It felt good to relax.

She had asked everyone to leave her, Val, and David alone for a bit. She needed some quiet time to recharge her batteries. Soon she would need to go in front of the cameras again and give a speech. Nicole had asked whether Monica wanted her to draft something, but Monica declined.

"I'll think of something," Monica had told her friend. "Go get some coffee and chill a bit."

"You okay, Mom?" David's careful question brought his mother out of her thoughts.

Monica looked up. "Yes, of course. Thank you so much for being here, sweets. There is no one else I would rather celebrate tonight with than you two."

She smiled, almost moved to tears. David had that look on his face that he had been giving her since he was a young child. It was an emotional look, both acknowledging his mother's love and sharing the connection with her. It made Monica's heart swell with pride, even though she knew she had been far from a perfect parent.

"Are *you* all right?" Monica asked him. "Do you need anything else to eat?"

"No, Mom. I ate so much pizza I'm gonna explode."

Monica smiled.

The door opened and Nicole entered. "Hey, you guys." She wore a broad smile, even if her eyes were lined and tired.

"Monica, are you good?" she asked. "I'm sorry to interrupt."

"No problem. Yeah, I'm good. What's up?"

"You should probably make the rounds here, thank the staff and everything —"

"Of course. I'm ready now."

"— you know, before you make your acceptance speech and then kick ass and take names."

Monica smiled ear-to-ear, feeling the fatigue in her face. "Couldn't have done it without you."

"Stop." Nicole hid her face in her elbow. "You're gonna make me cry."

In the hotel where the local GOP held its after-election party, a raucous blowout was going on in the ballroom downstairs. Staffers and volunteers had poured in after a long day's arduous work, and partook of wine and nachos. Typically, the candidates didn't mingle the entire evening; they were too wiped out by the end. They would, however, make appearances and give speeches.

Monica had made the rounds of her campaign staff, individually thanking and congratulating her closest staffers and advisors. She told them that she knew they had worked diligently, giving up time with their family and friends, in order to make her campaign a success. She acknowledged the problems that had happened in the campaign, including news of the affair, a topic that she refused to avoid with her own staff. She told them that, if anyone was interested in a position with her administration to please let her know, and she would try to accommodate as many as she could. She was heartened to learn that among her staff there was no lack of interest in working with her.

Monica approached the ballroom with David, Val, Nicole, and Don. As they entered, Monica instantly became overwhelmed and overstimulated, her brain quickly taking in every detail and practically shutting down from the overload. She had difficulty focusing on any one thing and didn't even have the presence of mind to recite the Litany Against Fear.

The crowd went wild with enthusiasm as soon as they saw her. Monica gave a tired smile and a friendly wave.

She allowed Don to lead her to the raised platform, and made sure that David and Val didn't get lost in the crowd while they followed her. She thought for a moment that everyone would notice that her husband was conspicuously absent, but then again, he had been absent throughout the entire campaign.

They formed a small group on the platform, smaller than those of other candidates, which, in Monica's opinion, made their victory all the sweeter.

Nicole gave her friend a helpful pat on the back, her signal that Monica should step forward and address the crowd.

What could I possibly say? she thought. Ugh, I should have agreed to let Nicole write something for me. I hate crowds.

"So I guess I should say something?" she spoke into the microphone, with a hint of upbeat sarcasm. She intended to come across as playful, and was happy that the crowd laughed before continuing to whoop in celebration.

When the noise died down, Monica took a breath, and found her words.

"I am in utter awe at the efforts you guys have made that allow me to be standing here with you today."

The crowd roared and clapped; Monica almost covered her ears.

"Everyone in this room knows what this campaign has been like," she continued. "It's been difficult; that's a bit of an understatement. And, frankly, there is no way I would be here without the support of Nicole and Don," here she motioned to them, "and all of my staffers and volunteers. They worked tirelessly, giving up their free time, and donating their money. I cannot thank them enough. Also, my son," she motioned to David, "has kept me sane throughout the past few months, no easy feat. And my sister," she winked at Val, "has been supportive from Day One." There was more laughter from the crowd.

"So thank you, to everyone. Thank you to all the volunteers who manned our polling stations today. You took a day off of work, and out of your lives, to help us. That is extremely appreciated." She paused to gather additional strength. "And I cannot tell you how much I look forward to representing the people of this district." Here she smiled genuinely, unable to contain her zeal.

The audience cheered again. She stayed on the platform until the noise receded, thanked everyone again, and told them to enjoy the party.

Chapter 57

Brian was obliged to make an appearance at his "victory" party but it was the last thing that he wanted to do. He gave a concession speech, thanking his competitor and congratulating her for running a successful campaign. He thanked his campaign team and his parents, and conspicuously (and unintentionally) left Abby out of his speech. In reality, it hadn't even occurred to him to mention her.

He felt shitty, as if he had lost everything that had been important to him. He had lost Abby, even though he wasn't sure he had ever really wanted her. He had lost the congressional seat he wanted. He had lost his standing in the party. Most importantly, he had lost Monica. She was a rock, strong through it all, and she didn't need him.

Mike and Sean weren't taking the defeat particularly well, especially Mike. Sean appeared more resigned.

"I can't believe this," Mike protested, pacing Brian's office. "We had this in the bag!"

"Nothing is ever *in the bag*," Sean responded. "We took this election for granted, which you should never do. Even with high turnout, which usually helps us, we lost. What does *that* tell you?"

"That she hoodwinked us."

"No," Brian interrupted. He stood, arms crossed and with

his fist to his chin. "She outsmarted us. She ran a fantastic campaign. She went and talked to people that Republicans would never think to talk to. She let people ask her questions. She was vulnerable, and it worked to her advantage."

"Yeah, because she's a woman," Mike scoffed.

"I don't think so," Brian countered, giving Mike a hard glare. "To paraphrase Churchill, she was going through hell, and she kept going, even when it was painful. We didn't."

"You didn't want to," Mike said accusatorily.

"You didn't help, Mike, with you calling her a slut and everything."

Sean nodded but remained silent.

Mike scoffed again and moved toward the door. "I've gotta go call our big donors and apologize, try to save something from this mess." He left quickly.

Sean and Brian remained in silence for a few moments. Brian was pensive and didn't feel like talking. He took a deep breath. At least all this was over. He could go back to — what, exactly? His old nonprofit job?

"You know why you didn't win, right?" Sean said gently to his friend.

Brian looked at Sean, uncertain and annoyed. "Enlighten me, please."

Sean sighed and leaned back into the sofa, his fatigue showing in the lines of his face. "Monica wanted to win; she had it in her bones. You didn't. In your heart of hearts, you didn't want it. Not really."

Brian looked at Sean and said nothing. Sean was right; he knew it, and Brian knew it.

Brian hadn't cared about winning. He hadn't felt it for the campaign. He felt it for Monica. In his heart of hearts, he wanted to be with her, but that possibility appeared to be slipping from his grasp.

Chapter 58

Monica tapped one dark red nail on the glass table of the hotel bar, looking out the window. People-watching had always been a favorite pastime of hers and David's; it was something the two introverts could do together without talking too much.

She sat at the small table gazing at the street, observing people rushing to the metro, trying to get to work on time. The occasional dog walker passed by.

Brian had invited her for a drink and she had accepted. For once, she had arrived a bit early, and was waiting for him. He had called her on election night to congratulate her, which was traditional for the losing candidate to do. He had then called her a few days later, and asked her out.

"I just want to see you and talk to you for a few minutes," he had told her.

She had scheduled their meeting for a few days after that, so that she had had time to rest and recover from the campaign. She still felt as if she could sleep for weeks.

"Hi."

She looked up into Brian's face. He looked tired, but she didn't say that.

"Hey, there. You look good," she said instead.

"So do you. But then, you always look good."

Monica smiled. "Thank you."

He sat down and straightened his tie. At the sight of his hands, she suddenly remembered what it had felt like to be held by him, to be *possessed* by him.

Can I handle this? she thought.

They ordered drinks. Monica sipped hers slowly. It warmed her from the near-December chill.

"What's going on?" Monica asked.

"I just wanted to see your face," Brian said, straightening his shoulders.

The directness of his statement surprised her.

Monica nodded and half-smiled.

"How are you doing?" he asked.

"I'm good." She weighed whether to tell him the latest news. What the hell, she thought.

"My husband and I are legally separated, and he plans to file for divorce as soon as he can."

"I'm sorry to hear that," Brian said, frowning.

"Yeah, well. I don't blame him. I'm going to try to agree with him on things. I don't want to fight him, or litigate anything."

Brian nodded. "I'm sorry," he repeated.

"I'm giving myself time to process it. We were together a long time. It's for the best, but it's still painful." Her voice trailed off.

"Yeah, I know. Breakups are always painful, doesn't matter why."

Their eyes met. Monica resisted the urge to lean over the table and kiss him.

"Anyway, what about you? How are *you* doing?"

"I'm all right. Abby and I broke up a while ago, as you know, and I'm talking with this consulting group in Denver about possibly working for them."

"That's awesome. You'd move there?"

"Yes."

"Denver's a nice town," Monica said wistfully, wishing for a moment that she could live anywhere other than in the outskirts of Washington, DC.

"We'll see what happens," Brian said. He appeared to be distracted. "It's not really — what I want to be doing." He looked at her. "And I didn't really want to run for office either, to be honest. I don't know —"

"What *do* you want to be doing?" Monica asked.

He looked at her and smiled, batting his eyelashes like a fool. "I don't really know."

"Well, you're young. You have time to figure it out."

They sat in comfortable silence for a few moments. Monica sipped her wine, enjoying the spicy flavor of it.

"Do you know why you won?" Brian asked her suddenly, leaning back in his chair.

Monica paused, wondering if he expected her to answer honestly. She had run a better campaign than he had, for sure. Was that what he wanted to hear?

"Why don't *you* tell *me*?" she finally asked.

"You constantly underestimate yourself. And because of that, you work thousands of times harder than everyone else, and you exceed everyone's expectations."

Monica paused, churning his comment over in her mind.

"People who think too much of themselves, who are too arrogant, they aren't usually the ones who succeed —"

"Is that what happened to *you*?" Monica interrupted.

"Kind of." Brian left it at that.

"You mean that *you* underestimated me," Monica said.

Brian shook his head. "No," he said with conviction. "My *team* underestimated you. I never did. You can ask them."

"Is that so?"

"Yes, that is very much so."

They sat in silence for a minute, gazing at each other.

"Monica, I want to see you."

"You're seeing me now."

"No, I mean, I want to keep seeing you."

Monica sighed. Damn, she thought. What to do now?

"I don't know," was her first response. "We're too different, aren't we? I mean, a Catholic and an atheist?"

"Well, I'm more of an agnostic, actually," Brian smiled his charming crooked smile.

"Oh, really?" Monica said, crossing her arms.

After a few moments, her tone became serious. "Look, I'm forty-four."

Brian leaned back and said smugly, "age is nothing but a number on a piece of government-issued plastic, and we all know how well the government can count, and what plastic is worth."

Monica laughed, and Brian's face lit up.

"Be very careful," she said. "You're starting to sound like a libertarian."

"Well, there's this intelligent libertarian lady I know, who, once in a while, makes some very good points."

Monica shook her head at him, amused. "Goofball," she said.

"I'm *your* goofball, if you'll have me," he said. "That's really all I wanted to say to you."

This is my cue to exit, she thought.

"I'm sorry, but I've got to get going. My son and I have Christmas shopping to do."

Monica rose from her chair, took some cash out of her wallet, placed her wallet back into her purse, and put the money on the table. Then she looked at Brian.

"As for your question —" she realized that she wasn't ready to make a decision on it. "I'll think about it."

She started to walk past him, and as she did so, she put her hand on his shoulder. "Best of luck with everything, Brian."

She left and didn't look back.

Chapter 59

"How's the team coming along?" Monica asked as soon as she answered the call from Don. She was at home cooking.

"Coming along great, boss. We're getting key positions lined up."

"Awesome."

"Nicole's going to some political happy hour downtown later tonight, and she's gonna report back on the scuttlebutt."

"Fantastic. Please thank her for me."

"Will do."

Monica paused before continuing. She had dreaded having this conversation with Don, but it had to be done. She had also preferred telling him to his face, but didn't know when she would see him again, since everyone would take off soon to celebrate the holidays.

"Look, Don, we already talked about you being Chief of Staff in my administration."

"Yeah," he said.

"You're gonna make an excellent Chief of Staff, and I'm lucky to have you on my team."

"And?"

"I gotta tell you, your past advances on me have made me nervous."

"I'm sorry, Monica."

"I absolutely, under no circumstances, will get involved romantically with you."

There was a pause before he said, "I got it."

Did he really? she thought.

"If anything like that ever happens again, if you make a pass at me, I will fire you on the spot. I do not want to be working with you if I can't trust you. And I don't care about the optics. I'm past caring about anything related to optics."

"I'm sorry —"

"That's all. Don't make me fire you, Don. Don't make me have to explain to people why I fired you. And I know you don't want to have to explain it either. I don't want to have to do that, but I will. No one will make me feel uncomfortable."

"Okay." He sounded crestfallen, but also sounded like he had really heard her.

"Okay. We're on the same page here?"

"Yes, boss. Absolutely."

"All right. Let me know what else you guys need from me, but I'll be laying low until after the holidays."

"Gotcha."

Monica felt as if she needed to clarify her statement. "That means, please do not contact me unless it is absolutely necessary."

"Understood," Don replied.

They hung up.

Chapter 60

Nicole walked into the political happy hour that night with low expectations, but it did not turn out to be as bad as she had expected.

Some people avoided her like the plague (she had, after all, helped a Republican win a congressional seat although she was technically a Democrat), but others were almost sycophantic in trying to get in her good graces.

She was surprised to see Mike and Sean there. She had assumed they would be at home nursing their wounds. She was even more surprised when they approached her.

"Congratulations," Mike said to Nicole derisively.

Nicole didn't respond. She could tell that Mike had had a few drinks. He was typically aggressive, but she was unsure how the alcohol would affect his behavior.

"Hey, there," Nicole said cheerfully, trying to lighten the mood.

"By the way, the only reason you won was because Brian, that idiot, refused to release that info about Monica."

"What?" Nicole asked, intrigued.

"That's right —"

"Come on, Mike, that's enough," Sean interrupted.

"We had that dirt on her, it would've been perfect, but stupid Brian — he must've been in love with her or something —"

"Jesus, Mike, shut it," Sean said, leaning closer toward Mike and making eye contact with him. "Go get another drink, why don't you? And get me one, too."

Mike shuffled away angrily and Nicole faced Sean.

"What's he talking about? What dirt could you have possibly had on her, I mean, other than —" she left it hanging.

Sean sighed. "Mike talked to someone Monica went to high school with. Apparently, she may have had an eating disorder or something." Sean looked sheepish.

"And?" Nicole prompted.

"Mike wanted to use it, release it to the media, and Brian wouldn't let him."

"What did *you* think?" Nicole asked.

Sean gave her an *are you serious?* look.

"Mike thought it was our last chance to turn the tables in the polls. I told Brian that it was risky, that it would probably look bad for us, that it had happened a long time ago. But I also told him that it was his choice whether to release the info or not."

"And he didn't want to?"

"Right. He refused."

Nicole inclined her head. "Wow."

"Sorry. We didn't mean for you to find out this way."

"I mean, this is how oppo works, right? Although I don't know if this counts as oppo. The idea of it is disgusting." She raised her eyebrows.

"I know, it happened a long time ago. Brian didn't think it was right."

"And it's personal. We all have our past demons."

"Yeah, that's definitely true." Sean raised a blond eyebrow.

Nicole looked directly at him. "Honestly, I don't think it would've made a difference for Brian, if that makes you feel better."

"Even if it would have, I think it would've been a rotten thing to do."

Nicole smiled, and thought that maybe Sean wasn't so bad after all.

The next morning, Nicole could hardly contain herself. Soon after she woke up, she called Monica.

"Hey, what's up?" Monica greeted her friend.

"You're not going to believe this."

"What?" Monica asked, concerned.

"Last night I went to this political thing. Sean and Mike were there."

"Really?"

"Yes. You will never guess what happened."

Nicole breathlessly recounted the story to her.

"Honestly, Monica, I don't think Brian's such a bad guy after all."

Chapter 61

Monica pounded on the townhouse door relentlessly. She knew he was in there.

The door opened quickly, and she was face-to-face with a sleepy-eyed Brian, who wore a T-shirt and sweatpants.

He squinted into the sunlight, his dark hair unruly and sticking straight up. "Hey, what's up?" he asked.

"I have a bone to pick with you."

"What's that?" Brian asked, suspicious. He put his hands at his waist.

"Nicole ran into Mike," Monica said, as she shouldered past him into the foyer.

Brian's shoulders fell. He closed the front door.

"What did he do now?" he asked.

Brian's question told Monica all she needed to know about Brian's opinion of his former campaign manager.

"He could've been lying but I'm not sure. He told me that you had dirt on me."

"No, we didn't. What's he talking about?" Brian asked, confused.

Monica weighed whether or not to spell it out. "That apparently your team knew that I was diagnosed with an eating disorder when I was in high school and that I saw a therapist."

319

Monica saw in his eyes when he decided to come clean to her.

"Oh, that." He sighed. "Yes, we did know."

"How'd you find out?"

"Mike talked to people and he found someone — I don't know who — who you apparently went to high school with, and who said that you had that. Yes, unfortunately, it's true."

"So why didn't you use the info? I mean — oppo is everything. That's the creed."

"Mike wanted to. Sean — Sean was noncommittal about it at first but thought it wasn't a good idea."

"And you?"

"I'm the reason it didn't go public. I thought it was ridiculous to out that about someone. It — it wasn't right."

Monica stared, uncertain what to believe anymore.

"What I'm saying is," he said, "Monica, I couldn't do that to you. I wouldn't have been able to live with myself."

Brian was surprised when Monica started crying, wiping furious tears from the corner of her eyes.

"You always do that. Just when I've convinced myself that I hate you, you come back and do something like that, that shows me that you're really a good person, even though you cheated on Abby with me and then broke my heart —"

Brian rushed toward her but Monica held up both hands and took two steps backward.

"I'm sorry," Brian began.

"What are you sorry for? You didn't do anything wrong. Withholding the info was the right thing to do. I'm just — I'm confused."

She was confused about her feelings for him. She wanted to make sure that she wasn't confusing the sexual feelings she had had for him the other day with feelings of actual love.

Monica regained her composure and took a deep breath. "I'm okay."

"I'm sorry. I didn't mean to make you upset."

"Not upset, really. Just — overwhelmed."

Monica left hurriedly before Brian could say anything else.

VII

DECEMBER

Chapter 62

"What's up?" Monica answered her cell phone when she saw that it was Nicole.

"Sorry to bother you on your days off," her friend said.

"No worries. I'm at home. My sister's sleeping upstairs."

Indeed, Monica and Val were enjoying a few peaceful days of doing nothing at all. Monica had taken David to school, although he hadn't been keen on going. It was almost winter vacation, and he, too, needed a break.

"How's Val doing?" Nicole asked.

"She's much better. She's back at work but has this week off. She's sleeping at my place. Still not comfortable being by herself."

"Oh, I understand that."

There was a pause and Monica allowed silence to fill the space.

"Monica, I'm calling because I heard some gossip about Brian," Nicole said.

Monica's heart began to race. "Oh, what's that?"

"He's leaving DC."

Monica took a few seconds to process what she heard. "You mean he took that job in Denver?"

"Yeah. Doing consulting work or something. Sean told me today."

"Really?" Monica said.

"Yeah, so you won't randomly run into him."

Monica looked out the window. "Huh."

"That's all. Just thought you wanted to know."

"Thanks. Yeah — thanks for letting me know."

They hung up.

Afterward, Monica took care of several housekeeping things while Val slept in until past noon.

When Val came downstairs and into the kitchen, Monica decided to talk to her about Brian.

"How you doin'?" Val asked.

"Doin' great," Monica answered. "How'd you sleep, Doc?"

"Stellar."

"I'll make you an omelet." Monica smiled.

"Oh, my God, I love you," Val said.

"Love you, too." Monica paused. "Hey, let me ask you something."

"Shoot."

Monica told Val about how Brian had withheld the information about her eating disorder from the media.

"Damn," was Val's response.

"I mean, it's crazy."

"Yeah," Val agreed, nodding.

"So what does it mean?"

"That he's not as much of a douchebag as we previously thought."

"Yeah, maybe," Monica said, pensive.

"Maybe he still cares about you." Val shrugged, as if it were a logical conclusion from the information provided.

Monica considered her sister's statement. "Look, it's after

noon. Fuck it. Let's do mimosas, if you care to join me."

Val's eyebrows shot up at her sister's swearing. "Damn straight. Don't have to tell me twice!"

Monica opened a bottle of good champagne and mixed the drinks, then poured two glasses.

When the sisters had their full glasses in hand, Monica said, "let's toast."

"I've got this," Val said, then continued. *"Salud, amor, y dinero, necesariamente en esa orden."*

Monica smiled warmly at Val's slight tweak of their mother's signature toast.

"So what are you gonna do about Brian?" Val asked.

Monica took a sip of her mimosa and shook her head. "I don't know."

Chapter 63

Monica watched the violet-tinged sunset with awe as she strolled along the cobblestone street, as if she were seeing it for the first time. She ambled slowly, as if she had all the time in the world, kicking a small rock along in front of her.

A few people hurried around her, trying to get wherever they needed to be. She relished her easy pace, without the need to be anywhere.

Her cell phone rang and she stopped, wondering whether or not to answer it. She sighed and decided to dig it out of her purse.

"Hey, hey," she greeted Nicole.

"Hey," her friend replied. "We have a couple of campaign staffers we need to find positions for."

"Okay."

"Well, I know these two in particular, you really wanted to make sure they got something permanent." She named the staffers.

"Yes, of course. Who have you talked to?"

Nicole filled Monica in on her progress. "I'm pretty sure we can find them something decent."

"Good. Let's make sure of it." Monica continued strolling, making sure to watch where she walked on the loose cobble-

328

stones.

"I'll send the info over to you later, so you can take a look."

"Great. Thanks."

"Otherwise, I'll let you rest."

Monica smiled, appreciative of her friend's comment. "Thank you. I need it."

"Hey, at least you don't have to worry about running into Brian. Word is that he's leaving for Denver really soon."

"Yeah." Monica sighed.

"Call me if you need anything."

"For sure. Thanks again."

"Anytime."

They hung up. Monica dropped her phone into her purse and stopped, staring across the street at Brian's front door.

Chapter 64

"So you're making a habit of coming by my house." Brian served up the statement with a charming smile after he opened the door and saw an impeccably dressed Monica standing on his front porch. She wore a thick black coat and a long, red cashmere scarf. Her hair hung loose in waves and she had no makeup on.

"Shut up," she said, and his eyes widened in surprise at her statement. "Don't worry, this'll be the last time I come by your house."

His sad expression made Monica soften a bit. "Can I talk to you — just for a few minutes?"

"Yeah — of course." He stood aside and Monica walked into his apartment.

"I have to tell you something," Monica said. She felt resigned, and at the same time she didn't understand why she had waited so long to tell him.

"I heard you're definitely going to Denver," she said tentatively.

"That's right." Brian said. He crossed his arms and raised a dark eyebrow.

Monica nodded. "It sounds like a good gig."

Brian shrugged. "It's a gig."

"I don't want you to go." She shook her head with determination.

Brian had been about to say something and stopped mid-sentence.

"I told you that I loved you, right? I mean, that I used to love you."

Brian hesitated. "Yes?"

Monica's expression was pained. She kept her distance from him.

"Brian, I still love you. I have always loved you. And frankly, I have no idea why I have ever felt that way about you. I mean, you're too young for me, and — I don't know —"

"But you said at the press conference that you didn't love me before."

"Yes, but I lied. I couldn't let the whole world know that I fell for you like an idiot!"

He smiled slightly at her words.

She went on. Her smile was sad, resigned. She figured that she had already lost him, and that she had nothing else to lose. It made her want to tell him everything.

"The thing is — you don't choose who you fall for. It's not a conscious choice. You don't look at someone and say, oh he's over six feet tall, he has the right job, he's the right age, the right education level, yeah, I think I'm going to have feelings for this person. It's not like that." Her hand sliced the air. "You either feel it for someone or you don't. And I feel it for *you*. God help me, but I do."

Monica's eyes met his, and she continued. "The truth is, Brian, I have no idea why I feel this way about you, but I do. Honestly, I kind of hate you for making me feel it." Her heart raced, and her palms were sweaty. "But I love you and I don't want you to go to Denver. I want you to stay here in DC, and I want you to be with me."

Brian opened her mouth to say something, but Monica held up her hand.

"I know that what I say now will have absolutely no effect on anything, that you will still leave, and that's fine. I just wanted to be fair, to be honest —"

Brian took two long strides toward her and pressed his body against hers until Monica was backed up against the door.

His lips were against her face, and the energy rolled off of him in waves.

"Are you done?" he whispered.

"Am I done what?" she retorted, staying absolutely still, while a sly smile played at the corner of her mouth.

"Are you done talking, so that I can take you into my bedroom?"

Monica reached under his T-shirt and traced his side with one finger. "Maybe you've never realized this before," she lowered her voice, "but I can talk and have sex at the same time."

With a low growl, Brian bent down and scooped Monica up in his arms, heading for the bedroom.

Chapter 65

The newscaster couldn't help the stupid grin on his face. It slightly irritated Monica, but she decided that she would give him a break.

"Here's your coffee." Brian handed her a steaming mug of coffee and she thanked him.

It was a chilly Sunday morning, and Brian had come over to read the paper and watch television with her, while David slept the lazy sleep of teenagers on a weekend.

"Look at this," Monica said to him, motioning toward the television. One of the cable news channels was on.

"The drama between Virginia's Eighth District congressional campaign heated up the other day, ending in what looked like a reconciliation."

The story then cut to Monica and Brian walking on a dark street in Old Town.

"And to think, I thought no one would notice us," Monica sighed.

The video then showed the two of them kissing.

"This is *your* fault," Monica looked at Brian.

"What?"

"You can't keep your hands off of me."

"Well, can you stop being so hot?"

"No," Monica said flatly as she lay her feet on Brian's lap.

He laughed.

"Can't believe we made the national news." Monica shook her head and smiled.

"There's no hiding it now," Brian said, smiling.

The newscaster continued. "The only question now is, will he accompany her to her swearing-in ceremony?"

Monica and Brian looked at each other.

"Will you?" Monica asked coyly over the rim of her coffee cup.

"Yes," Brian said with mock formality, dark eyes twinkling, "I will."

Epilogue

"When is Mom coming home again?" Ariel asked her father, who drove.

"I've already told you three times," Brian said, slightly irritated. Were all teenagers like this? he thought.

"Well, I forgot."

Brian looked at his daughter, who sat next to him. "She'll be home in a couple of days. This particular client needs a lot of hand-holding."

"And when's David coming?"

"Your brother will be here to visit about a week after your Mom gets home."

"Awesome!"

Brian had to brake as the car in front of him slowed down, and he took the opportunity to check his phone.

"Dad, you know it pisses Mom off when you text and drive."

"I know, I know. It's just that — I'm waiting for her to text me back."

"What? Why?"

"You see," Brian said to his daughter, who looked at him curiously, "every morning, when your mother is away, I text her good morning. Every morning."

"So?" she shrugged, not understanding the significance.

Brian sighed. "Maybe you're too young to understand this." He hesitated, searching for the right words. "It's like — I text

335

her first, and when she texts me back, that first time, first thing in the morning — when she texts me good morning back, then I know that everything is okay."

"What do you mean, everything is okay?"

"I know that life is okay, that whatever is going on with us, and in the world, that everything is okay."

"You mean you know that you're okay with Mom." It wasn't a question. "Aren't you always okay with Mom?"

"Yes, but — your mother — I never take her time, or her love for me, for granted. So every morning, when she's not with me, I text her —"

"*Say Anything.*"

"Say what?" Brian asked his daughter, confused.

"Like the movie, when John Cusack, at the end, tells his girlfriend that everything will be okay."

Brian searched the files of his mind. "John Cusack?"

"In the movie *Say Anything,*" Ariel insisted.

Brian suddenly remembered watching it with Monica.

Ariel went on. "At the end, they're going to London, and she's paranoid of flying; she's never flown before."

Brian listened, amazed at how perceptive his daughter was. Just like her mother.

"And John Cusack, he tells her that everything will be okay when the seatbelt sign turns off, because if anything happens to the plane, statistically it will happen during the first few minutes of the flight."

"Okay," Brian nodded, stopping for a red light.

"So you know everything is okay when Mom texts you, when you get that first text in the morning."

"Yes." Brian was almost speechless.

"In the movie, when she hears the ping of the seatbelt sign

going off, she knows that everything is okay. And that's how the movie ends."

"Right, so — it's about 7:45am, and I texted your mother good morning before we left the house —"

"So you're waiting for her text —"

"Yes."

"So you know that everything is all right."

"Yes. As soon as I get that text, I know that everything is okay." And all is right with the world, Brian thought.

"I think I get it."

Brian smiled and pulled up to his daughter's high school.

"Love you, Dad," Ariel told him, getting out of the car, dragging her backpack behind her.

"Love you, too," Brian told his daughter. "Have a great day, sweetheart."

The car door slammed shut and Brian sat there, looking ahead.

"Hmm," he said aloud, "*Say Anything*." Ariel must have watched that movie with her mother. Interestingly, Monica had been the last person whom he had seen it with.

"*Say Anything*," he repeated to himself.

Ping.

Brian felt his phone vibrate in his pocket. He looked at it carefully. Then, reading the text, he grinned like a teenager, mentally counting down the hours until his wife came home, until he could hold her in his arms again.

THE END

Thank you for reading. I would very much appreciate an honest review on Amazon and/or Goodreads.

You can follow me on Amazon and/or Goodreads to get updates regarding my next novel. You may also enjoy Miscalculated Risks and Acceptable Misconduct, Books 1 and 2 of the Law School Heretic series, a contemporary romance series set in a Washington, DC-area law school.

About the Author

Maria Riegger is based in the Washington, DC area. She is a banking/corporate attorney by day (but please don't hold that against her), and an author by night.

Maria is a Gemini whose head has always been in the clouds. From a young age, her mother scolded her for not paying attention; when she was bored, she would make up stories in her head. She has been writing since she was about thirteen years old. A lover of languages, she speaks French, Spanish, and Catalan.

She has been caught air-guitaring in public. She loves to laugh, and is the "go-to" person if a friend needs someone to laugh at his lame jokes. In true Gemini fashion, she indulges both her logical personality as an attorney as well as her creative fiction-writing personality. She loved law school and even misses it, which led her friends to conclude that she is certifiable.

An irreverent Gen X'er, she writes gritty contemporary romance, with plenty of sarcasm, as well as nonfiction.

You can connect with me on:

- http://www.lawschoolheretic.com
- http://www.twitter.com/RieggerM
- http://www.facebook.com/lawschoolheretic
- http://www.instagram.com/rieggemr

Subscribe to my newsletter:

- http://eepurl.com/dAz9HH

Also by Maria R. Riegger

Miscalculated Risks

She's an overachieving law student who's not looking for love, so why can't she resist the mysterious newcomer?

Outspoken and abrasive, law student Isabel enjoys arguing with just about everyone, including her friends. Her strained relationship with her mother, less-than-stellar job prospects and frustrations with the conformist culture of Washington, DC have left her resentful and unfulfilled. When she meets Tarek, a new fellow student who dares to challenge her, she is intrigued but skeptical. While Isabel is risk-averse where her feelings are concerned, she is also becoming increasingly curious. She's afraid to get close, because being vulnerable always lead to being hurt, doesn't it?

Acceptable Misconduct

In the sequel to Miscalculated Risks, antagonistic Washington DC law student Isabel must face her unsettled past and navigate the final weeks of the semester while figuring out fellow student Tarek's feelings for her before he slips away. Will Isabel be willing and able to reveal her painful secret, at the risk of losing the one man who truly understands her?

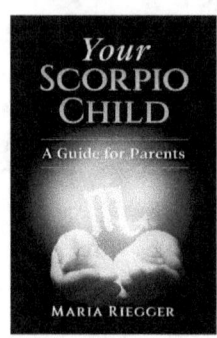

Your Scorpio Child: A Guide for Parents
Want to know all the secrets for handling your intense Scorpio child?

Scorpio is the most misunderstood and enigmatic of all the signs in the zodiac. Much has been written about Scorpio men and women. However, the Scorpio child remains elusive, mostly because Scorpio children do not usually say what is on their mind. Scorpio children are dramatic, suspicious, manipulative, and can seriously try parents' patience. They are also sensitive, intuitive, and loyal. The key to having the relationship with your Scorpio child that you want lies in knowing how to handle his innate characteristics. I hope that you find the information in this book useful.

Self-Publishing Primer
https://lawschoolheretic.com/free-stuff
I'm giving away a self-publishing guide FOR FREE. I'm a self-published author who's been in the trenches. Let me help you. You'll get all the relevant info in one spot! I learned how to self-publish on the fly, and I'd like to let you in on what I know. This information is so essential that I want you to have it for FREE.